"I've always been so grateful to you."

He met her eyes, trying to convey his sincerity. "You have no idea what he means to me. I love him so much. It's...indescribable, the intensity of that love."

"I think I do have an idea," Adeline said. "I felt it the moment I held him for the first time."

Their gazes locked in that moment. Jeremy felt a bond cement between them, one only a mother and a father could have. He let the feeling take him without concern over consequences.

He leaned toward her, turning his head to bring his lips to hers. The first featherlight touch seared him with sensation. When she put her hand on his face, he deepened the kiss.

An instant later, she answered his passion. He leaned more, pressing her down onto the oversize sofa. She bent one knee and his hardening erection found itself against her groin. The shock of sensation pushed him to the brink of no control.

Jeremy went still. If they took this any further...

* * *

**The Coltons of Shadow Creek:
Only family can keep you safe...**

* * *

**If you're on Twitter, tell us what you think of Harlequin Romantic Suspense!
#harlequinromsuspense**

Dear Reader,

Welcome to the latest book in The Coltons of Shadow Creek series, where Livia Colton lives on—even though she is believed dead. Enter the tantalizing world of scandal and love in *Mission: Colton Justice*.

The most appealing aspect of this story for me was the hero's entrepreneurial spirit and his penchant for honor and, yes, justice. The heroine is his perfect counterpart, with equal zest for success and a deep desire to belong to her very own family. May you be drawn in from page one and enjoy the rest of the series!

Sincerely,

Jennifer

MISSION: COLTON JUSTICE

Jennifer Morey

HARLEQUIN®ROMANTIC SUSPENSE

Special thanks and acknowledgment are given to
Jennifer Morey for her contribution to
The Coltons of Shadow Creek miniseries.

ISBN-13: 978-0-373-40226-7

Mission: Colton Justice

Copyright © 2017 by Harlequin Books S.A.

Recycling programs
for this product may
not exist in your area.

This edition published by arrangement with Harlequin Books S.A.

For questions and comments about the quality of this book, please contact us at CustomerService@Harlequin.com.

HARLEQUIN®
www.Harlequin.com

Printed in U.S.A.

Two-time RITA® Award nominee and Golden Quill award-winner **Jennifer Morey** writes single-title contemporary romance and page-turning romantic suspense. She has a geology degree and has managed export programs in compliance with the International Traffic in Arms Regulations (ITAR) for the aerospace industry. She lives at the foot of the Rocky Mountains in Denver, Colorado, and loves to hear from readers through her website, jennifermorey.com, or Facebook.

Books by Jennifer Morey

Harlequin Romantic Suspense

The Coltons of Shadow Creek

Mission: Colton Justice

Cold Case Detectives

A Wanted Man
Justice Hunter
Cold Case Recruit
Taming Deputy Harlow
Runaway Heiress

The Coltons of Texas

A Baby for Agent Colton

Ivy Avengers

Front Page Affair
Armed and Famous
One Secret Night
The Eligible Suspect

All McQueen's Men

The Secret Soldier
Heiress Under Fire
Unmasking the Mercenary
Special Ops Affair
Seducing the Accomplice
Seducing the Colonel's Daughter

Visit Jennifer's Author Profile page at Harlequin.com, or jennifermorey.com, for more titles.

For Allie, my adorable, loyal and loving
Australian shepherd,
who is always by my side.

Chapter 1

The vision that walked toward his open office door differed mightily from the broke college student he'd last seen a few years ago. Jeremy Kincaid forgot all about the exciting new investment opportunity in a high-tech night vision equipment start-up. Adeline Winters seemed to float with each smooth, graceful stride. She could just as easily be on a catwalk as in his reception area.

Her endlessly long legs made the light gray trousers wave as she moved. The open lapels of her knee-length black trench coat offered glimpses of slender hips beneath the fitted hem of a gray button-up vest. Modest cleavage peeked out from above a soft, silky yellow shirt, very business-like. Thick, shoulder-length blond hair fanned out. He drank in the sight of her. By the time she stopped at his office door, her porcelain skin and naturally pink lips arrested him next, and then her keen, light blue eyes snapped him out of his trance.

He stood, feeling as though he might have to control his drool. Clearing his throat, he got a hold of himself and stepped away from his chair. Did she have the same reaction to seeing him again? She held a leather pad-folio in one arm. Her gaze took in his form as he came around the desk, but he couldn't be sure the same electric sexual awareness afflicted her.

"Ms. Winters. Thank you for coming." He shook her soft hand.

"Adeline. Thank you for inviting me, Mr. Kincaid."

"Jeremy." He smiled as he looked down at her attire. "College seems to have agreed with you."

A slight answering smile curved her perfect lips. "My business is growing. Maybe after this meeting, it will grow even more."

She'd turned her criminal justice degree into her own private investigation agency. When he'd learned that, the wheels in his head had started spinning. Not only did he admire anyone with the know-how and courage to blaze their own path—he'd built his own business on the same steam—he could use her expertise.

Putting the padfolio down on one of two plush brown leather chairs facing his big, cherrywood desk, she removed her coat and draped it over the arm. She had a gun holster and an ammo pouch fastened to her belt. While he wondered about that, she looked up at his thirty-six-by-forty-eight black-and-white picture of the moon, half in sunlight and half in shadow.

"That was taken by an imaging satellite," he explained. "The founder of a start-up I invested in sent it to me."

She looked over the rest of his office. A whiteboard covered one wall and pictures of ranch land accented a conference table. A credenza took up the space behind his desk.

After taking those in, she returned her attention to him. "You like ranching and stargazing?"

"Ranching is in the family. Not me. I'm a businessman." He looked over the photos. "I like investing in technological concepts, seeing entrepreneurs take an idea and turn it into a success. I built my first company from nothing and started investing after I sold it."

"To the moon and back." She smiled wider than before. "I knew you invested but I didn't know you sold your first company. Tess never mentioned that." She wandered to the whiteboard where he kept a list of tasks and an unclassified flowchart of a new night vision scope for a military rifle.

"I didn't have much money. I had my engineering degree and a partner with an innovative idea to make a garage door opener that could read license plates. Kind of like electronic toll optics."

She nodded. "Yeah, I know some people who have one of those." She turned to face him. "Fascinating."

"My partner bought my share of the company. That's what I used to build this." He opened his arms.

She met his eyes with softening warmth. He hadn't known her long before his wife had died. He and Tess had chosen her from a donor pool.

He suspected she was thinking of that time along similar lines, perhaps how she didn't really know him, either.

Tess had been so excited with the prospect of having a baby. He had been thrilled to make her that happy. The sting of loss caught him as it often did. He still could not let her go.

Lingering too long on the sparkle in her glowing eyes, he gestured to the chairs. "Please, have a seat."

He stepped back and then around to his chair behind the desk. She adjusted herself until she found a comfortable position, crossing her sexy legs and leaning back to patiently await his purpose in inviting her to his office.

"Is there a reason you're armed?" he asked. The college student he once knew wouldn't have packed heat.

"Only when I work cases that make me nervous."

"Hopefully that doesn't mean me." He kept his tone light. If she had any idea why he'd asked her to meet, she'd have a good reason to be armed.

A brief breath left her, seeming to stem partly from a response to his lightness and partly from patient tolerance. "No. A mother hired me to track down a drug dealer her son has gotten mixed up with."

"Ah." He leaned back with his fingers to his jaw. "You do target practice?"

"I wouldn't have a gun if I didn't. I assure you, I'm legal and qualified."

"I wasn't questioning your experience as an investigator." He knew nothing about her experience. Her website had glowing reviews from clients, and everything about her presented professionalism. He'd take a chance on her, which was better than he'd get from the local sheriff's department. Other than Knox Colton, he didn't trust anyone.

"Why did you ask me here, Mr. Kincaid?"

"Jeremy. I want to talk to you about Tess."

Adeline's gaze faltered with the mention of Tess, making him wonder if that part of her past bothered her, being an egg donor and surrogate to fund her college tuition, giving up her baby.

"It's hard to believe it's been two years," she said.

"Yes. The first year was pretty hard on me and

Jamie." He'd spent the next year trying to get deputies to look into the car accident that had killed her. That had proved futile.

Her eyes lifted and he saw the hungry need for more information about the boy. Jeremy couldn't deny her link to him, and Jamie had influenced his decision to call her.

"He's doing much better now. He misses his mother, but he's adjusting," Jeremy said.

Adeline only met his eyes, seeming to be caught in ponderous thought.

"He looks like you." Jeremy didn't know why he'd said that. After Jamie had been born he'd focused on thinking of him as his and Tess's baby. But it had been difficult not to make the comparison. "He's got blond hair and blue eyes." He breathed a laugh and pointed to his dark, short cropped hair and brown eyes. Tess had dark hair and gray eyes.

Adeline made no comment and lowered her gaze. Talking about Jamie must make her uncomfortable.

He used to tell himself that Jamie's bright blue eyes resembled Tess's. Jamie had a lot of his own features, but the blond hair and blue eyes were always Adeline's. He'd often felt he had to convince himself that Jamie was his and Tess's and not his and Adeline's.

"Sometimes I wish I wouldn't have been so impulsive," Adeline said at last. "Being an egg donor and surrogate for Tess." She shook her head. "I wanted and needed to finish college, but...wow."

Jeremy wasn't sure what she meant by "wow." "You regret it?" She'd given him and Tess a priceless gift. Why would she be anything but proud?

"No, not regret. I know how much Tess wanted a baby. I saw that when I met her. And the money did get me through college. It was worth it just for those two things."

He heard the *but* she didn't say. Giving up a baby would be hard but she'd gotten past that…hadn't she?

Tess had lost her ability to have children due to polyps in her uterus. When she had found out, she had been devastated.

Catapulted back in time, he remembered certain key things about the in vitro fertilization process. Using his sperm and Adeline's egg and implanting the fertilized embryo into Adeline, her growing stomach through the pregnancy, and then giving birth to Jamie—to all accounts, his son with Tess. He'd tried to experience it all with Tess, but there had been moments when he felt connected to Adeline in an intimate way only a man and woman who produced a life could understand. That's why he'd kept his distance from Adeline as much as possible. Adeline had spent most of her time with Tess when visiting them during her pregnancy. Thankfully he'd had work to fall back on.

"Why don't we talk about the reason you asked me here?" Adeline said.

"Of course." They'd ventured a little too far into the past. He sat forward and placed his hands on the desk. "There is no easing into what I have to say. So I'll just say it." He watched anticipation brighten her eyes. "I think Tess was murdered."

Adeline's head moved back in unexpected surprise. "Murdered? She drove into a pole."

She hadn't injected herself into his and Tess's lives after giving birth, but she had attended the funeral. She had also done her research before meeting him. He liked that. "Yes, and her blood alcohol level was high. But a few months ago I spoke with a local who said he saw Tess having lunch with a man the day of her accident. She left upset over whatever the two discussed. Her death always bothered me but I didn't start thinking there might be more going on than a simple accident until then. What if she had relations with people I didn't know about? Why did she meet this stranger and what made her upset? It's too much of a coincidence that she died the same day."

"Who is the man?"

"The local didn't know. I tried to get the sheriff's office to look into it but they haven't. I get a brush-off every time I go there." Renowned local criminal Livia Colton had her tentacles buried deep into the department in Shadow Creek, Texas. Jeremy knew her through his ties with other Coltons. He wouldn't put it past Livia having something to do with the lackadaisical mindset of the sheriff's department.

"I don't see how Tess's lunch could have anything to do with her accident. She may have been upset and that may have contributed, but…murder?"

Adeline clearly thought he was taking a leap. Jeremy expected her to be analytical.

"Even in prison Livia still had contact with a few of her followers. Someone I know heard one of them talking at a cocktail party, saying how she'd love to see Tess suffer somehow. 'Like some kind of terrible accident, something to mess up her perfect, fortuitous life so she can see how the rest of the world lives,' she said. Livia did not like Tess. She hated her youth and goodness."

"Why do you think she had motive to kill? And from prison? Tess was young and beautiful and she married you. Maybe Livia was just jealous."

Jealousy was enough. She didn't know Livia well enough if she didn't agree. "I know there has to be more and I don't have much to go on right now, but Livia is capable of paying lackeys to do her dirty work. She could have paid someone in the sheriff's department to cover it up. She's a sociopath. Matthew Colton was her brother, remember, and a serial killer. Even he feared her. She worked in the highest ranks of an organized crime group, trafficked drugs—and people. She's been convicted of murder before, so why not do it again if it made her feel better or gave her some kind of gain?"

"I agree she's capable, I just need more of a motive."

"I agree with that, too. That's why I called you. I want you to find out, either way. Was Tess murdered and if so, did Livia do it? Tess's accident report said her car swerved off the road and there were no skid marks before she hit the pole."

"She was drunk."

"Something Livia would capitalize on."

Adeline seemed to ponder that awhile. "Who is she to you?"

"Livia? Wrecker of my friends' lives." He knew several of the Colton clan. "Destroyer of a community I love. And someone who I know for a fact hated my wife—for whatever reason."

"You talk as though you know she's still alive."

"I believe she is."

Again, she fell quiet and considered him. "Livia is dead, Jeremy."

"Livia has escaped capture before. She was on the run for months until she was found hiding in her La Bonne Vie estate. Her kids all thought she would finally go back to jail when the vehicle crashed and went into the river. Her body was never recovered."

"The SUV was swept downstream during a heavy storm. She's probably buried in mud somewhere."

He enjoyed visualizing Livia dead under several feet of gooey mud. "Right where she belongs." Was there a more fitting demise? "Ever since Tess's accident, I've had a feeling she shouldn't have died, that the accident seemed too staged, that she wouldn't have driven into a pole. Livia never liked her. Now I find out Tess met with a man she never told me about. I just need answers. I need someone I can trust to look into it, to make sure she wasn't murdered."

Her expression eased of skepticism. "All right. I can do that." She picked up the padfolio and opened it. "What's the local's name? I'll start there."

He sat back. "Good. Why don't you pack some things and stay at my house until this is over?"

She looked up from the padfolio. "Excuse me?"

"If Livia is involved, this could put you in danger. Besides, when you aren't busy investigating, I thought you could help me with Jamie. Spend some time with him. I had to let his nanny go for stealing some of Tess's jewelry. Emily Stanton seemed like a nice woman, but I had her pegged all wrong."

"I'm not… I'm a private investigator, not a nanny."

He suspected she might react this way. She hadn't seen Jamie in a long time. As his biological mother, she would have to have some kind of feelings on the matter, wouldn't she? While he didn't want to push too hard, concern for her safety was his primary motive. If Livia was involved, he needed to know Adeline and Jamie were safe and the only way to do that was to have her close to him.

"I'll pay you," he said. "In addition to your investigation fee."

She looked down with a befuddled grunt.

"Jamie would love to meet you." His son had gone too long without a mother figure around.

She looked up with only her eyes and he saw her reluctance. Is that the reason she stayed away after giving Jamie to him and Tess? Was it too painful to be with Jamie and know the boy didn't belong to her? He'd often wondered. Not that he would have wanted her to be a permanent fixture. That might have been awkward, but a friendly visit every now and then would have been just fine.

"Please." He had to convince her. "You're the only person who's capable of helping me. I don't trust anyone else."

After several seconds she closed her padfolio. "I'll think about it."

"Then come over for dinner tonight. We can talk about strategy going forward. I'll give you the name of the local then."

She half smiled, wry. "Are you bribing me?"

He answered her smile with a grin. "Just giving you a little incentive." If he was honest, he'd have just said yes.

Jeremy's handsome grin stayed with Adeline long after she left his office. Dark stubble had begun to make its presence known and matched the black color of his hair and arches of his eyebrows. His playful but determined brown eyes and the deeper crease on the right side of his mouth haunted her thoughts most. Sitting in her four-door Audi A3 with the headlights off in case Jeremy watched for her, she gripped the steering wheel and looked at his house. She hadn't driven up to the gated entry yet, just parked on the street to be sure of whether to do so.

She could see his house through a stone pillar and iron fence, a veritable mansion by her standards. She had a nice house but it wasn't big, just a fixed-up older colonial with two bedrooms, a living room and a kitchen. She could get lost in Jeremy's house. On a huge plot of land where the nearest neighbor was a tee shot away, the modern English country manor had no front yard. Exterior light lit the impressive home. She pictured a carriage rolling to a stop before the arched front entrance, over square stone slabs that extended right up to the house with some kind of ground cover growing in the spaces between. Four symmetrical casement windows lined the first and second levels on each side of the door. This part of the house was made of varying earth-toned sedimentary stone blocks that gave it a rough texture. Three attic windows jutted out from a dark slate roof. The front of the house stood out from a recessed back portion made of much smoother, monotone stone.

Was she really going to do this?

Reaching over to her laptop case, she unzipped a pouch along the outer side. Pulling out the last photo Tess had sent her of Jamie, she stared at his one-year-old face. At the time, she'd thought sending the surrogate and egg donor a picture of her son odd. Why had Tess done it? Her note had said something to the effect of, "Thought you'd want to see what an angel we have, thanks to you." She'd been tempted many times to reach out to Jeremy just so she could see her son again, but doing so would only make her want more. Had Tess sent the photo as a warning not to try to come see her baby? The original photo showed all three of them, Jeremy and Tess smiling, Jamie in Tess's arms. Tess hadn't struck her as that type of person, and she had to admit her reluctance to see Jamie had been the only thing that had kept her away—nothing Tess had done either intentionally or unintentionally.

Now here she was, parked outside Jeremy's house, knowing full well that she'd go inside and not leave, help him investigate Tess's accident while they both watched over Jamie. The drug dealer she'd investigated had been arrested just this afternoon, so she had no other cases. That had only given her another reason to come here.

Putting the photo back into the pouch, she was about to drive to the gated entry and onto the stone slabs when she noticed a car across the street. It hadn't been there when she'd pulled up. In fact, it must have just pulled up. The headlights went out and no one left the vehicle.

Adeline stayed in her car and watched.

A few minutes later, a man got out and walked toward Jeremy's property.

Removing her pistol, Adeline loaded it and got out of her car. The man disappeared into the darkness along the fence lining Jeremy's property.

Adeline ran after him. Seeing him clear the fence, she did the same. On the other side, she saw the man go into a cluster of trees between Jeremy's house and the one next door. At the trees, she hid behind a trunk and spotted the man continuing along the same line. He reached the backyard and stopped. Looking at the house where light shone from an upper level window. Jamie's room?

"Hey, you!" Adeline raised her weapon. "Don't

move!" She stepped out from the tree and walked toward the man.

He ducked into the trees and ran.

She ran into the trees after him, hoping to cut him off. She heard him crashing through the trees, breaking branches and shuffling leaves. When he stopped, so did she, taking cover behind a tree. Peering out, she searched the wooded area. She heard water flowing through a small stream. Jeremy lived on a large parcel of land in a wooded area of Shadow Creek. She moved forward slowly, listening and looking for a sign of the man.

At the stream, she stopped. Downstream she saw several boulders rose above the surface of the water. He could have crossed there. She ran to the spot and hopped rocks to the other side. Lighting her flashlight, she searched the ground until she found a fresh footprint. Following them until they reached the fence. Climbing over, she ran back to her car. Before she reached the road, she heard the revving engine of a vehicle driving away. Just as she made it to the street, she saw the car that had parked across the street racing away in the other direction, too far to get a plate number.

Why had that man been here? What would he have done if she hadn't interfered? Hurt Jamie? Motherly instinct she could never shed after giving birth raced through her.

Putting her gun back in its holster, she went to her car and drove through the open gate and parked on the stone slabs near the front door. No question about staying with them now…

She took her luggage and laptop case to his door, ringing the bell. Jeremy answered and then smiled when he saw her luggage. He'd removed his suit jacket and tie, the top three buttons of his blue dress shirt undone to reveal a tantalizing glimpse of his chest. He looked stunning in a suit. She'd always thought so, but he wore more relaxed just as well.

"I just chased a man through the trees." She stepped inside as his pleased look faded; she took in the curving staircase to one side of the wide and high entry and the formal living room to the other. She could see a little of the grand family room through one archway and a dining room through the other. A huge, colorful abstract painting hung on the wall across from the front door, a light shining on it, and a console table beneath with a vase full of fresh flowers and a stack of books about art.

"You what?"

"Yeah." She walked toward the family room, nervous over seeing Jamie again. "He got away before I could find out who he was." But she would.

"And you went after him yourself?"

His house wasn't anything she didn't expect from someone with his kind of money. Functional leather furniture and a few tables were well placed with dashes of color. A large, round hanging light broke up the cavernous space and floor-to-ceiling windows would allow ample light in the morning. A table lined most of the back of the couch that separated this room from the magazine-worthy open kitchen with stainless steel appliances, white cabinets and marble countertops. The kitchen island sat six. Clean. Tidy. No clutter. She liked it.

She completed her circle. "Should I have rung your bell first?"

"Very funny."

She told him what happened, how she had seen the man and followed until he had raced away.

"Someone must have started watching me. Maybe after discovering I hired you."

That could be true. Seeing his house for the first time had diverted her attention—that, and nervousness over seeing Jamie.

"Nice place," she said, more as a conversational statement, unable to ward off the impending moment when she'd meet Jamie, see him for the first time in two years.

"Thanks."

His delayed response made her aware that he noticed her discomfort.

"Daddy?"

With a sharp pang bursting in her core, Adeline looked up at the railing of the loft and saw a three-year-old boy clutching one of the spindles. He wore jeans and a superhero T-shirt.

Her chest froze. She struggled to breathe, or maybe her body had automatically made her conscious of the fact that she had to take deeper breaths and the reaction might be obvious to the astute observer. She didn't care. She gobbled up the sight of the little boy, his full head of ruffled blond hair that reminded her of painful combings after a shower, his light blue eyes shaped like Jeremy's but the exact color of hers. So much more, intangible and strumming a lovely tune in her.

"Who's that?" Jamie pointed to Adeline.

She sensed his curiosity and it warmed her. Was he curious because she was a woman? He was too young when Tess died. Did he remember her at all? She doubted he remembered enough to make a significant conscious impact. He had to have dealt with some subliminal effects. Instinctually he'd feel the loss.

"Hey, buddy, this is Adeline."

Jamie eyed Adeline and then turned to his father. "Can I have ice cream?"

"Sure, come on down."

Adeline wondered if he said yes just to get the boy to come down and greet her. Her heart drummed anxiously until she put herself in check. She was there to help with a case, not take over the role of Jamie's mother. She stood stiffly as he came down the stairs and emerged through the front entry. His little steps carried him toward her and he stared in shy absorption.

"I don't bring women here much," Jeremy said. "I haven't dated or anything."

After he lost his wife, Adeline could well understand. She wouldn't think too long on why he hadn't seen any women.

"I'm a bit younger than his grandparents," she said.

"You're not my grandma," Jamie said, all in fun. He went to the freezer.

Jeremy got a bowl and went about the task of scooping a small amount of ice cream while Adeline took advantage of the time to just stare at her son.

Tess had been Jamie's mother, but he was *her* son. She'd felt proud and sometimes sad because she wasn't part of his life. She didn't like thinking of Jamie as Tess's son. She couldn't quite let go of the fact that she'd had a son and he was being raised by his father and another woman. Tess hadn't been able to have children of her own because of undiagnosed endometriosis. Adeline should be completely happy that she'd given the woman such a gift, not envious or regretful. Why did those thoughts plague her so much? She hadn't been at a point in her life to care for a child. She had college ahead of her. She'd made the right decision, despite the occasional doubt that seized her.

The only thing she might doubt...and even more, regret...was letting her fantasies of Jeremy take flight.

Chapter 2

"Jamie, Adeline was...my and your mom's friend."

Jamie looked up from his spoonful of ice cream, his chewing slowing. He sat on a high stool at the kitchen island. Did the mention of his mother make him sad?

"Ice cream?" Jeremy asked her as he headed toward the refrigerator.

Why not? "I'd love some."

"Chocolate with chocolate chunks or vanilla caramel?"

"It's got to be the chocolate chunks." She smiled at Jamie, who still stared at her as he shoveled ice cream into his mouth.

She went around the island and sat to one side of the boy, catching a whiff of his kid scent.

Jeremy placed a bowl in front of her and sat on the other side of Jamie.

Adeline put a spoonful of ice cream into her mouth, the rich chocolate flavor bursting. Delicious. She couldn't remember the last time she'd had ice cream.

Beside her Jamie started to laugh, almost a giggle. She glanced at him and he pointed.

"You got ice cream on your face." His young voice tripped over the words *ice cream*, spending more time on them.

Smiling, she licked. "Did I get it?"

"Yeah." Jamie laughed some more, swinging his feet and piling in another heaping bite.

He rested his forearm on the edge of the counter and Adeline noticed Jeremy doing the same thing. They held their spoons the same, Jamie's fingers a much smaller version. Jeremy glanced at her and so did Jamie and she felt a pang of affection.

"All right, buddy. Time for pajamas. By the time all that sugar wears off, I want you in bed."

"I don't wanna go to bed."

"I'll read you a story." Jeremy cleared his and Jamie's bowls and took them to the sink.

"Will Adda read, too?"

He called her Adda. How adorable. She took her bowl to the sink where Jeremy withdrew from rinsing his and Jamie's. Her hand brushed his. In an instant, awareness of how close she stood to him inundated her senses. The unexpectedness of it threw her off balance. For a few seconds all that existed was him, his nearly six-foot height, fit build, dark lashes around his warm, confident eyes...and the smell of him, spicy but subtle.

Jamie tugged on Jeremy's sleeve. "Read."

"Go get into your jammies. We'll be up in a second." Jamie hopped off.

Adeline listened to his feet patter up the stairs, thinking she could hear the sound every day and never tire of it.

"We have about two minutes to get up there before he starts hollering." Jeremy rinsed her bowl and put the dishes into the dishwasher.

He didn't have a housekeeper?

He turned and headed for the stairs. Feeling a little awkward participating in this family activity, she followed. He stopped in the entryway to pick up her luggage and carried it upstairs.

At the top he paused and let her catch up. "You don't have to do this, you know. I can show you to your room and you can get settled in."

"What's so tough about reading to a kid?" She kept the mood light, not comfortable revealing how this affected her. She was about to read to her son for the first time.

She took in the huge landing area, a loft with a seating area and desk. There were two halls sprouting off the room, one to the left and one to the right.

Jeremy led her down the hall to the right and entered the first room. Spacious with a love seat and chair and queen bed, blues and greens and carved white crown molding, it invited coziness. A five-piece bath with a walk-in closet was more than she needed.

"How many rooms do you have here?"

"Eight. This one's closest to the stairs." He pointed toward the opposite hall. "Jamie's room is the first one on that side. Mine's at the end. It's a suite. More than I need, but it was nice to share with Tess on those lazy days."

He seemed to catch himself talking inappropriately and scratched his temple. "Not…er…for watching movies on rainy days is what I meant."

"It's okay if you spent days in your room with your wife, Jeremy."

"I know but…"

She held up her hand. "I got it." She did not need to hear about how much he enjoyed those days with Tess. And she berated herself for even feeling a tinge of envy.

In Jamie's room, the boy had a book out and was bouncing into position, getting under the covers.

"I want Adda to read first."

"It's Adeline, Jamie." Jeremy picked up the book and sat on the bed. "You're not very shy today, are you?"

"Adda Lion."

"Adda-leen."

"Adda."

Adeline laughed along with Jeremy, making Jamie laugh, too. "It's okay, I can read to him." She stepped forward, taking the book from Jeremy and shooing him off the bed.

Taking his place, she opened the book and began reading, aware of Jeremy sitting on the chair in the corner. The story was about a big, hairy golden retriever named Doug. Doug was a girl dog who struggled socially at doggy day care. The other dogs teased her because she had a boy dog name.

"*On the way home from doggy day care, Doug ran into three other dogs,*" Adeline read from the book. "*They had no home so they didn't get to go to doggy day care. 'Look. Here comes Doug,' one of the dog bullies said.*"

Jamie touched the drawing of a black Doberman between a medium-sized brown terrier and a pit bull. "They're mean."

"*'She's got a boy name,' said the brown terrier,*" Adeline went on. "*'Why'd your people name you Doug?' Doug held her tail high and said, 'They love me.' Then the three dog bullies passed. The Doberman didn't say anything. He knew Doug had a nice home and he had none.*" Adeline turned the page. "*Doug overcame her fear of the dog bullies. She felt sorry for them instead. They teased her but she didn't have to let them hurt her.*"

"Why are dog bullies mean?"

"They're jealous," Adeline said.

"What's 'jell-us'?"

She'd have to get used to talking to a three-year-old. "They just want what Doug has."

Adeline read about Doug going home to her people. Then Doug and the bullies ran into each other at a birthday party. The bullies found a home and they all started to become friends. At that point, Adeline finished to "The End."

She closed the book. "That was a good story."

"Yeah. I feel sorry for the dog bullies."

"Why do you feel sorry for them?"

"They didn't have a home."

"Well, then you got the message of the story right. And they ended up getting a home." She smiled down at him as he looked thoughtfully up at her.

"Do you have a mommy?" Jamie asked.

The question came so out of the blue she had to take a moment to assemble her reply. "Yes."

Jamie wore such a serious face for one so young. "Did she go away?"

Did he ask very many people this? He must have noticed other kids his age had both a mother and a father. Did he remember Tess? He'd only been a year old when she died. "No, but my dad did."

"You don't have a daddy?"

He couldn't possibly know what a hard question that was. "I do but he went away when I was a baby."

Jamie stared up at her, his crystal clear blue eyes wide with absorption. "Is he dead?"

"No. He didn't want to stay with me and my mother."

With that, Jamie turned and lowered his head. After a time he looked back up at her. "My mommy left me. Daddy said she had to go away."

"She didn't want to leave, sweetie. She died. I know she would have never left you if she had any say in the matter." She put her hand over his tiny one on the comforter. "It's okay. Your daddy loves you very much, just like my mommy loves me. Some of us don't have both parents, that's all."

Jeremy appeared by the bed. "Time for sleep, buddy."

Adeline stood while he tucked Jamie into the covers.

"Love you." Jeremy kissed Jamie's forehead.

"Love you too, Daddy."

Jamie's eyes closed and he began to slip into sleep. Precious. Children could fall asleep so easily.

Jeremy headed for the door and Adeline left ahead of him. Out of the room, he stopped in the loft.

"Sorry about that. I didn't mean to throw you into that on your first day here."

"It's all right. I enjoyed it." She tried to sound nonchalant, as though reading to her son and handling a serious question were no big deal. That wouldn't affect her when it came time to leave…not.

The next day, Jeremy stepped into his office building with concern weighing down his brow. He and Adeline had just dropped Jamie off at Camille and Oscar Biggs's house. Camille had offered to watch Jamie temporarily until Jeremy could find a new nanny. He and Oscar were friends as well as colleagues. Camille had told them Oscar would want to talk to Jeremy when he arrived in the office. Jeremy had received a text saying the equivalent from Oscar himself. His general counsel wouldn't relay a message like that if it wasn't important.

He guided Adeline into the elevator, vaguely aware of how she took everything in around her, from the marble lobby to the security desk and the sign in the elevator mapping out businesses on each floor. She wore her professional PI attire again, this time in a man-torturing black pencil skirt with matching vest over a white shirt. She had her trench coat over her arm, and runnable heel-height ankle boots, showcasing her leggy strides.

The elevator opened on the top floor. He walked out with her into the open reception area flanked on three sides by cubicles, the windowed walls lined with the executive offices. Adeline's heels tapped against the gray slate tile.

"Good morning, Mr. Kincaid," the receptionist greeted from behind the marble-plated half wall from her desk. She wore her black hair pulled tight into a bun. A vase of white lilies and a large round bronze clock added a touch of warmth. Light streamed through windows on each side, and irregularly placed tables with white chairs provided books and magazines catering to a variety of interests.

Jeremy guided Adeline down a hall between cubicles to the west side of the floor and his corner office.

His assistant rose from her chair when she saw him. "Oscar said to get him as soon as you arrived."

"Send him in."

"I'll wait out here." Adeline stopped near the assistant.

She and Jeremy were going to go over Tess's accident this morning and strategize on how to take his lead further. But now they had another meeting with Oscar to squeeze in.

"Oscar said to include your PI," the assistant said.

That brought both his and Adeline's head turning.

Was this related to Tess?

"I'll go get him."

Jeremy met Adeline's eyes, hers likely less astounded than his. She might expect the unexpected while working cases. In business he could handle that. This was personal, though. Oscar never insisted on talking to him so urgently. If something important came up, he usually just stopped by his office.

He remained standing with her as Oscar appeared at his assistant's desk. A shade over six feet, Oscar dressed in a suit and tie every day and kept his body in good physical condition. He wore scholarly glasses and still had a head of dark hair, clipped short and peppered with gray.

He came into the office with a curious glance at Adeline.

Jeremy introduced them.

"The PI," Oscar said, shaking her hand and giving her form a quick, purely observational once-over. "Not quite what I expected."

"Did you expect a man, Mr. Biggs?"

Jeremy couldn't tell if she sounded defensive. She didn't strike him as a woman who'd let anyone get away with treating her with anything other than respect.

"I'm not sure what I expected, Ms. Winters, but it wasn't a woman with such a fine presence."

She had a way of balancing social etiquette with a serious question, her smile engaging and, yes, her presence *was* fine…very fine. Whatever she'd sought to find out must have satisfied her.

"Thank you… I think."

Oscar put his hands together in a soft clap. "On to the purpose of this meeting."

"Coffee." Jeremy's assistant entered with a tray and put it down on a conference table.

Jeremy sat at one end, Oscar to his right, Adeline to his left. She didn't take a cup of coffee, just a glass of water. Oscar sipped from a steaming cup and Jeremy waited for his to cool.

Then Oscar put his cup down and, after a lengthy silence, finally turned to Jeremy. "What I have to say isn't easy, Jeremy."

Jeremy didn't get uptight over that announcement. He'd already anticipated something big. That it wasn't easy to say suggested this was personal. Nothing related to his business would be that shocking. Oscar must know something. No matter what, Jeremy preferred he tell him.

"You know how people talk around here. I heard you suspect Livia Colton may have something to do with Tess's accident," Oscar said.

Jeremy grew instantly more alert. Did Oscar know something about Livia that could help his case? "Yes." Why had he brought that up? Had he found a connection? Jeremy contained his flaring hope.

"How long have you suspected her?"

"Not seriously until recently. Why?"

"Why didn't you tell me?" Oscar asked.

Why would he? "I had nothing to go on, only a hunch." He waited for Oscar to tell him what he'd come to say, which seemed more and more to be a confession of some sort—a confession related to Livia's involvement in Tess's accident.

Oscar lowered his head briefly, uncharacteristic of such a powerful man. He had major difficulty with his declaration. He must have kept this secret for some time and something had compelled him to come forward.

"Before I came to work for you, I was involved with Livia," Oscar finally said, not sounding or seeming proud.

"You had an affair?" Adeline asked.

He nodded. Jeremy could see how Oscar might be ashamed of that.

"What might make you think that is related to Tess's accident?" Adeline asked.

The way Oscar turned to her and then slowly, reluctantly, met Jeremy's eyes, warned of what was about to come next.

"I was the man your witness saw meeting Tess the day of her accident."

Of all the things. Jeremy leaned back against his chair, needing the support to keep steady. Beside him, Adeline leaned over and removed her padfolio and a pen from her case. Putting them on the table, she began to write, asking, "Did you tell law enforcement this, Mr. Biggs?"

"No. I didn't see the need. Tess's accident wasn't determined to be a homicide." He turned to Jeremy. "But I see a need now. The next day when I heard she died in a car accident, I felt I was to blame."

"Her blood alcohol level was well over the legal limit," Adeline said, jotting down more on her notepad, her handwriting neat and uniform. He read her observations on Oscar's appearance. *Well-groomed. Anxious but forthright...*

Jeremy got the idea she didn't do anything halfway. Her attire was as neat and precise as her writing. Her blond hair was down but combed to a smooth, silky shine. Even her pen had the stamp of detail, with a monogram of her initials.

"Why did you meet her?" she asked, bringing Jeremy's attention back to the purpose of this meeting.

Oscar looked intent, as though working up to plead his case. "Tess asked me to. I refused the first few times, but she wouldn't stop until finally I agreed to meet her for a late lunch."

A few times? She'd had a relationship with Oscar before Jeremy met her. Had she wanted to get back together with Oscar?

Jeremy was stunned. How had he missed her unhappiness? Sure, her drinking had caused problems in their marriage. She had gone to rehab but Jeremy had always worried she might relapse. It wasn't until she died that he'd he realized she had. She hadn't been dissatisfied with him as a husband…had she?

"Jeremy, I didn't get involved with her."

"Why did she meet you?" he asked again.

In his side vision he saw Adeline carefully put down her pen, pausing in taking notes and only listening intently now.

Oscar's breath sighed out long and full of reluctance. "She wanted to start up with me again. When I refused, she left upset. I didn't know she was drinking until I heard about her accident. If I'd have known, I would have stopped her."

Looking straight ahead, Jeremy searched his memory for signs that Tess had drifted away from him to the point where she'd seek out other men. None came to mind, but the idea stung. He'd always been busy at work. Sometimes he didn't get home until after eight. They had shared many evenings together, though. She hadn't seemed unhappy.

Then he began recalling the weeks leading up to her accident. They hadn't talked much. They'd had family dinners and done things together on the weekends, but now that he thought back in more detail, he and Tess hadn't said much to each other. When they'd first met, they'd talked all the time. She hadn't had to work and used to wait for him to get home so she could eat dinner with him. Somewhere along the way she'd stopped doing that. After they brought Jamie home, the sex had almost stopped, too.

"She was drinking again, Jeremy," Oscar said in his lengthy silence. "She wasn't thinking straight."

Jeremy turned to him, a trusted employee, a trusted top executive. "You've been a good friend to me, Oscar. If she strayed, it wasn't your fault."

"I'm sorry. You've been a good friend to me, too. I should have told you sooner." He bent his head above his coffee cup and shook his head before looking back at Jeremy. "But with her dying… I… I just couldn't. I could see how much you were grieving. If I'd have been the one in your shoes, I'd have wanted the same. Time."

Two years was a long wait.

Adeline picked up her pen again. "Tess died two years ago."

Oscar didn't falter as she pinned him with that fact. "Yes. And that's why I'm sorry," he said to her. Then to Jeremy he added, "But to be honest, I don't think you've stopped grieving. When I heard about your suspicion of Livia, it dawned on me why. You've always thought Tess was murdered."

Jeremy nodded. "I've told the deputy who worked the accident but he has done nothing. That only supports my theory about Livia."

"She did have long tentacles into the community, and they didn't stop at law enforcement."

"How do you know that?" Adeline asked.

Oscar seemed to catch himself, remembering who she was, a PI Jeremy hired to look into Tess's death. And he could have possibly implicated himself. "People talk."

"She never said anything to you? You weren't aware of her meeting with anyone on the force?"

He shook his head. "No. She had lots of meetings she didn't tell me about. She wasn't an open book. She was a walking secret factory."

Adeline nodded as though she agreed. She must have heard things herself, although she had never been close enough to feel Livia's evil.

"How long did you see her?" Adeline asked.

"Six months. She never got over me breaking things off, and was always jealous when I was with other women."

"Did Livia know you met Tess?" Jeremy took up the questioning from Adeline.

"Not at first. Then she sent me a letter. Threatening me. That's another reason I wanted to meet with you, why it was so important."

"What kind of threats?" Adeline asked.

"If I didn't break up with Tess, I might start having some accidents. She said she'd haunt me from prison. Her words exactly."

Jeremy met Adeline's glance. Livia had somehow managed to get a threatening letter delivered to Oscar. Did that bring her closer to believing Livia had enough reason to go after Tess?

"When did all of this happen?" Adeline asked.

"Years after Livia and I were together. I never understood why she hung on to so much resentment for so long."

"Because she's that crazy," Jeremy said.

"What happened after she threatened you?" Adeline asked. "Did she ever haunt you?"

Oscar shook his head, propping his ankle on his knee, looking much more relaxed. "Tess broke up with me a few weeks later. Nothing unusual happened. I thought Livia finally let it go, like she was glad Tess and I split up. Tess met Jeremy about a month later. Jeremy was a good man about it. He made sure I had no hard feelings. I didn't. I knew Tess and I weren't right for each other." He looked directly at Jeremy. "I could see she loved you. I could see you loved her. It was obvious. If Livia held a grudge for years over me and Tess, she might have disliked Tess enough to go after her when she met you, a successful man who made her happy."

"I appreciate you telling me." Jeremy really was thankful for his candor. And he was relieved he hadn't been wrong about keeping him on as his general counsel. He also felt reassured that he'd let his wife, Camille, watch Jamie when he or Adeline couldn't be with him.

As he turned to see how Adeline was taking all this, he saw her scrutinizing Oscar, as though she felt the man was either a smooth talker or hiding something.

Chapter 3

"You dress differently when you go on stakeouts?" Jeremy asked.

After talking to Oscar, they decided to track down the deputy Jeremy had gone to for help on his suspicions regarding Tess's accident, the one who had brushed him off. Had Livia paid the deputy to help her go after Tess? They had picked up Jamie and then the next day found the man and followed him here, to this café. He sat by himself drinking coffee and hadn't noticed them.

Adeline glanced down at her black slacks with white-and-black patterned blouse. She'd draped her trench coat over the back of the chair. "I don't always wear vests." She did like the Sherlock Holmes kind of feeling she had when she did wear them, though.

"Maybe that's what looks so different."

She knew why when she saw him look down at her cleavage, which was modest, she knew. She never dressed sexy when she worked, but she did have some sexy clothes in her closet.

"Does it bother you?" she asked, hearing her own flirty tone.

"No. The opposite," he said with answering flirtation.

The waitress came to their table, and she and Jeremy ordered coffee.

"Who are you, Adeline Winters?" Jeremy said. "I want to know more about you, more than they tell you about family history of a surrogate mother, anyway."

Did he? Would she be wise in telling him? The tickle in her heart wouldn't allow her to decide.

"I'm just a girl from Austin, Texas, who grew up wanting to fight bad guys."

He grinned with enchantment lighting his soft, smart, daring eyes. "You must have had someone in your life who made you interested in fighting bad guys."

Like a man who'd taught her to fight? She wished her past had been that fanciful. She had to avert her face, not see his eyes.

"No," she finally said.

"No one?"

"My mom worked two day jobs, came home for a couple of hours after I got off school, then left for her night job. Every day. Seven days a week. My grandparents lived in Arizona and had given up on her before I was born. She didn't know my paternal grandparents because my dad hightailed it a few months after I was born…which you already knew." Adeline turned to the deputy sitting at the table, vaguely registering he was still alone.

"You're bitter about your childhood?"

He was really going to pry? "No. My mother was an only child. Her mother was too messed up to raise a child properly. It was just me and my mother. We only needed each other." Adeline often wished she could be part of a family of her own. She'd never experienced that.

"Is that why your mom gave up on her? Or did she abandon her?"

"She kicked her out for following in her footsteps. Mom got herself into trouble a lot and got herself pregnant. But she cleaned herself up when I was conceived. Not being like her mother was important to her."

The waitress arrived with their coffees. Adeline smelled the flavorful aroma and reached for some creamer.

"I bet your mother would have liked your dad to stick around to help." Jeremy picked up their conversation.

Adeline stirred the creamer. "She was glad my dad left. My mother is not a weak person. She didn't need anyone to take care of her. She wasn't afraid to work. She wasn't lazy. She liked hard work because it provided for me. And her. She taught me not to depend on anyone, least of all a man. Why depend on someone who won't be there when it counts?" Adeline couldn't stop the angry emotion. She hated how hard her mother had lived to provide for her daughter. It wasn't fair. Adeline took care of her mother now, but the years of hardship had taken their toll. Her mother had aged before her time. She had circles under her eyes that hadn't gone away with her lightened load, as though the man who'd gotten her pregnant had tattooed her.

As Jeremy dumped creamer into his coffee, he asked, "She talked bad about your dad?"

Adeline sipped her coffee before responding. "No, but he abandoned us. There's a difference between a father who doesn't *want* his kids and one who does but struggles to pay child support or find time outside work hours to see them or whatever. My dad didn't want me. He didn't love me and had no interest in loving me. I get it. I'm good with that. It taught me to choose the people I want in my life and not tolerate those who aren't good for me." She set down her cup, growing uncomfortable. "My father wasn't good for me or my mother."

"Do you know where he is?" He sipped his coffee.

"Yes." But she didn't care. That had been the point in finding out. She knew where her biological father was. Now she didn't have to care.

"Where? What's he doing?"

She just shook her head. Not going there. It wasn't completely true she didn't care. She hated what her father had done. She hated what he represented, the kind of man who had no heart. Maybe he was a serial killer.

"It sounds like your mother did well," he said. "Worked hard but did the right thing."

"Yes, she did." But she was lonely and unhappy, and… "I barely ever saw her, especially when I was old enough to take care of myself, which started about when I was nine. She helped me go to college. Not financially, but she helped me find and apply for scholarships." She smiled softly with the memory. "That was important to her, too." Her mother loved her daughter. Adeline had never felt the lack of that. The few quality times they'd had together were all special.

"Why didn't she find someone else? If she looks anything like you, she should have had no trouble."

That often bothered Adeline. She worried her mother had never gotten over him.

"She didn't want to. Being a mother was enough for her."

After several seconds where Adeline felt Jeremy's

doubt, he finally said, "What did your mother think of you giving Tess and I a baby?"

"She had a very open mind about it. She supported me."

He got a thoughtful look. He must come from a different kind of family. Wealthy. Elite college education. A mom *and* a dad. He had no trouble talking about his family because he came from a solid unit. While she'd come from a solid unit as well, hers was just two people: her mother and herself. She and her mother were close friends, made closer by the parental bond. She encountered few people who truly understood what it meant to be raised by a struggling single parent—at least, not that resembled her experience. And most she did encounter didn't struggle to make a living. Adeline could now count herself among that demographic. She'd risen above what her mother had endured.

"I'm sorry," Jeremy said. "I didn't mean to make you talk about anything that upsets you."

"No. I'm not upset. Don't be sorry." She warmed to his sensitivity. Had she ever met such a nice man before? "Your turn."

He chuckled softly. "All right. Well…as you know, I had a dad. He was demanding. Started teaching us at a young age. I could read junior high level by the time I was six. Forget the baseball bat and glove. It was all brains for my dad." He glanced away, the memory not seeming to sit great with him.

"No wonder you're so successful in tech start-ups," she said.

He looked at her again. "He wanted me to be a lawyer. He was so disappointed in me I joked with him that I should star in a family drama movie where the mother or father tries to force their child to be a mini version of them."

"Are you bitter?"

His discomfort eased in his eyes. "No. I'm grateful my father pushed me. I didn't like it as a kid, but I wouldn't have been as successful if I hadn't been shown the way of the world from early on."

Her mother had done similarly with her. "I can't imagine it's unusual for fathers to want their kids to be raging successes."

"No. Mothers, too. My mother stayed home to raise us. She was the supporter and my dad was the enforcer. But I wish he would have let the kid in me discover things on his own. Teach. Don't cram education down kid's throats."

She nodded. She'd had a little of both worlds. "I didn't start reading junior high level until junior high, but I was cleaning house and cooking dinner by the time I was eleven." She sipped her coffee, taking her time, then putting the cup down. "Are you from Shadow Creek?"

"No, Austin, but I've always liked Shadow Creek and moved here after college."

He must like smaller towns. So did she, as long as authorities cleaned out the people like Livia Colton. "What about brothers and sisters?"

"I have a younger sister. She's a lawyer," he said.

"Is she nice?" she asked in a teasing way.

"Yes, as long as you agree with her."

Now Adeline laughed briefly. Most lawyers she knew or heard of bulldozed their way through life—Oscar aside. He seemed nice. They might have nice qualities to their personalities but hospitality workers, they were not.

"She's single. Incurable workaholic. But she makes Dad proud."

"You adore her, don't you?" She could see his eyes and heard his tone.

"Yes. She's a lot of fun when she isn't wearing her lawyer hat."

He had the same outlook as her and Adeline wondered how many other ideas they shared in common. "Isn't your dad proud of you?"

"I think he's jealous. I followed my own path and I'm more successful than him." He didn't brag, only stated the truth. Adeline liked that. Straight shooters always appealed to her most. She'd mark that as another characteristic they had in common.

"Maybe you should remind him he taught you to read junior high level by the time you were six," she said.

"I have. Except I wouldn't say 'I remind him.' It's more like 'I accuse him.'"

She smiled at his light tone. "But you love him, don't you?"

"Of course I do. I love my whole family. We just have hot buttons like every other family."

Adeline wouldn't comment on that. She didn't know what it was like to have a dad and feel love for the man. She felt nothing but disrespect for her dad.

She checked on the deputy, amazed that she'd almost forgotten him. He'd finished eating his Danish and coffee. Was it a break and a snack or was this breakfast?

"Our friend is going to be leaving soon," she said.

"Did you ever hook up with a guy?" Jeremy asked, apparently not finished quenching his curiosity. "You're what…twenty-seven now?"

He was thirty-four. Adeline remembered when Tess

had told her about when she'd first met him, all bubbly with infatuation. Adeline had been a little green with envy over it, wanting that for herself but never having found it.

"I've had boyfriends." This was another thing she didn't talk about.

"Didn't rise to the bar?" he teased.

"I'm picky."

As he met her gaze, she felt him about to probe into why when their subject paid and stood.

"He's on the move," she said.

Jeremy had already put down cash to cover their ticket. She was relieved to be finished with their conversation, and wondered why it had begun anyway.

After three more hours watching the Nicholson's house, it had become clear the man wasn't going anywhere else. His two young kids had bounced out of the house when he'd pulled into the driveway and his wife waited with a smile in the open doorway, watching as the deputy knelt with open arms and his little girls crashed into him. Jeremy was a pretty good read on people and this guy didn't strike him as a criminal or anyone who'd associate themselves with Livia, but appearances could be misleading.

He'd driven Adeline back to his place.

Parked in front on the stone slab drive area, he wasn't ready to go inside. Once they did, she'd go off on her own. He'd keep her nearby for a while longer.

"Let's take a walk," he said. "The sun is setting. There's a lake not far from here. I want to show you."

After staring at him briefly, probably wondering why, she got out and said, "I need to change."

"We won't go far. What you have on is fine." The air had begun to chill but she had her coat. He started walking.

"Tomorrow we should hang out by the station to see if there's any connection between them and Livia," Adeline said as they walked. "I need to find evidence to support a reason that deputy might hide any involvement in causing Tess's accident."

"Okay." He was more interested in the sky changing colors than another boring day watching a clean deputy. He was also much more interested in her. The spark that had been there when he'd first met her and returned when she'd come to his office had grown into something more. Something about her drew him in. When this day ended he might address that. Right now he just wanted to take in a sunset with her.

"Nicholson may be working with someone who doesn't live as nice as he does," she said. "If he is as clean as he seems, maybe there is another who is not. That won't explain why the deputy you dealt with brushed you off, though."

She seemed to ramble on. He didn't think she was convinced any deputies were connected in any way to Tess's accident. While that rubbed him wrong, he let it go. He heard the awkwardness in her voice, as though she talked just for something to say. She was affected by their day as much as him. That pushed away any opinion she had about the accident and gave him an alluring thrill instead.

Spending time with her, talking, sharing, had kept a fire burning. Her passion talking about her family—her mother—made him curious. What about that upset her? Her mother had worked a lot of hours. Maybe she regretted not having more time together.

Her upbringing was so different from his. Different from Tess's, too. They'd both had two parents and siblings. Money.

"No more talk about surveillance." He stopped where the neighborhood ended, at a park with a lake. "Look." He pointed to the setting sun's reflection on the water, a painting of trees and a blue-and-orange sky.

"Nice." She watched with him as the colors deepened. "Why is this more important than trying to find out if Livia still has connections to dirty deputies?"

"It isn't. It's called taking a break. Unwinding."

She watched the sky a few moments longer. "Do you do this often?"

"I haven't been here since before…" He couldn't finish, or say his dead wife's name.

"You watched sunsets with Tess?"

"All the time."

"How romantic." Adeline turned her head.

"She wasn't as appreciative as I was about them."

"Sunsets?" She gave his a quizzical look, and then her expression smoothed. "Tess wasn't much for idle moments."

She faced the setting sun again. "My favorite time of day is when the sun rises, those first moments when light chases the quiet darkness away."

With a soft curve to her mouth, she turned to him again.

Their eyes met and he forgot everything but her. Wasn't this exactly why he'd brought her here? If he faced the honest truth, yes. He craved a quiet, intimate moment with her. He missed them with Tess, and now he realized he missed them in general, that close connection, the stirrings of loving feelings, companionship.

Taking her hand, he pulled her toward him, on autopilot, letting instinct guide him. She seemed to do the same, her hands going to his chest, blue eyes communicating her own rising desire. So beautiful.

He slid his other hand behind her head. "I don't know why I'm doing this. I just know I have to." With that, he kissed her, a light, warm touch that ignited more feeling than he anticipated. She responded instantly, pressing against him for more. If he gave her more, they could create something he wasn't sure he was ready to handle.

Withdrawing, he said, "We better get back."

The sky had darkened and the chill in the air had increased in the few moments that followed the setting sun.

"Yeah." She sounded relieved as she began walking ahead of him toward his house.

Flustered all the way back to Jeremy's house, Adeline still felt her lips tingle when she stepped inside through the garage. Leaving the entryway, she went into the spacious living room, the floor-to-ceiling windows dark now that the sun had set. She went to the open kitchen, removed her jacket and draped it over one of the kitchen island chairs.

"Are you hungry?" Jeremy asked, placing his jacket next to hers.

"Not terribly."

"I can order something delivered. Pizza?"

"Sure." The distraction would help get her mind off Jeremy kissing her.

As he removed his cell, a sound from upstairs made her turn and Jeremy pause.

"Did you hear that?" she asked.

"Yes. It sounded like something dropped."

"When is your mother dropping Jamie off?" he asked.

"In about an hour," she said.

"Stay here."

"Hey. I'm the one who's armed." She removed her pistol and put her other hand on his chest.

"Adeline, no. I'll go first." He took the pistol from her, making her suck in a startled breath.

Following him, she asked, "When did you learn how to shoot?"

"Shh. When I was a teenager."

She climbed the stairs after him. In the open loft, she stopped with him to listen. The sound came from here and she saw Jeremy's desk was messy and a stapler had fallen to the floor. No one had come downstairs. Did that mean someone was still up here?

Another sound coming from a bedroom down the hall made Jeremy rush in that direction. He first checked Jamie's room, and then ran to the next. Filmy curtains blew in from an open window; the screen was cut and also moving in the breeze.

Adeline rushed to look through the window and saw a man running across Jeremy's property. He had the same stature as the one she'd seen the first time she'd arrived there.

"Is that the man you chased off my property?" Jeremy asked.

"Yes, I think so. He has the same build, but it's hard to say. It's pretty dark." She left the window as Jeremy closed and locked the latch, going back into the office where things had been disturbed.

"What was he looking for?"

Jeremy sifted through the papers that had been disturbed and shook his mouse. A locked screen came up on his desktop computer.

"He couldn't have cracked my password," Jeremy said.

"Do you have anything on Tess's accident?" she asked.

He opened a file drawer and withdrew a folder. Together they looked into its contents. All he had were documents for insurance covering her accident and death, just auto and life.

"Nothing is missing," Jeremy said. "But he might have taken pictures."

"Why? None of this proves anything other than Tess died in an accident." What else could this relate to, though, if not Jeremy's action in taking a look at Tess's accident as a possible murder?

Jeremy put the file away and stood still, looking across the loft. "He must have bypassed my security."

When they'd entered she had seen him disarm the alarm and reset it. Someone had disarmed it. Had they known the code? Or somehow discovered it?

Chapter 4

Later that night, Jeremy tucked Jamie into bed and went back downstairs, where Knox Colton questioned Adeline about the break-in and the man she'd chased off Jeremy's property. Broad-shouldered and just over six feet, he now wore a sheriff's uniform and a hat over his light brown hair and blue eyes. He'd recently been elected sheriff of Shadow Creek. He had a couple of his trusted deputies searching the house for any evidence.

Sheriff Colton saw Jeremy and smiled.

Knox was one of several Coltons Jeremy had befriended over time. He knew all about their local trials and tribulations, particularly when it came to Knox's mother, Livia Colton. Without her in town, the other Coltons had a good name.

Jeremy shook his hand. "Good to see you again."

"Wish it was under other circumstances. Adeline just told me you hired her to look into Tess's accident?"

He nodded. "I can't believe she'd drive into a pole without even trying to stop or swerve, drinking or not.

It's also known Livia didn't like her, and had held a long grudge against her…"

Knox ran his hand down his stubbly face. "Yeah, I have to admit that's bothered me, too—her body not being found. And it wasn't hard to incite her wrath."

Jeremy didn't miss how he used the past tense, as though he considered Livia dead. She hadn't been much of a mother to Knox. He'd basically written her off long before she'd been sent to prison. He, as much as anyone, and maybe more, had reason to despise the woman and never trust her. She had escaped once from a maximum security prison. What would stop her from using an accident in her favor?

"What about it bothers you?" Adeline asked.

He turned patient blue eyes to her. "Growing up with Livia as a mother taught me many things about deceitful people, but she was a special case. She had an assortment of husbands she used to her advantage, worked with a criminal organization, and trafficked drugs and people."

"People?"

"Don't forget murder," Jeremy added. She may have added Tess to her list of victims.

"Yes, that, as well. I often wonder how she ended up so evil," Knox said. "Her half brother was a serial killer. Maybe that's what turned her into a sociopath. Maybe it's in her blood."

"If she's still alive, she's definitely capable of evil," Adeline said.

What hadn't that woman done? Hearing Adeline's skepticism, Jeremy subdued his rising irritation. Didn't she see why he and Knox were so concerned that Livia still walked the earth?

"That's putting it mildly. Her family history is only

part of her character," Knox said. "On top of murder and trafficking, you can add kidnapping. She kidnapped my sister Claudia's mother and took Claudia from her real Russian family. As an adult Claudia hired a PI and is now reunited with them."

"She fell in love with the PI," Jeremy added.

"Yes, she did. Hawk Huntley. He's a good man. I'm glad she found happiness after all she's been through."

"You've all been through a lot because of Livia," Jeremy said.

Adeline looked thoughtfully at Jeremy. Would she finally buy into his reason for thinking Livia could have killed Tess? He wondered if asking her to investigate had been a mistake. But then he remembered her pregnancy and the secret feelings he'd had back then, and the feelings that had renewed when he first saw her come into his office. Desire. The mother of his child...

No matter how many times he told himself the real reason he'd asked her here was for her expertise, he couldn't get past the secret feelings. Guilt stabbed as always whenever he thought of Adeline that way. He'd loved Tess.

"Your security company said someone entered the code around the time the burglar broke in," Knox said.

That's what Jeremy had figured. "Then we should talk to my ex-nanny, and maybe my general counsel, Oscar Biggs. He came to me and confessed he had an affair with Livia long before he also had an affair with Tess, and that he met with Tess the day of her accident. He said she wanted to get back together and he declined. She supposedly left upset because of that."

"When did they meet?" Knox asked.

"Oscar said for a late lunch the day of her accident," Adeline answered.

"Her accident happened later than that," Jeremy said.

"Much later," Knox added.

"Excuse me, Sheriff."

Jeremy turned to see one of the deputies holding a small device in his palm. "We found three of these planted throughout the house. We're searching for others."

Knox took the object and held it up. "It's a listening device." He looked at Jeremy. "Whoever planted them wants to know what you're doing."

"With Tess's accident?" Adeline asked, her voice full of disbelief.

"What other reason could there be?" Knox asked. "This has the earmark of Livia if I've ever seen one."

Jeremy nodded, glad he at least had the sheriff on his side. "Have you or your siblings heard from her?"

Knox scoffed. "If I had, do you think any of us wouldn't let the Feds know?"

Jeremy didn't doubt they would, but he might ask anyway.

Late the next afternoon, Adeline walked with Jeremy down the sidewalk downtown. They were going to stop in Claudia's boutique to ask her about Livia when they saw her leave and duck into an Italian restaurant. They followed.

Jeremy held the door for her and Adeline couldn't help a tiny warm smile at his considerate gesture. Claudia went to the bar area and sat with a menu. Adeline admired her black lace, fit-and-flare dress with horizontal stripe detail breaking up the floral pattern.

Adeline stopped just behind Claudia, Jeremy to her other side. Claudia didn't seem to notice them, too involved in the menu.

"The usual to go?" the bartender asked her.

"I think I'll try something new this time." She closed the menu and looked up at the bartender. "What do you recommend?"

"The chicken piccata and the herb-grilled salmon are my favorites. The salmon comes with broccoli and is a lighter option, which you seem to prefer."

"Great. I'll try the salmon, but I'd better get Hawk something else. How about the chicken for him?"

"You got it." The bartender took the menu and poured her a glass of water. "Can I help you folks?" he asked Adeline and Jeremy.

"No, thanks, we're here to see her." Jeremy pointed to Claudia, who paused as she lifted the glass to look at him.

"Jeremy Kincaid?" Swiveling the bar stool, she smiled up at him and then caught sight of Adeline. "And a friend."

He smiled. "Hello, Claudia."

She put her hands on her thighs. "Knox told me you had an eventful night."

"Someone broke in and tried to plant some bugs," Jeremy said.

"That's what Knox said. He also told me you might come talk to the rest of the Colton clan. I haven't heard from Livia and I'm sorry to say that I'm very glad about that."

"When is the last time you did hear from her?" Adeline asked.

"I'm sorry again, I didn't get your name." She tucked a few strands of her long, blond hair behind her ear.

"I'm being rude," Jeremy said apologetically. "This is Adeline Winters. She's a private investigator."

"Ah." Claudia frowned. "Did you hire her or do the two of you have a thing going?"

"I hired her."

Why had she asked if they had a thing? Was their attraction that obvious? Or maybe they looked good together.

Claudia eyed Adeline and then Jeremy. "But possibly something going on?" She winked. "It's been a while since Tess's accident. We all would love to see you moving on. Such a tragedy. How are you and Jamie doing?"

"We're doing quite well. Even better now that Adeline is here."

Claudia sipped her water through a straw and then put down the glass. "Having her around is probably good for Jamie. And you. But why the need for a private investigator?"

"He thinks Tess was murdered and Livia might have been behind it," Adeline said, hoping she didn't sound too cynical. She caught Jeremy's look and felt his offense. She didn't mean to be offensive; she just thought Livia killing Tess was a little far-fetched. She needed proof. That's why she'd become a PI. Her brain was hardwired that way. He was just going to have to adjust.

"Oh." Claudia glanced at Adeline and then stared at Jeremy. "Why do you think Livia killed her?"

"She had relations with a man Tess saw before she met me and frequently made comments about how much she disliked Tess."

"So you think she was jealous?" When Jeremy let his

original statement answer for him, she went on. "That woman has haunted us all and we've thought her responsible for many bad deeds, not all of them attributable to her."

"Which is why I need to check her out."

"Why do you think I would know anything about her? I'm hoping she's dead like the sheriff's department has assumed."

"She hasn't contacted you? She still thinks of you as one of her own, most likely," Jeremy said.

"She hasn't contacted me. If she survived that accident, she'd be careful not to get caught," Claudia said.

Adeline couldn't agree more.

"Unless I see her body, I'm not making any assumptions," Jeremy said.

"You're right. Unless there is a body, we can't be sure." Claudia's shoulders trembled. "The idea of that makes me shiver."

Claudia had likely come a long way since reuniting with her biological family. Adeline saw the pretty ring on her left finger and surmised her life had blossomed in other ways, as well. Life without Livia had grown rather rosy for her. Adeline wished she could find a real family and have her very own happy ending.

"What if she did survive?" Claudia asked, looking back at Jeremy.

"Then I'd like to find her," Jeremy said.

"And if she didn't kill Tess?" Adeline had to ask.

"Then I'd still feel good about helping to bring her back to prison."

Adeline wondered. He seemed hell-bent on proving Livia killed his wife, as though that would somehow heal the injustice of her death. Losing a loved one so abruptly couldn't be easy, but she thought perhaps he dealt with other issues. Maybe he'd gone through the grieving process but still hadn't gotten past Tess's alcoholism.

"No one else has heard from her, either," Claudia said. "Knox already asked everyone in the family. He said he was going to call and let you know. We'll see if there's any indication Livia still has deputies on her payroll, too."

"Thanks."

"And we'll let you know if we do hear from her or find out she's lurking somewhere."

Hiding out. Jeremy had a powerful sense that's exactly what she was doing. Laying low somewhere.

The bartender appeared from the kitchen carrying a bag. As he put it on the counter, Adeline smelled the food and her stomach growled.

Claudia paid for her order and then stood with the bag. "I'd stay and chat, but Hawk is waiting for me."

"Good seeing you again." Jeremy stepped back and out of her way.

"Nice meeting you," Claudia said to Adeline. "We should get together sometime." She held up the bag of food. "Maybe dinner?"

"We'd love that," Adeline said, feeling Jeremy's head jerk her way as though her ready and eager response had surprised him.

Maybe she'd even surprised herself. Meeting up with Claudia and Hawk seemed like a good idea, maybe because Claudia seemed so nice. Adeline liked real people like her. She sensed no pretense from the woman, only genuine friendliness.

When Claudia disappeared from view, she glanced at

Jeremy. Why did they remain standing there? Claudia's air had left them in the wake of her loveliness.

"Why don't we stay for dinner?" Jeremy asked. They'd found a sitter for Jamie, who wouldn't expect them until later.

"I haven't had Italian in a long time. Sure." She was starving anyway.

They approached the hostess, who led them to a cozy, white-linen-covered table nestled in a corner booth. This began to have a romantic feel. Adeline sat across from Jeremy and put her attention to the menu. The grilled salmon had smelled wonderful but she had a hunger for more traditional Italian fare tonight.

The waiter brought warm bread and Jeremy ordered a bottle of white wine that would go well with her chicken marsala.

"I think Jamie is improving with you in the house," Jeremy said.

He'd ascertained that so soon? "Really? How so?"

"He's having pancakes for the first time since Tess died. I tell him things about his mother so he grows up with a sense of who she was. She used to love pancakes."

Adeline had made pancakes for breakfast this morning. She also loved them and felt odd that Tess also had. Even more, she felt odd that Jeremy had called Tess Jamie's mother.

"He perked right up when he smelled them. Didn't you notice how happy he was?"

Yes, she had. Sometimes she just stared at his adorable face. She wanted to permanently imprint the images in her brain.

"I thought he must be like that all the time." She buried the spark of good feeling and the desire to remember Jamie's cuteness. Memories like that would become painful if she couldn't be with him as his real mother.

"No. He's been quiet and unsocial. I've been thinking about taking him to therapy, but now I don't think I need to anymore."

He thought she was therapeutic? And did she really have that much of an effect on Jamie? More of those good feelings surged up. If Jamie responded so positively, he must sense—even subconsciously—that she was someone close. Or maybe the way she treated him gave him that message. He was her son and she loved him. He must feel that love.

Should she be alarmed? She neither wanted to lead him to believe she'd be around nor allow herself to become too accustomed to being with him. In the end, if she had to give him up again, she'd go through agony, more than she had when she'd given birth to him.

She caught him watching her and saw his awkward glance away. He'd made the comment but now must wish he hadn't. Her having such a positive influence on his son suggested she might be a good addition to his recently reduced family. That presented a contemplation too serious for the near future.

The waiter delivered the wine and poured them each a glass. Adeline relaxed back against her chair and enjoyed a slow sip along with a break in conversation.

"Why haven't you had any kids of your own?" he asked.

So much for avoiding this kind of talk. Had he recovered so quickly from his last observation? Why did he ask that? Putting her glass down, she said, "I...don't really want kids." That wasn't entirely true.

"Really? Why not?"

She couldn't say that giving up Jamie had been too painful to consider having another. She'd feel as though she were trying to replace him. Did they have to talk about such a sensitive topic?

"I want to focus on my career."

"But you seem like such a natural with Jamie."

"Well… I did give birth to him."

That drew a smile from him and he didn't comment further.

"Why haven't you seen any other women?" she asked. She'd been curious of that for a while now. "It's been a long time since Tess died."

His smile vanished and he put his glass of wine down. He rested his hands on the table and looked at her as though thinking how best to respond. She doubted he did anything without doing that, without thinking things through. That's probably how he'd become so successful.

"I guess I didn't want to see any other women," he said at last. "I loved Tess, and to have that taken away so abruptly, so unexpectedly, changes a person."

She could certainly see that. She also felt a little disconcerted, being attracted to him and hearing him profess his love for his wife. Competing with the memory of another woman didn't seem wise.

"Are you afraid to give love a second chance?" she asked.

"I'm not sure I'd call it fear. I don't have any desire to feel like that again."

"Love?"

"No, the pain of losing the love."

She lowered her eyes, no longer able to meet his, and fingered her silverware. Could she say she'd been in love? She'd thought she had been, once. Then he had shown his true self and she couldn't possibly have loved that person. She'd loved the man he'd presented to her, though, a kind, mild-tempered man.

In Jeremy's case, she had some reservations that perhaps what he experienced might be magnified by the way he'd lost Tess, so suddenly and with a young child. Did he really love Tess that much? If so, she wanted no part in competing with that.

"I have to admit," Jeremy went on, surprising Adeline, "I held back with Tess because I knew she was a recovering alcoholic and I worried if she'd truly conquered that. She attended AA meetings but that started to taper off. I worried mostly for Jamie's sake. Now that she's gone and I discovered she had lost that battle, I feel partly to blame but also angry with her for keeping that a secret and for not getting help. It makes me wonder if she ever really loved Jamie as much as I did."

"I'm sure she did. Alcoholism is a disease. Maybe she wouldn't have drunk if she could have helped it, especially with Jamie in her life. I don't think she was irresponsible. She had a problem and, yes, she should have gotten help. Maybe she would have if the accident hadn't robbed her of the chance." She looked around the restaurant as the few memories of Tess came to her, smiling, sunny Tess. She faced Jeremy again. "She seemed so much stronger, like she could beat it."

He nodded. "She was strong, up until she started drinking again. I should have seen the signs."

"You can't hold on to regret." Was that what he was doing? He professed his love for Tess, but in the next breath had confessed he hadn't trusted her. He'd even said he'd held back.

Adeline grew uncomfortable with the way she internally rationalized his thoughts in a way that might open a door for her to pursue him romantically. That could come with some ramifications. He seemed reluctant to love, period.

"Why haven't you ever married?" he asked, startling her some. Why had he asked such a question?

"I'm only twenty-seven."

"That's marriage age. You've gone to college, you're established in your career. Aren't you ready yet?"

Was he asking for himself or in general? She found she hoped for the former. "I was in a serious relationship for a while. I met him in college. He told me he was going on to law school. After we graduated, we lived together. I got to work and he never went to law school. He also didn't get a job—not *any* job."

"You supported him?"

"Yes. He was looking for an easy way out. I don't think he ever really wanted to work. I think he looked for a free ride, and I was it. I heard him talking to one of his friends who must have asked why he wasn't working and he said he didn't have to because his girlfriend made enough money. I asked him to leave the next day. He refused, so the next time he left to go out, I threw all his things outside, changed the locks and got a restraining order. He tried to beat the door in. He did break a window. Luckily the police arrived right after that, or he might have climbed in and attacked me. Scariest night of my life."

Jeremy's jaw had opened farther as he listened. "Did he abuse you?"

"No, never. He never lost his temper before that, either. And I never saw him again after that night. I heard a few months later that he was working as a waiter some-where and living with his parents."

"Everybody's got to start somewhere."

She laughed shortly at his sarcasm. "I sometimes shudder to think I almost married him."

"He asked you?"

"All the time. But I didn't trust his unemployment. I didn't really mind making all the money. I actually felt proud, accomplished, empowered as a woman. I just didn't like feeling used."

Jeremy's mouth had closed by now and he looked fondly at her, turning his wineglass in a circle. "Did you love him?"

"I think I did when we moved in together."

"But then he showed his true colors?"

She liked that he was so intuitive. "Yes, I suppose so."

"How long ago was that?"

"Gosh. Four years now."

"And you tell me it's been a long time since I lost Tess." He chuckled softly, and then sipped his wine.

Their food arrived. Adeline started eating, all the while wondering how much her experience with her ex-boyfriend had tainted her appetite for love…or men. She looked across the table at Jeremy. She certainly had noth-ing to fear from him in the way of finances. With him, her apprehension in getting involved centered on Jamie and Tess. Even now a chill seized her when she thought of the day she'd have to leave. She'd lose her son all over again. She didn't think she could survive that.

Chapter 5

Driving up to sprawling Bluewood Ranch a few days later, Jeremy parked where many other townspeople had already gathered. A white tent sheltered picnic tables. Heat lamps had been placed as a precautionary measure, maybe for the evening crowd. Shadow Creek enjoyed mild winters and today's mid-October forecast called for seventy-five and sunny. A giant inflated pumpkin set the mood for the festival. While they'd come for the pony rides, the pumpkin patch would provide more excitement for Jamie.

"Ponies!" Jamie grabbed Adeline's hand and pulled. He missed Jeremy's. "Come on!"

Adeline laughed lightly and walked fast beside Jamie's short, clumsily running legs.

He had taken Adeline to her office so she could catch up on a few things and direct her deputy investigator to handle some tasks for her. Now they had the rest of the day to relax and have fun.

Jeremy spotted Halle Ford outside a corral, finishing with the saddle of one of four horses: a black mare, two chestnuts and a smaller Appaloosa mix, a breed also called Pony of the Americas.

"Jamie!" Halle crouched to greet the excited boy, her long, thick, auburn hair pulled back and wide, her cheek-creasing smile revealing perfect white teeth.

He pointed to the Appaloosa mix. "That's my pony."

"Yes, it certainly is." Halle messed up the top of his blond hair, then lifted him and plopped him on top of the pony. "Hold on."

Jamie gripped the saddle horn and petted the animal's neck with his free hand.

"Applejack is one of our most docile ponies," Halle said.

"Jamie's ridden before," Jeremy said. "Not that he's ready for a wild stallion."

Halle laughed and so did Adeline. Jeremy saw Adeline watching Jamie, seeing how balanced he was. He had an agile little body and would probably stay seated better than him.

"I haven't," Adeline said.

Jeremy stepped forward to introduce them, Jamie preoccupied with the pony. "Halle, this is Adeline Winters. I'm not sure if you've met before."

"We haven't, not formally. I've seen you in town and heard about your investigations business. Very impressive."

"Hello." Adeline smiled, seeming to like the woman instantly. There wasn't much not to like about Halle.

"Is this your ranch?" Adeline glanced around the beautiful property, so alive with activity today.

"Yes." Halle's smile faded. "I inherited Bluewood after my father was killed in a hit and run."

"Oh, I'm so sorry," Adeline said.

"Livia killed him," Jeremy said with a glance at his son, who had leaned down with a smile, his face in the pony's mane.

"She bribed the arresting officer and basically got away with murder," Halle added.

"Something she's good at," Jeremy said, seeing how Adeline caught his look and frowned back in admonishment. Surely by now she could see why he suspected Livia in his wife's death. But she still needed proof. He supposed she wouldn't be a good investigator otherwise.

Halle handed her the reins to one of the chestnuts, and Jeremy took the reins of the other and led the animal to Jamie's side.

"Are you sure we're not taking you away from your festival?" Jeremy asked as he mounted.

"I've got plenty of help. Trail rides are part of the activities today. Besides, I like going out on rides every now and then." She climbed onto the black mare and Adeline awkwardly did the same with the chestnut.

"Just grab a hold of the reins and follow Jamie," Halle said to her. "Riding horses is easy. You just tap their sides when you want to move or go faster and tug the reins left or right for turning. Pull back on the reins to stop or slow. You don't have to tug or pull very hard."

"Okay, I don't want to hurt the animal."

"You won't. These horses are very well mannered."

"That's reassuring," Adeline said, giving the horse a tug to move away from the corral fence and tapping lightly to follow Jamie's pony.

Jeremy kept his horse next to Jamie and told him to stay beside him. Halle sent her horse into a trot to take over. Then she twisted on the saddle to say, "We'll go on an easy ride. No steep hills or rivers."

"Thank you."

Jamie made giddyap chants and swung his feet out of the stirrups.

"Jamie, put your feet in the stirrups and stop fidgeting on the horse," Jeremy said.

The boy calmed and did as he was told. "It's a pony."

They reached a narrow dirt road lined with trees. Adeline rode beside Jamie, allowing Jeremy to ride beside Halle ahead of them.

"Your ranch is beautiful," Adeline said.

"Thanks." Halle twisted to look back at her. "My father loved this place. It's my goal to keep his memory alive by making it thrive. It's been a challenge but I believe it will work out."

"Did Livia bribe deputies often?" Adeline asked.

Jeremy was glad she'd decided to dig for information. Anything to make her believe Livia capable of murdering Tess. If she believed, then she'd prove Livia's guilt.

"It's pretty common knowledge around these parts that she had several dirty deputies on her payroll. If any of them looked into Tess's accident, and Livia had anything to do with it, you can bet they didn't look close enough."

"We've checked into the deputy who wrote the accident report," Adeline said. "So far nothing suspicious has come up."

"If she can cover up a hit and run, she can cover up an accident." Halle looked over at Jeremy.

Halle might be a little biased when it came to Livia, but Jeremy had to agree. Livia could cover up almost anything. He looked back at Adeline, who averted her face as though taking in her surroundings. She'd stick to her process and let the evidence tell her what had really happened. Jeremy would settle for that—for now.

Adeline grimaced as she dismounted from the horse. They had only gone for an hour-long ride but that was enough to have an impact on her muscles. Jeremy grinned over at her as he handed his reins to a groom.

"I don't wanna get off yet," Jamie whined. He'd complained as soon as he saw they were headed back to the corral.

"We still have the pumpkin patch to visit," Jeremy said, lifting the boy off the horse.

"But I like Apple," Jamie protested, his blue eyes a well of young sorrow.

Jeremy chuckled, having seen the same as Adeline had. "Let's go see what else we can do here. It'll be fun."

A groom led the pony away and Adeline thought Jamie would tear up. She took his hand. "Come on. I heard they have games and cotton candy."

"Cotton candy?" Jamie skipped alongside her, and they headed for the tent, where grills smoked and the aroma of burgers, brats and dogs filled the air.

"Nothing like a fall barbecue," she said.

"The climate is good here," Jeremy said.

"Really good today." She lifted her head to the sun, closing her eyes briefly.

At the cotton candy kiosk, Adeline retrieved one for Jamie and handed it to him. He happily ate away at the sweet confection.

Jeremy steered them toward a face-painting canopy. Jamie insisted on having his done as a horse head. Adeline chose to have a sunflower, with her nose the center and petals fanning out from her eyes, cheeks and chin. Jeremy asked for a scary pumpkin face.

Adeline laughed at the jagged teeth the artist painted, making Jamie laugh with her. Seeing a photo booth, she took the boy's hand and pulled him inside, Jeremy following. She made a funny face as the camera began shooting. Jamie's high-pitched laugh rang in her ear along with the deep baritone of Jeremy's.

The photos dispensed and she took them outside, where the three of them looked and laughed some more. Next they picked out pumpkins and went into the tent for lunch.

Adeline noticed certain people staring at them, mostly women who wore fond, admiring expressions. She and Jeremy did make an attractive couple, if she could say so herself. Add a cute kid and they were a stunning family. Jamie did look a lot like her, as he should. He was her living, breathing, real-life son. She looked at him a long time, marveling over that.

He took notice and after a bit, between messy mouthfuls of a ketchup-loaded hotdog, made a face at her. Loving his playfulness, she made one back. He shoved a huge bite into his mouth, ketchup oozing from the corners. Adeline took a big bite, too. Jamie laughed and for a moment she feared he'd choke, but his little mouth worked to chew.

Jeremy reached over with his finger and wiped the corner of her mouth. She lifted her napkin and wiped just in case.

"You two are having too much fun."

She looked up to see sheriff Knox Colton approach with his pretty wife, Allison and adorable son, Cody.

Allison's long, dark blond hair was pulled back and her hazel eyes sparkled in complement to her green shirt.

"It's so nice to see you with someone, Jeremy," Allison said. "What a handsome family you make."

"Careful, honey, Adeline here is a private investigator, not his girlfriend."

"She's Jamie's mother." Obviously realizing what she'd just said, Allison put her hand to her mouth with a "whoops."

Jamie looked at Adeline. "You're not my mommy,"

"No, but I'd consider myself lucky if I was," Adeline said in an attempt to buffer the blunder. She winked at Jamie, who hesitantly smiled.

"We'll leave you two to your private moment," Knox said, putting an arm around his wife's waist. "Let's go get some lunch, honey."

"Okay, darling."

Adeline admired them as a couple as they walked away. Their love was so obvious, even without the sweet talk.

As Adeline and Jeremy picked up their things to leave, she spotted Claudia talking to Knox. Adeline waved, Jeremy doing the same before he took Jamie's hand. As they left the tent area, he took the other pumpkin from Adeline. She took Jamie's hand since both of his were now full. They walked toward the parked vehicles.

Holding Jamie's hand and watching his little legs take him along between her and Jeremy, and then looking up at Jeremy's handsome profile, she began to feel as though she truly belonged in this family. She felt like Jamie's mother, and Jeremy... She caught him looking at her with manly appreciation. She dared not finish her thought. That precarious trail would not lead anywhere safe.

The ride home and entering Jeremy's home like a family left Adeline quiet with an increasing sense of dread. What if she couldn't control her feelings toward Jeremy? They had a definite physical attraction and a growing intellectual connection. Add their son into the mix and things became complicated.

They baked cookies and let Jamie watch a movie after dinner. Family time. Now Jeremy took their son upstairs. Adeline had planned to wait downstairs, but the tug in her heart brought her upstairs and to the open door.

Jeremy finished reading a story, stopping before the ending because Jamie fell asleep. Then he joined her in the doorway. Adeline wasn't ready to stop looking at the boy. She'd made that cute little bundle.

"He's such a good kid," she said.

"Yeah."

"That says a lot about his daddy." Tess hadn't lived long after Jamie was born. A lot of who Jamie was must have been shaped by Jeremy. He appeared to be doing a wonderful job as a single dad.

"He had a nanny, too."

The nanny hadn't sounded like a very good influence. "Don't be shy. Jamie is good because of you."

Jeremy looked toward the bed with her and she could feel his love for the boy. Adeline felt the same, even though she hadn't been close, only gave birth to him. The powerful seed had rooted, though. She felt a strong connection to Jamie that had only cemented itself inside her ever since arriving there.

"He does look a lot like you. Sometimes he reminded me of you."

His confession surprised her. He'd thought of her while he was married to Tess? Only because she'd been Jamie's biological mother. He couldn't have had romantic thoughts about her...could he?

"I see you in him, too," she said. Then made the mistake of turning to look at him in this warm, intimate moment.

His eyes took on that same look she'd seen at the festival. Sharing a child together had cast some sort of mysterious spell on her. Him, too, as he showed when he slid his hand to her waist and pulled her closer while he brought his head down. Just before his lips touched hers, Jamie said, "Daddy?"

Adeline jerked back and so did Jeremy.

"Is that Mommy?"

"It's Adeline, sweetie," she said.

After a brief pause, Jamie propped himself up on his elbows, blinking sleepily. "Why was Daddy holding you like a mommy?"

He must have seen other parents embrace.

"Go to sleep, buddy." Jeremy walked into the room and bent to press a kiss to Jamie's forehead.

Adeline left the doorway and went to her bedroom. She would read or something, anything to get her mind off Jeremy.

Later that night, Jeremy gave up trying to sleep and threw the covers off himself. He got up and left the room in his underwear. Maybe some milk would help him get to sleep. And maybe getting up and moving around would redirect his thoughts. All he could think about was the way Adeline had smelled and the warmth radiating from her soft body when he'd pulled her close. That, and imagining what her mouth would feel like if he kissed her...really kissed her.

Getting a glass of milk, he saw rain falling through one of the kitchen windows, reflected beneath the outer lighting at the end of his driveway. Taking his drink, he left the kitchen and passed through the family room to double doors leading to a sunroom. The doors were already open. Slowing, he approached.

He didn't hear anyone inside, so he peered in and saw Adeline sitting with her legs curled up, leaning back against an oversize sofa. She jerked when she grew aware of him.

"Sorry. I didn't mean to sneak up on you." He entered the room, putting down his milk on a side table.

"Can't sleep, either?" she asked.

"No." If she only knew why. Maybe she did. Maybe her reason matched his.

She leaned her head back against the sofa. He changed the furniture in the room during the fall and winter months for warmth. During the summer, he had more patio-like furniture installed.

"I love the rain," she said.

"Me, too. That's why I had this room added." Going to a standing patio heater, he turned it on and then slid open the door, leaving the screen door shut. Then he went to the sofa and sat beside her.

Rolling her head, she looked at him. "What do you love about it?"

"It's peaceful."

"I love the sound and the smell." She breathed in and

looked up at the glass ceiling, peppered with drops of rain and rivulets.

Rainwater ran through the downspouts and trickled onto the rock border around the house. The soggy patter on glass and grass added to the melody.

"Today was nice," he said.

"Yes."

She sounded noncommittal. He'd noticed a few times when she'd gone from enjoying the day to thoughtful and silent. What had been on her mind?

"Can I ask you something?" He saw her relaxed eyes widen a bit and she turned to him.

"Sure."

"Was it difficult to give up Jamie?"

She stared at him awhile and then turned her face away. "What kind of person would I be if it wasn't?"

That wasn't really an answer. She seemed to make light of something she felt strongly about.

"I was glad he was going to a good home," she said.

"But you questioned giving him up?"

"That was the agreement. I needed money, and you and Tess wanted a baby. She told me once how much she wanted one of her own."

"She did." Sometimes he wondered if Tess had felt threatened that Adeline had been Jamie's biological mother. Could she tell he'd thought of Adeline at all? He hoped not.

He didn't press Adeline for a more direct answer. By her evasiveness, he knew giving up Jamie must have been hard.

"I did go through some postpartum depression," she finally said.

"I'm sorry." He still didn't understand how any

woman could give up their child, but he was glad she had. Jamie was everything to him.

"I'm glad you didn't." Her eyes blinked with unpretentiousness. "I don't regret being your egg donor and surrogate. Jamie had two good parents. And if I hadn't done it, he wouldn't be here. He's adorable and precious."

Jeremy chuckled. "He is." But he also only had one parent. The last two years had been rocky for him. Only one thing worked in his favor—if anything good could come of such tragedy, his son had been too young to really know what he'd lost. Having his biological mother still alive might help him later in life.

Thinking along those lines unsettled Jeremy. Every time he contemplated finding another woman to share the rest of his life, he felt sick. Dread described the feeling well. He never wanted to feel like that again, that loss and being left to raise a young child alone. He worried a lot over how Tess's death would affect Jamie, over whether or not he'd be a good father.

"I've always been so grateful to you." He met her eyes, trying to convey his sincerity. "You have no idea what he means to me. I love him so much. It's…indescribable, the intensity of that love."

"I think I do have an idea," she said. "I felt it the moment I held him for the first time."

Their gazes locked in that moment. Jeremy felt a bond cement between them, one only a mother and a father could have. He let the feeling take him without concern over consequences.

He leaned toward her, turning his head to bring his lips to hers. The first featherlight touch seared him with sensation. When she put her hand on his face, he deepened the kiss.

An instant later, she answered his passion. He leaned more, pressing her down onto the sofa. She bent one knee and his hardening erection found itself against her groin. The shock of sensation pushed him to the brink of no control.

Jeremy went still. If they took this any further...

"Jeremy?"

He heard her alarm and moved back. She seemed to have snapped out of the spell with him.

"I'm sorry... I..."

"It's okay." She swung her legs over the sofa and stood, hurrying off toward the stairs. "Good night."

It would be a long night for him. He wouldn't be able to fall asleep anytime soon. Not with a hurricane of passion urging him to go after her and seduce her into finishing what they'd started.

Chapter 6

Breakfast with Jeremy and Jamie had become a delight-
ful routine over the last several days. Jamie loved pancakes and a fair amount of discipline had to be applied
to keep him from demanding them every day. Adeline's
disconcertion had intensified after dropping the boy off
at her mother's house.

Now she sat with Jeremy at a downtown café, where
he had asked her to meet. She had some down time
while she had assigned her assistant to look into Tess's
activities prior to her accident. This felt like a date,
which made her uncomfortable. Alone with Jeremy, she
couldn't ease the invisible and powerful awareness of
him as a man, and remember every detail of last night.
How close they'd come to making love...

"I should get going," Adeline said. "I need to check
in at the office."

"Okay." He seemed equally uncomfortable.

Adeline began to gather her things when she caught
a glimpse of a man entering the café. Tall and well built
for a man of about sixty, he had close-shaved gray hair

and steel blue eyes in a blocky, masculine face. He approached a table where she recognized the deputy who had brushed Jeremy off over Tess's accident.

"Look," she said to Jeremy.

Jeremy looked at the deputy and then the man approaching the table.

"I don't believe it," Jeremy said.

"What?"

"That's Evan Sigurdsson. My former CFO. I fired him for sexual harassment."

This had gotten much more interesting. She abandoned gathering her things. "How long ago?"

"A little more than a year."

Then he couldn't have had motive to kill Tess, could he? Tess had died two years ago. Unless Tess had known something that threatened him, Oscar had no motive. That left Livia. If Tess had been murdered, it seemed she'd turn out to be the most likely suspect.

Together they watched Evan sit with the deputy awhile.

"I had trouble with Evan before Tess's accident," Jeremy said, bringing Adeline's attention swinging back to him. "The first time someone accused him of sexual harassment, I gave him a warning. He didn't take it well. He argued that I took the side of subordinates who were trying to sabotage him. I threatened to fire him right then if he didn't stop. That was about a week before Tess's accident."

So he'd gone less than a year before getting caught again? He must have harassed other women before that.

"What happened?" This could mean something to her investigation. Now he might give her some kind of motive.

"Evan has a very personable way about him. He can be charming and funny. At first impression he's a harmless guy. I was stunned to learn what he did. Then I realized he is a man who works hard to hide what he really is. By the time the accountant came forward, she had been harassed for several months. The last straw came when Evan made her work late, not an unusual occurrence, but he became much more aggressive. He asked if she ever fantasized about having sex on a conference room table. When she tried to leave, he said they still had work to do and touched her rear. She managed to get away with him threatening she'd lose her job. The next day she went to Human Resources. Human Resources informed me and I hauled Evan into my office. After I explained everything, I told him he'd apologize to the accountant and if he so much as smiled wrong at her I'd fire him."

"How did he take that?"

"Not well. He denied everything. I told him he was lucky I was giving him a second chance. I wanted to fire him but took the recommendation of my head of HR to give him one warning, since the employee had agreed not to press charges. I said he'd be watched from then on."

"He must have done it again."

"Yes. Unfortunately, I didn't have cameras inside offices and conference rooms. He behaved wherever security could keep an eye on him. He never harassed the accountant again and I moved her to another manager so she wouldn't have to work with Evan. As it turns out, she ended up finding another job a few months later. I did give her a bonus and a raise but she wasn't comfortable working at the same company as Evan."

Adeline wasn't sure how she'd react if she was in the same situation. Give him a good knee to the groin. Press charges. Yes, she'd press serious charges. But some women didn't want the trouble or the disruption to their lives. It wasn't worth the unhappiness. Adeline had aspired to work in law enforcement, so bringing the law down on a man like Evan would have been no trouble for her.

"Then his executive assistant came forward," Jeremy said. "Evan chose her for his next target when he couldn't pick on the accountant anymore. She was much more vulnerable, lower on the pay grade in a role that had her doing whatever he asked. I brought her into my office a few times to see if he was treating her well. Although she never revealed anything untoward, I sensed some fear in her. I gave her the name of someone in HR to contact if Evan did anything inappropriate. I gave her examples, too. It could be anything from telling her she looked pretty to threatening her job if she turned him in. I reassured her Evan would not be allowed to fire her and if he did anything to her that made her uncomfortable he'd be the one fired. I told her he'd already been warned. He wouldn't get a second chance.

"A few days later she'd reached out to the HR contact. Turned out he was threatening her. He also made her wear low-cut dresses or shirts and just before my meeting with her he cornered her in a conference room and made advances. She managed to get away, again with Evan threatening her job."

"That's when you fired him?"

"That same day. I had Security haul him out the door in front of everyone."

"How did he react to that?"

"He shouted threats to me the whole way. Apparently he didn't think I could—or would—fire him. I encouraged the assistant to file charges but she refused. Instead, I did the same as I did with the accountant, gave her a bonus and a raise."

She stared at Jeremy awhile.

"Do you think he could have killed Tess?" she finally asked.

He shook his head. "Why? He wasn't fired back then. He got away with harassing the accountant. He and I didn't get along well after that, but I don't think he had reason to go after my wife."

She agreed. If Tess's accident had been staged, Livia made a better suspect. She had motive. The timing for Evan's motive was off.

Checking on Evan and the deputy, Adeline noticed Evan had grown agitated and the two talked in low tones. The deputy leaned forward and said something back to Evan through gritted teeth.

Evan reached inside his jacket and retrieved an envelope, sliding it across the table toward the deputy. Nicholson took it and stood, saying something to Evan before walking out of the café.

"Let's go find out what's in that envelope." As Adeline stood, she caught Evan glancing over at them. His eyes narrowed when they landed on Jeremy. Naturally, he wouldn't be fond of the man who'd canned him.

She slung her briefcase over her shoulder and started for the door. Evan watched them go with unfriendly eyes. He had a chilling look to him, that direct stare, strong and full of animosity.

She and Jeremy left the café.

"Why did you bring that thing?" Jeremy nodded toward the briefcase she often carried with her during investigations.

"The documents you have on Tess's accident. I found a crash expert I want to go see. I've got an appointment for later today."

"Why a crash expert?"

"I want to see if we have a good reason to suspect foul play." She didn't sugarcoat.

As expected Jeremy became annoyed. "We have good reason, Adeline."

"I want an expert's opinion." She would not sacrifice her detective work to placate his adamancy that Tess was murdered. He was too personally tied to the accident and the loss of his wife. Adeline had studied everything Jeremy had collected, including the accident report and the insurance claim.

Outside, Adeline spotted the deputy getting into his marked car. She walked close to the curb as they passed the parallel-parked vehicle. Nicholson opened the envelope and took out some cash. Adeline saw enough to recognize they were one-hundred dollar bills. Not an alarming amount but the fact that it was cash indicated something nefarious. The deputy put the money back into the envelope and dropped it onto the passenger seat, looking up through the window as she and Jeremy passed. He didn't seem affected by her, but when he looked at Jeremy, his brow lowered a fraction. He hadn't noticed them in the café. She walked on, as though thinking nothing of seeing him inspect an envelope full of cash.

Why had Jeremy's former CFO given a deputy cash? They'd met in public so neither man had feared being seen. Maybe they were just friends and Nicholson had done Evan a favor. But maybe the favor hadn't been legal.

The crash expert ran his own agency and handled cases for insurance companies and individuals seeking to prove liability in court proceedings. He also had handled a handful of homicides, which was why Adeline had chosen him.

A short, plump man who resembled Danny DeVito smiled wide and shook first her hand, then Jeremy's.

"I did a little reading before you arrived." The crash expert held Jeremy's hand a moment longer than typical. "I'm very sorry for your loss."

"Thank you."

The man stepped back and gave them an exuberant welcome to his office with a sweeping hand gesture.

Adeline sat before his desk beside Jeremy.

He sat across from them. "I understand you suspect your wife may have been murdered?"

"Are you familiar with Livia Colton?" Jeremy asked.

The man's brow rose, creasing his high forehead. "Ah. Why, yes. Is there anyone in this town who isn't familiar with that name? I read in the news she drowned when the prison transport vehicle was washed downstream. Good riddance, wouldn't you say?"

"Her body was never recovered," Jeremy said.

After a few seconds, the man said, "And you think…"

Adeline sensed the crash expert's skepticism and knew that wouldn't settle well with Jeremy.

"I discovered my wife had an affair with one of my employees, who also happened to have been with Livia long before this," Jeremy said.

He didn't sound defensive. Jeremy's confidence didn't allow intimidation or irrational emotion, not that she'd seen so far. He had his conviction and stood by it, a steadfast, stoic man. One more thing to admire about him—and to attract her.

"You suspect that perhaps Livia took her revenge and tampered with Tess's car?" the crash expert asked.

"I suspect she arranged for someone to do something to cause her accident," Jeremy said definitively. "Livia was in prison."

The crash expert put on a very businesslike face and folded his hands together on the desk. "I've gone over everything you sent me." He glanced at Adeline as though he found allegiance with her. "The report is thorough. The officer questioned witnesses and captured all their information along with insurance information. None actually saw the accident itself, only saw the car pass unsteadily and faster than the speed limit. There were no skid marks, and it appears the driver lost control and crashed into the light pole."

"Yes, that appears to be what happened," she said.

"The weather was clear that night and the road well lit."

"Yes."

"The officer noted he smelled alcohol in the car."

"She was drinking," Jeremy admitted. "Would you mind telling me your background? I only just today learned we were meeting." He glanced accusingly at Adeline.

She remained quiet but used her eyes to say he should know why.

"I'm an engineer and an automotive technologist. I

specialize in recreating crashes. I've been doing this for more than twenty years now."

Adeline saw how Jeremy couldn't refute the man's experience. He said nothing.

"Now, before we go on, I'd like to develop a computer-generated scale diagram. The report included a vehicle inspection, which documented the measurement of the amount of damage and the damage profile. I see an independent mechanical inspection was done."

"Yes," Jeremy said. "I had a mechanic go over the car."

"That's good. He was very meticulous and his report was very useful to me. The brakes, steering, tires, suspension and lights were all in good working condition, but there was a lot of contents in the vehicle."

"Tess went shopping the day before," Jeremy said. "She must not have brought the items into the house."

The crash expert nodded. "Cause of death was blunt force trauma to the head. The mechanic noted the headrest had broken off during the accident. One could speculate the headrest had been tampered with and caused the death. However, reconstructing the crash, I find it highly unlikely this was deliberate. I used the damage profile to calculate the speed at which the vehicle struck the tree. Analyzing other things along with this—the vehicle's position during the accident sequence, direction of travel, the absence of skid marks, point of impact, impact angle and weights of the vehicle—all of these point to a driver not braking when they lost control of the vehicle and crashed into the tree. The headrest was damaged from the door frame bending inward. That's what struck the victim's head. A heavy item in the back of the car passed by the damaged headrest and struck the windshield. The only other way I can see this could be a homicide is if the suspect were present at the crash site. Perhaps he or she was in the road or driving on the road. However, none of the witnesses reported seeing anyone or anything like that. There were no other cars near the victim's. There were no other pedestrians."

"So, in your opinion, you don't suspect foul play," Adeline said.

"No, I don't, but there was a dent in the back wheel well panel that doesn't fit a head-on crash with a pole. Did you see it?"

"No." Adeline saw Jeremy's rising enthusiasm that the crash expert had found something significant. "Does that indicate someone could have driven her into that pole?"

"Maybe, but why in that location? She could have easily driven into someone's yard. I agree the dent might be enough to cause some suspicion, but it might not be enough to indicate someone tried to drive her into a pole. Something like that would be difficult to plan, much less execute. How does anyone deliberately send another car head-on into a pole of their choosing? I'm not saying it's impossible, I just think it's unlikely. It's also hard to tell from the photos, but the dent appears to have been caused with less force than you'd expect from a car running into the side in an attempt to crash it."

"But it's not impossible," Adeline said, more to placate Jeremy. "Someone like Livia would try to drive an enemy into anything. City streets have lots of objects to run into. It didn't have to be that particular pole."

"A very good point. It's not impossible."

He still wasn't convinced, though. Adeline didn't comment further.

"There was no dent in her car the morning I left the house, the last time I saw her alive," Jeremy said.

"I'm sorry, but I don't think it is related to the accident that killed your wife, Mr. Kincaid."

"So you think it magically appeared sometime before that?"

Adeline could tell Jeremy was becoming annoyed and almost couldn't blame him. The crash expert had decided he didn't believe Tess's accident was caused by someone who meant her harm. He wouldn't be swayed.

On the other hand, Jeremy bulldozed his way into making others agree with him that Livia killed Tess. She was afraid he'd overlook evidence in his stubbornness.

The crash expert didn't engage Jeremy. He only said, "Again, I'm very sorry for your loss."

Jeremy abruptly stood. "Livia could have been there. She would have made sure no one saw her. And if I know Livia—and I do—she *could* have planned to run Tess off the road."

"I understand," the expert said neutrally. "But I have to look at the evidence at hand, and in my opinion, none of that points to murder."

"That's the nature of murder." Jeremy's voice rose. "The killer doesn't want to get caught!" He stormed out, heading for the door.

Adeline thanked the crash expert, who handed her a copy of his findings, and then hurried after Jeremy. She felt for him, but he had to see he might be reaching here.

"I'll go over the reports and question the witnesses again," she said, fumbling to get the crash analysis report into her briefcase. "And I'll talk to Tess's friends. They might know something." She saw him relax a little.

"You should have told me you contacted a crash expert," he said.

"It's standard procedure for me. I work with evidence, just like that man said. We have to rely on the evidence. Without it, we have nothing, Jeremy. Please try and understand that."

He relaxed further and stopped outside on the sidewalk, facing her. "I do. I'm sorry. I don't mean to be difficult."

Her heart melted at his easy softening. He was so even-tempered. She smiled. "Don't worry about it." She stepped closer and elbowed his arm. "Just let me do my job, handsome."

He grinned and the moment switched back to where they'd left off last night. Then she caught herself in this flirtation and started walking.

"You really think I'm handsome?"

A handsome widower who still mourned his wife's death. She sent him a look that should let him know she wasn't playing.

"I think you're beautiful," he said.

Why was he talking this way? Was he happy she'd keep investigating? Maybe romancing her into doing a thorough job? He should know by now that she would. Or had their near sexual encounter gotten him thinking?

"Have you changed your mind about seeing other women?" She had to ask to protect herself. She needed to know where he stood in that regard.

He walked a few steps without answering, as though the flirtation had been fun but now she'd asked a serious question.

"I don't know. I haven't really given it much thought."

She walked beside him awhile.

"I'm not ready to feel that way for anyone yet. Losing her..." He trailed off.

Adeline felt the pain he must have gone through, losing his wife with such a young child. Those months leading up to her death must have been magical, a new baby with a woman he loved. How could he and Tess have been anything but floating in the clouds with happiness? And then to have that ripped apart so suddenly must have been terrible, unimaginable.

Was he afraid to fall in love again?

Adeline didn't fear love. She had a healthy respect for it. Trust the wrong man and love would end up hurting her. Trust the right man and love would flourish. She'd have what Jeremy had with Tess.

The more her thoughts took her down that path, the more a sense of foreboding mushroomed, blooming from her core into a full-fledged warning.

She could not allow herself to have any feelings for him, not until she knew she could trust him.

"I also won't risk Jamie's well-being," Jeremy said.

Why not make her apprehension worse?

He did when he went on. "He doesn't remember his mother. Someday that's going to be tough on him."

"Maybe. Are you going to tell him about me?"

Jeremy stopped at the car and faced her. "I hadn't really thought about it. Tess and I talked about it and didn't come to a decision. And then she died. I'm not sure how that will affect him."

"Well, if you never marry again, it might affect him a great deal."

"It would have to be the right woman."

"I couldn't agree more." She could be blatantly honest on this. "I won't make the same mistake I made before. If

I ever fall in love again, I'll trust the man." She'd never told anyone that before. Why had she confided in him?

Moving around him, she got into the passenger seat.

Jeremy went around to the driver's side. When he closed the door, he started the engine but didn't drive anywhere.

"You said you loved the man who used you," he said.

"I also said I didn't trust him." And she hadn't. She'd loved the man she met in college, not the man she'd lived with. Blindly. Impulsively. Now she knew she had to wait, to know for sure she could trust.

"Do you trust me?"

What a loaded question. She turned to study his face, which he kept straight forward. Was he testing her? For Jamie? Checking to see if she was worthy? Adeline couldn't be sure. She could only be honest.

"I don't know you well enough to say."

Then he turned, his eyes soft and warm. "Maybe we should rectify that."

Did he intend to do some exploring? Adeline felt herself recoil, that earlier foreboding returning. She didn't mind getting to know him and he her, but this wasn't going anywhere beyond friendly unless she had some assurances.

Chapter 7

Jamie finished eating his chocolate chip pancake topped with whipped cream and more chocolate chips. Adeline finished cleaning up the mess they'd just made. She was beginning to really love the mornings when she and Jamie shared pancake breakfast. Those were her favorites as a kid, too.

"Are we going to the park today?"

She turned from the sink, drying her hands. Why had that idea popped into his head?

"You want to go to the park?"

Jamie swung his little legs from the island stool, having to think of his answer. "Daddy said Mommy took me there."

"Oh. Do you remember going with her?" She went to him and smoothed his hair.

"No."

"Did you hear your daddy talk about going there?"

"Yeah. He said Mommy liked it."

She wondered if he wanted to go to see what it was like, maybe so he could imagine going with his mother as he must have done with his father or nanny, whom he hadn't had a chance to know. If only she could tell him Tess wasn't his biological mother. She wished Jamie knew who she was.

And along with that powerful desire came another wave of foreboding.

"Let's get you cleaned up. I've got some errands to run and maybe we'll have time to stop by the park on the way to see your dad." Jeremy had invited them to his office for lunch today. And wouldn't that be a family affair? She got tickles in her stomach that subdued her foreboding, which could be a dangerous thing.

Jamie bounded up the stairs ahead of her. She followed him into the bathroom first and ran some water. In his superhero PJs, he started making faces at himself in the mirror.

Adeline wet a cloth with warm water and scrubbed all the chocolate off his face and hands. She made a face with him in the mirror. She stuck her tongue out the side of her mouth and made her eyes cross.

Jamie laughed and did the same. He looked so much like her she laughed with him. Instinctively, she leaned over and kissed the top of his head.

Their fun eased and Jamie continued to observe her in the mirror.

"Are you going to be my mommy?" he asked.

Shock rendered her speechless for a second. "I don't know. Would you like that?"

"Other kids have mommies."

"Yes, they sure do." She crouched in front of him. "Tell you what. Let's get you cleaned up and dressed and then we'll decide later, okay?"

"Okay."

* * *

Ready for her day in a chain-trimmed bouclé tweed, light gray-and-black collarless jacket over a white silk camisole and straight-legged black pants, Adeline still floated on a cloud of bliss as she drove with Jamie in the backseat. She'd dressed him in jeans and a superhero long-sleeved T-shirt under his sporty blue windbreaker. She felt so good she didn't even attempt caution. The damage to her heart could be devastating if she continued, however. If she became too attached to this child—to her child—what would she do when the time came to part ways?

Through the rearview mirror she noticed a black Suburban followed her too closely. She turned on her blinker and moved into the right lane. The Suburban moved behind her, not using a blinker.

"What the…"

Adeline slowed down. Maybe the driver would tire of following her. He didn't. She tried to get a good look at him but he wore a black hat and sunglasses. He had the same build as the man she'd chased from Jeremy's property, from what she could see of his upper torso.

Heading into a turn in the road, Adeline drove past a stand of trees. The landscape opened up after that, with a hill sloping off on the right. As the hill steepened, the Suburban switched lanes. Finally. Maybe that flash of apprehension had been nothing, after all.

The Suburban drove up alongside her. She glanced over just as it veered into her lane. With a gasp, she steered to the right. The road dropped off at the steep slope. She couldn't move over any more.

The Suburban hit the driver's side. Adeline lost a little control, braking to get out of the way. From the backseat, Jamie screeched. The Suburban braked with her, and the driver steered into her vehicle again. She narrowly missed the edge of the road and the steep drop-off. Braking harder, she reached into her jacket and retrieved her pistol as the car came to a stop. She kept the gun hidden from Jamie but carried anyway because of her other client.

Ahead of her, the Suburban backed toward her; as he passed beside her, she rolled her window down and stuck the pistol out. The man saw her and sped faster backward. She fired and missed.

Adeline pressed on the gas and drove fast down the road. The Suburban chased behind. The landscape evened out and the first sign of the town came into view. The Suburban grew more and more distant, and then stopped altogether and turned around on the road.

"Why did that man hit us?" Jamie asked.

"Are you all right?" She twisted briefly to check on him, anger rising fast and intense that someone had tried to run her off the road with a small child in the car. Her child.

"Yeah."

Putting her gun away, she slowed to a stop along the side of the road and dug out her cell phone. She called 9-1-1 and explained what had just happened. The dispatcher told her to stay where she was.

Less than three minutes later, a sheriff's car drove up. It was Knox.

"Stay in the car, Jamie." Adeline got out and met Knox as he did the same. "A man just tried to run us off the road." She pointed. "Back there where the slope gets steep down to the river."

Knox glanced back and then faced her again. "Are you okay?"

"Yes, we're both fine." But they almost hadn't been. "It was a man in a black Suburban, a newer model."

"You didn't happen to get the plate on it, did you?"

"No." She'd been too busy keeping the car on the road and getting away from the man.

Knox inspected her damaged car and then went back to his car and radioed for backup, instructing his deputy to drive the road to see if they could find the Suburban. After that, he started making notes for his report.

Adeline called Jeremy and let him know what had happened. He'd been earnest in asking if they were okay and then said he'd come and get them. The car would be towed for repairs. While she was still on the phone, another car drove up and she recognized the deputy who had dismissed Jeremy's concern that Tess had been murdered, seeing his name tag. Nicholson. She already knew his first name was Rusty.

He walked toward her and Knox. Ending the call with Jeremy, she faced the other deputy with Knox.

"Any trouble here?" the deputy asked.

"A man driving a black Suburban tried to run this woman and her young boy off the road," Knox said, surprising her by referring to Jamie as her boy. "I've got my deputy looking for him."

"That driver is long gone by now."

Was he just a pessimist or did he not want the driver of the Suburban found? Adeline watched him closely awhile. He saw her and met her look and Adeline thought she detected wariness in the man.

"Why did you think Tess Kincaid's accident couldn't

have been deliberate?" she asked, drawing a look from Knox.

Nicholson appeared to have to search his memory.

"Jeremy Kincaid's late wife?" Adeline helped him out.

"Yes. There was no evidence of foul play. None of the witnesses saw anything unusual and Mrs. Kincaid had an elevated blood alcohol level."

"How well did you know Livia Colton?"

He drew his head back as though he thought that a strange question. "I knew of her. Everyone knows about Livia Colton."

"Maybe you're trying to protect her by not looking into Tess's accident as a possible homicide."

"There was no need to look into a possible homicide. The accident was an accident and nothing more. I'm sorry for Mr. Kincaid's loss, but there's nothing I or anyone else can do."

He seemed sincere, if a little dismissive. She could see why Jeremy had thought that about him.

"I just stopped to make sure everything was all right." He gave a nod to Knox and went back to his car.

He left rather abruptly, as though he preferred to avoid any talk involving Livia. She glanced at Knox, whose dark eyebrows had lowered as he watched the deputy drive away.

"You think he's dirty?" she asked.

"Anything's possible, I suppose. He hasn't done anything to raise my suspicion, but Livia is my mother. I know her. She could talk a paper clip into doing what she asks." He turned a wry smile at her.

Just then, Jeremy pulled up. Adeline went to get Jamie, who'd gotten busy with a superhero action figure.

"Come on, little guy." She unclipped him from his car seat and helped him out. Taking his hand, she led him to Jeremy, who crouched before him and took him into his arms.

"I'm fine, Dad," Jamie complained.

He stood and leaned over to put his arm around Adeline and kissed her cheek. "I'm so glad you're okay. And I'm so sorry I pulled you into this."

Still tingling from his touch and warm greeting, she said, "I'm more convinced than ever that you need me to look into Tess's accident." She still needed proof but she felt more purpose now.

That pleased him but didn't clear the concern from his eyes.

The tow truck arrived and interrupted the intimate moment. Adeline saw Knox's knowing smile and chose to ignore him.

Jeremy shared a lunch with Adeline and Jamie. It had taken a long time for his worry to subside. He kept imagining Jamie injured or killed if Adeline had been driven off the road. Her quick thinking and reaction could have saved both her and Jamie's lives.

"Daddy?" Jamie asked from across the office table in Jeremy's office, his jean-clad legs dangling off the chair. His blond hair was messy and he had ketchup on the corner of his mouth.

Jeremy finished the last of his sandwich. "Yes?" Jamie had opted for a hot dog. They'd brought takeout back to his office.

"Can I have a dog?"

"Since when do you want a dog?" He had never asked for one before, but then he was only three.

He swung his feet back and forth. "I was in a ax-dent—don't I get a present?"

"You weren't hurt."

Jamie lifted his blue eyes up, doing a poor job of hiding his mischief. "I coulda been."

"What kind of dog do you want?" Adeline asked.

Jeremy saw her adoration and felt her having a maternal moment. More and more Jeremy thought of her that way, as Jamie's mother, his biological mother.

"A big one," Jamie said excitedly.

"And why do you want one?" Adeline asked.

"Because they're cute and other kids have them."

"Dogs require a lot of responsibility," Adeline asked. "Are you sure you're ready for that? You'd have to feed him and make sure he went out to go potty."

"We'd have to get food."

"Yes, we sure would."

"Do they eat the same food all the time because they don't like our food?"

Jeremy met Adeline's look and smiled with her, then laughed a little. "Dogs don't eat people food. There's all kinds of different flavors of dog food."

A knock on the open door made Jeremy look up to see his assistant.

"You said to let you know when Oscar came in. He just went into his office."

"Thank you." Jeremy turned to Adeline. Oscar had been out of the office all morning and hadn't answered his home phone or cell. "Will you stay here with Jamie?"

"Sure."

Jeremy left his office and headed a couple down to Oscar's. Oscar connected his laptop to the docking station and sat as Jeremy entered and closed the door.

"Jeremy," Oscar greeted. "I took the morning off. I hope you weren't looking for me earlier."

Oscar reported to the chief executive officer, not Jeremy. Jeremy held the position of chairman of the board and worked as the chief technical officer. While he also reported to the CEO, no one was under any illusion Kincaid Enterprises was his company.

"Where were you?" He walked farther into the office and stood closer to the desk, leaning on the back of one of the chairs.

"This morning?" Oscar seemed taken off guard as he booted his computer. "I stayed home." He smiled but Jeremy didn't feel any sincerity. "Honey Do List was getting a little long."

"Did you go anywhere?"

"No. I was home. Why?"

"Someone tried to run Adeline and Jamie off the road this morning."

Oscar blanched slightly and this time Jeremy couldn't be sure of his sincerity. "Are you serious? Why would anyone do anything like that?"

"She's looking into Tess's accident for me. Maybe someone is getting nervous."

"Wow. So Tess was really murdered?" Oscar leaned back and contemplated Jeremy. "Wait a minute. Why are you asking me where I was this morning? You don't think…" His eyes narrowed. "Is that why you haven't brought Jamie over for my wife to watch? You think I tried to run Adeline off the road? You think I killed Tess?"

"I don't think anything yet. You had a relationship with Tess, and Livia might have wanted revenge. Have you seen Livia at all? Talked with her?"

"No. She hasn't contacted me in any way. I swear it. Jeremy, I can't believe you don't trust me."

"I don't trust anyone connected with Livia. Don't take it personally." If he was innocent. Jeremy had no reason not to trust Oscar, but his absence this morning did warrant a closer look.

"Just making sure?" Oscar seemed to relax a little. "I suppose that makes a difference, given we're talking about Livia."

"Thanks for understanding." Jeremy left the office and when he reached his, he saw Adeline sitting close to Jamie and getting him set up with some toys. She looked up and watched him close his office door and go to his phone. He found Oscar's home number and called Camille.

She answered on the third ring.

"Hello, Camille. It's Jeremy."

"Yes, Jeremy. Are you bringing Jamie by today?"

"No. Adeline is watching him for me. You remember she donated her eggs and was our surrogate?"

"Ah. Yes. That must be special for her. And maybe a little difficult?"

"She's a natural with him." He wouldn't comment on whether being with Jamie caused Adeline any discomfort or unease. He didn't want to think about that. He didn't want to take that time away from her but the two of them would go back to their lives once Tess's killer was caught.

"Oscar wasn't at work this morning. Did he stay home with you today?" He didn't say that Oscar was at work right now.

"Oscar wasn't at work?"

A sinking feeling ran through him. "No."

"He wasn't home, either. He got ready like he always does and took his briefcase. He didn't say he was going anywhere else."

"He's here now, but he claims he stayed home this morning to work on a Honey Do List."

Camille fell silent but Jeremy could hear her breathing. "He lied."

"I'm sorry. I don't mean to be the bearer of bad or unexpected news. What did he drive this morning?"

"I didn't look but he normally drives the BMW."

"Do you own a black Suburban?"

"No, why?"

He wouldn't get into that. "I thought I saw him driving one this morning."

"Well. It looks like my husband and I will have a lot to talk about over dinner tonight." She sounded a little choked. "I'm not surprised, though. I've suspected this for a while now."

"You think he's having an affair?" Is that where he'd gone? Adeline had been attacked on the road in the morning. He hadn't shown up to work until much later. He still had time.

Oscar would walk into a confrontation when he got home. How would he react? Would he attempt to harm Adeline again? Or would he go straight for Jeremy this time?

Chapter 8

Adeline had just put Jamie to bed when Knox arrived. He'd called earlier, saying he had some things to discuss about the case. She heard him talking to Jeremy downstairs. She descended and joined them in the family room, catching the warmth in Jeremy's eyes when he saw her. Knox turned and said hello. He stood tall and confident, his light hair trimmed short and blue eyes following her as she came to stand before them. His wife had caught herself a fine, nice man. He fit the role of sheriff, too. There was just something about him.

"I was just explaining to Jeremy that Claudia saw Oscar with another woman yesterday morning. They were coming out of the local B and B about two hours before you were nearly driven off the road."

What was Oscar doing coming out of a hotel in the morning with a strange woman? Had he spent the night with her or had he met the woman for early morning sex? After the two had parted ways, what had Oscar done with the rest of his morning? Had he spent it with his mistress or had they parted ways then?

"What was Claudia doing outside the hotel?" Adeline asked.

"Her boutique is near there," Jeremy said. "She sometimes walks to run errands."

"She owns a boutique?" Claudia was an entrepreneur. Adeline loved hearing about women like that. They gave women in general a boost in credibility. Better to be self-sufficient than rely on others to make a living.

"Quite successful," Knox said.

"How does Claudia know Oscar?" Oscar worked for Jeremy, so she turned to him.

"She's been to my house for gatherings. I invited Oscar on occasion," Jeremy said. "We should talk to him again."

"I want to talk to Rusty Nicholson, too." She didn't want to rule out any potential suspects. "Evan won't talk to us. You fired him."

"What about this deputy?" Knox asked, giving the side of his mouth a scratch and then resting his hands on his hips.

Jeremy explained how Rusty Nicholson handled Tess's accident, how he had minimized Jeremy's concern that Livia may have caused the crash on purpose.

"We've long suspected there are some crooked deputies in the department. With Livia missing—at least her body—there has been no activity that I can see."

No nefarious activity he meant.

"Who is Evan?" Knox asked.

"Jeremy's former chief financial officer. We saw him meet with the deputy and give him money," Adeline said.

Knox looked from Jeremy to Adeline. "You two have been busy. Anyone else come up on the radar?"

Adeline thought a moment. "Did Tess have any enemies?" She hadn't asked that question before, mainly because Tess had seemed like such a good person.

"Not that I'm aware," Jeremy said. "Everyone loved her." Then he appeared to consider a little longer.

A thought came to Adeline, a memory of conversations she'd had with Tess, girl-talk during Adeline's pregnancy. Tess had fond memories of high school. The smile and light in her eyes left, though, when she brought up one girl.

"Most everyone," Adeline said. "In high school there was one girl who couldn't stand her. Your typical green with envy syndrome."

"She told me about her, not long before she died," Jeremy said, seeming to search his mind for a name. "Holly something."

The conflict had bothered Tess. She'd tried to be friendly to the girl but she refused to accept Tess as anything but a rival.

"She competed with her in sports and cheerleading. She said the woman disliked her to an extreme. She didn't understand why and chalked it up to just what you said—jealousy."

Adeline found that possibly significant. "What made her tell you about her so long after high school?" Adeline would think, as his wife, she'd have told him long before she had.

"She saw her in town. Later that day, she told me. The woman moved back to Shadow Creek. Tess said she still looked at her the same way, with so much animosity. I wouldn't say Tess was scared, but I think she had a bad feeling."

Bad feeling as in, *really don't want to deal with that*

icky person, or *I think that person might try to kill me*?
The rational investigator in her went with the former.

"Realizing Tess married you must not have gone over
well, I bet." A successful businessman—a handsome,
sexy businessman.

"What's her last name?" Knox asked.

Adeline tried to recall. "I don't remember."

"I don't, either," Jeremy said.

"I'll ask Claudia. I bet she can find out," Knox said.
"She said she recognized the woman with Oscar. She
came in to Claudia's boutique not long ago."

"Good. Thanks for all your help on this," Jeremy said.

"Yes, thank you. I feel like you're doing what Jeremy
hired me to do."

Knox grinned. "I'm glad to help a fellow law-enforce-
ment type. And I promise I won't step on your toes."

"My toes are fine. And I can stop by Claudia's shop
tomorrow."

Knox turned to Jeremy. "Humble and pretty. You
scored big."

Jeremy didn't seem uncomfortable but Adeline was.
Had Knox seen something between the two of them?
She recalled how Jeremy had looked at her when she
came into the room.

"I don't think Adeline is the scoring kind," Jeremy
said.

He touched her with the way he said those words.
He considered her someone who deserved more than a
score. She deserved a good man. Did he consider himself that man? Or maybe he could…?

The following morning, a friend called about stopping by later that day. Jeremy finished with a meeting

and headed back to his office. He spotted Alastair Buchanan standing before his executive assistant. He could tell Alastair must be flirting with her, because he smiled crookedly. By the way her eyes rolled up to look at him, she wasn't impressed. Usually his Scottish accent and tall and lean good looks captivated women, as did his light eyes and clean-cut hair. But his assistant was in a relationship.

Adeline was stopping by on her way back from talking with Claudia to get Tess's high school nemesis's name. She had his car today.

Alastair saw him and gave up whatever he'd attempted with Jeremy's assistant.

"Jeremy." He stepped toward him and they shook hands.

"Good to see you again. What brings you by?"

"Catch up with a friend and ask him about some technology investments."

"You're looking to invest?" Heir to the multibillion-dollar Clyde Whiskey fortune, Alastair could certainly afford to invest. "Are you bored with whiskey?"

Alastair chuckled. "I'm always looking for something new."

Jeremy started toward his office and closed the door after Alastair.

"You're always up on what's new, so I thought I'd come by for a visit."

Jeremy sat behind his desk and Alastair sat across from him, propping his ankle on his knee and looking relaxed with his elbow on the arm of the chair.

"It so happens your timing is perfect. I've been looking into two start-ups, one that's coming up with new software for automobiles and another that's developing a virtual reality headset."

"Do they seem like sound ventures to you?"

"Software is a multibillion-dollar industry. I'd go with that over networking-type investments. That type seems to follow economic trends like recessions. If business trails off, then companies are most likely to cut budgets in their information technology divisions."

"Small start-ups are risky, though, aren't they?"

"Especially the high-tech start-ups." He smiled. "But that's what makes them exciting." And what kept his business exciting. "I look for companies that come up with outside-the-box products that consumers will love. What you have to watch is whether the company is capable of providing adequate software support after the sale. In many cases, none of them can."

"And the software start-up you have in mind can?"

"Not at the moment but they have a plan in place to implement as soon as revenue flows."

Alastair sat in silence awhile, seeming to think that over. "What about the virtual reality company?"

"I like that one better. They take virtual gaming to the next level. Their product is going to be a big seller."

"How do I find out more?"

"I'm arranging some meetings with them now. They aren't quite ready to make a presentation to us but they're close. How long do you have?"

"As long as it takes."

"Maybe you could check out the sights of Shadow Creek. Adeline and I took Jamie to Bluewood Ranch. There's a lot to do there, and the owner is right in your age range. Maybe you can flirt with her, too."

Alastair laughed low and brief. "Who is Adeline? You didn't mention a woman in your life."

He walked right into that one. "It's not what you think. I hired her to look into Tess's accident."

"But you took her to the ranch with your son. That sounds personal."

This could lead into some sensitive areas. "She's helping me with Jamie, too. I had to fire my nanny, remember?"

That seemed to satisfy Alastair. "Ah. Yes. You had me worried there. I thought I might lose one of my best single friends."

Jeremy covered his discomfort with a smile.

"But it is time to start putting yourself out there," Alastair said, lowering his foot. "What does Adeline look like?"

He *would* ask that. Hot. Beautiful. Sharply dressed. "She's attractive." He kept his tone as neutral as possible.

"Are you interested in her? She's a PI, so she must be smart."

"She is."

"So…you're not interested?"

He wouldn't let it go until Jeremy answered. "I don't know if I'm ready for that. And I have to be careful with Jamie."

"Why? He needs a mother. And…isn't Adeline the surrogate?"

He *would* remember that.

"Yes."

"Jamie is her son. The three of you could make a family together."

In a perfect world, sure.

"Daddy!" Jamie came bounding into the office. Adeline stood in the open doorway, her hand still on the knob. Had she heard them talking? His assistant must have told her to go on in.

He swiveled his chair as Jamie reached him and took the boy up onto his lap. "How was your day?"

"Good. We went to a girls' shop."

"A girls' shop?" He looked up at Adeline, whose expression hadn't changed as she entered the office. She seemed immersed in her private thoughts. "You mean Claudia's?"

"Yeah. I don't like it there."

The way he said that put light in his heart. "Kinda boring for a boy, huh?"

"Yeah. But Adda got me a chocolate shake after."

"Oh, yeah? She did, huh?" He looked up at her sparkling eyes as she watched and listened along with Alastair.

Jamie picked at Jeremy's shirt collar. He often did things like that when he was about to ask a manipulative question.

"Daddy?"

Love for his son burst inside him. "Yes?"

"Is Adda going to stay with us forever?"

"Forever's a long time, sport. Do you like Adeline?"

He nodded. "Is she going to be my mommy?"

There was the manipulative question, except it was not really manipulative. More direct than that. His son's young eyes met his with his innocent, heartfelt question.

"Let's talk about that later, okay?" Jeremy said, glancing at Alastair's amused face and then over to Adeline. He couldn't tell what kind of reaction Jamie's question elicited in her.

Alastair slapped his thighs. "Well, I'll leave you alone now." He stood.

"You don't have to go so soon."

"It's getting late. You're probably about to go home for a family dinner, aren't you?"

Jeremy was sure he'd injected the word *family* on purpose. "That was the plan." Adeline would meet here at the end of Jeremy's workday and they'd drive home together. He wanted to be with her as much as possible, in case someone tried to hurt her again. And Jamie...

Alastair headed for the door with a greeting for Adeline.

"Think about going to Bluewood," Jeremy said.

Alastair paused in the entry. "You know I'm more of a city man. I'm no cowboy. What's there that would interest me?"

"Fresh air and horses. Get a flavor for Shadow Creek. You might take a liking to it. Besides, what else will you do while we wait for the investment briefings?"

"Work."

"Precisely." Jeremy put Jamie down and stood to get ready to leave. "You do too much of that. Stop working for a while. Relax. Go to Bluewood."

"I'll think about it." He gave a salute and left.

Alastair worked hard and didn't play hard enough. While Jeremy had always had hard work in common with his friend, he recognized the need for downtime. Maybe the difference was Jeremy had a son at home.

Jeremy began packing up his laptop while Jamie went over to Adeline and took her hand.

Tipping his head up at her, he asked, "Can we have pancakes for dinner?"

She smiled big. "We had pancakes for breakfast."

"Why can't we have them again?"

Adeline laughed lightly. "Because that's too much syrup and chocolate for a boy your age. You need to grow into a strong young man and that's done with a balanced diet."

Jamie just stared up at her with a pouting lower lip.

That night, Adeline finished the last of a child's memory game. With eight pictures on each card, the object was to match one image with the same on another card. So far Jeremy had beaten her and Jamie the most. He'd let Jamie win once, though, and Adeline had beaten him once. Right now. She tossed down her last card with a picture of a pair of glasses.

"I don't like this game," Jamie complained.

"It's your bedtime, anyway," Jeremy said, standing. "Come on. Let's tuck you in."

"I don't wanna go to bed. I'm not tired."

"Upstairs." Jeremy lifted him up over his shoulder, letting his head dangle down on his back, pulling laughter from the boy.

Adeline followed, going upstairs and down the hall to Jamie's bedroom, watching Jeremy swing Jamie down and back up again. In the room, he lay the boy on the bed. Already in his PJs, Jamie wiggled himself under the covers and Jeremy pulled the blankets up.

Adeline stayed in the doorway, watching as Jeremy read a little from a book. He didn't have to read long. Jamie slipped into sweet sleep moments later. Jeremy kissed his son's forehead and turned out the light.

Then he walked back toward her. Adeline felt the lightness of love mushroom inside her. Not for Jeremy. For Jamie. She couldn't subdue the feeling. With her hand on the door frame, she left enough room for Jeremy to pass by. He did but stopped in the hall when she continued to look at Jamie. She couldn't believe she'd created such an angel. She felt a strong bond to him, one that kept growing the longer she spent with him.

A sinking feeling chased the lightness away and logic took over. She was in this too deep. She had to get out of there, get away before it was too late.

Turning from the door and the sight of her precious son, she hurriedly walked past Jeremy toward her room. Compelled by rising panic, she retrieved her suitcase from the closet and put it on the bed, flipping the top open.

As she went to the dresser, she saw Jeremy in the doorway.

"Adeline?" he said, his voice full of concern.

He should be concerned. She brought handfuls of socks to her suitcase and dumped them inside. She could investigate from her own house.

She went back to the dresser. "Don't try and stop me." She opened another drawer and took out some jeans. Why had she packed so many clothes, anyway? Wishful thinking?

"What are you doing?" He came into the room as she carried the jeans to the suitcase.

He took her hand and she dropped the jeans. They landed haphazardly inside the luggage.

She looked at him. "I can't do this anymore."

"Do what? Investigate Tess's murder?"

"We don't know if she was murdered yet."

"I do."

She pulled her hand away and went to get tops from the closet. Way too many clothes.

"Why are you packing? I don't want you to leave. Tess's accident…"

She hurried back to the suitcase. "Well, what you want isn't important to me right now. I can't stay here anymore. I can investigate Tess's accident from my house. You and I can talk on the phone."

He stood aside and watched her pack for a few seconds. A quick glance confirmed his perplexity.

Really? He didn't get it? She turned from the luggage and put her hand on her hip.

"Jamie is my son, Jeremy."

He stared at her blankly. She began to realize he hadn't completely thought about that, not outside her being a surrogate and donor. He hadn't thought of how she might feel spending time with her biological son. If he had, he must have blocked it out.

"I didn't consider that when I hired you," he finally admitted.

No, he'd thought of Jamie as his and Tess's. That hurt. Now that she felt like Jamie's mother all the way through her soul, she disliked the thought of any other woman posing as his mother. Tess hadn't posed. Back then, she felt she'd done the right thing and Tess would make a wonderful mother. But now…now she wanted Jamie all to herself. And maybe… Jeremy, too. And that was just too dangerous.

"What were you thinking?" As soon as she asked, she regretted doing so. "Never mind." She lowered her hand and returned to packing.

Jeremy took the handful of underwear from her and put it in the suitcase, which she found rather funny. He was trying to stop her from leaving and he'd just helped her pack her underwear.

He put his hands on her arms. "Adeline. I was thinking you were a private investigator and you were Jamie's biological mother. I thought I'd give you a chance to see what a great kid he is and help me prove Livia killed Tess."

She moved back from him, out of reach. "But you were married to Tess. You loved her. How could you bring me into your home and let me get close to Jamie?"

With that, Jeremy ran his hand through his hair and sighed. "Yeah. That part confuses me, too." Rubbing his hand down his face, he looked at her as though what he were about to say would be difficult.

"What do you mean?" She had to know.

After a long hesitation, he finally said, "After Jamie was born, I kept thinking of you pregnant and then the way you looked at him when you held him for the first time. I never forgot that, even after Tess and I brought the baby home."

Stunned he'd confessed such a thing, Adeline had to take time thinking it through. Was he saying he'd had some kind of feelings for her when she was pregnant? Or had the idea of her pregnant with his child beguiled him? He'd had a complete family with Tess and Jamie. Maybe that had satisfied him until Tess died. Did he miss having a family unit? Mother, father, baby? By having Adeline in his house, did he get some kind of relief from his grief?

That made her even more apprehensive about staying. She wouldn't stay and be a surrogate mother, not again.

"Don't go," he said.

"Why?" She still didn't understand why he'd brought her into his home. "Why show me what a great kid he is when you know I'll have to leave some day?"

"You gave him to me and Tess. You're someone I

can trust, and…" He hesitated. "And… I couldn't stop remembering."

Remembering her pregnant and never forgetting who Jamie's biological mother was. On a subliminal level, he had desired to have her with him and Jamie. He did miss having a complete family.

"Can you see now why I have to leave?" she asked. "I can't stay here and fill a void for you. I deserve more than that."

After several seconds, he finally said, "I don't want you to fill a void."

"Then you see why I have to leave."

"Yes, but I'm asking you not to."

"I'm starting to have feelings for you and Jamie." She had to be honest. "I don't trust you with that. You're still mourning Tess."

He didn't respond, which told her he could say nothing to reassure her, nor could he say he felt anything for her. She saw his confusion, which marginally made her feel better. He wasn't 100 percent certain he had no feelings for her.

Was it guilt that held him back? Did he still have a sense of loyalty to Tess? Adeline felt his attraction to her, but attraction had little meaning on the surface. What lay deeper inside mattered most, but therein lay the problem. He couldn't sort out what he felt deep inside. His only certainty was his loyalty to Tess, and the loss he felt. He needed closure, and who knew how long that would take?

"Stay," he said.

"Aside from loving my son, that's too much for me to handle," she said.

"I'll respect your space."

Would he be able to do that? Their physical desire for each other might interfere.

"It's too dangerous for you on your own."

She smiled. "That's part of my job." She carried a gun. She could probably do a better job of protecting herself than he could.

"Then stay for me. I'll go crazy worrying about you alone at night. The security here is good."

He did have something of a point there. Her house didn't have a security system. She needed more assurances, though.

"Will getting answers about Tess's accident help you move on?" she asked.

"Yes."

He sounded confident. Adeline felt a flicker of hope. If he could move on from Tess's accident, he'd be free to open his heart to other women. They'd have a chance to test their physical attraction for each other. As the prospect of being with Jeremy expanded, she leashed in the temptation. A chance wasn't enough for her. She wouldn't take any chances on love anymore.

"I also can't help thinking having you here is good for him. Even if you eventually have to go, his time with you is needed. Surely you've seen how he responds to you."

Adeline agreed having a mother figure around did benefit Jamie. But taking that away in the end would cause him pain. Could she mitigate that? The sooner she solved Tess's accident, the sooner she could go and therefore minimize the impact on Jamie. Despite the flimsy excuse that gave her, being a mother figure overruled. She could not turn away from that.

While logic and apprehension compelled her to finish packing, the promise of spending more time with

Jamie prevented her. She had a chance to get to know him, the baby boy she gave birth to and held in her arms only once. She'd stayed away from him as much as possible that first year, and even after Tess died. Now she didn't have to.

Her heart gave in.

She'd see this to the end. If something developed between her and Jeremy, she would have no regrets. She had a chance to be with her son. She'd risk anything for that.

Chapter 9

The next day, Jeremy couldn't stop thinking about his talk with Adeline. When she'd told him she had feelings for him, he'd almost said he had some for her, too. The still fresh loss of Tess had prevented him. He'd known she had grown distant and he'd suspected she'd lapsed back into her addiction, but he had loved her. He'd been attracted to her from the day he'd met her. When he'd married her, he'd devoted himself to her for the rest of his life. He was not a straying man. He took marriage seriously. Maybe resolving his questions over her death would help him move on, but what did that mean? Move on to what? A life with Adeline? A bolt of desire struck him right that instant. Quickly following was guilt. He'd felt the same when Adeline was pregnant with Jamie. Guilty for having such inappropriate thoughts about a woman not his wife.

He wouldn't betray Tess, even in death. Not until he was sure he was ready for someone new. Honestly and honorably. He'd built his corporation on integrity—and a lot of hard work and determination. Adeline had given

Tess a baby, an invaluable gift. How could he start up an intimate relationship with Adeline? Right now he couldn't. He had to bury Tess first. Once and for all. And he had to think of Jamie. Having Adeline around did help him, but too long would have adverse effects. What if Jamie started thinking of her as his mother?

"Sheriff Colton is here to see you."

Jeremy looked up to see his assistant in the doorway.

Having caught him in the middle of his wandering thoughts, she eyed him peculiarly. "Are you okay?"

He wouldn't even cogitate the answer to himself. "Send him in."

"Also, Oscar isn't in yet. No one's heard from him all morning."

With his marriage likely crumbling, that came as no surprise. "Thanks."

Knox appeared in the doorway next. He entered the office and shut the door.

"A closed-door meeting?" Jeremy asked. Something must be up.

He stopped near Jeremy's desk. "I've done some checking on Evan and Oscar. Oscar checks out but some interesting things came up from Evan's background." Taking a seat across from the desk, he adjusted his light-weather jacket as he got comfortable. "He's had financial trouble since you fired him. I expected that, but what I didn't expect is he's running an escort service now."

That gave Jeremy a jolt. "As in...prostitution?"

Knox's mouth curved in a wry grin. "Disguised as a professional escort service. They don't advertise sex, but you have to assume it's offered. It isn't illegal as long as the sex is consensual. Obviously, a hooker will consent. She just works under a different title."

Jeremy recalled Evan had given Deputy Nicholson money. "Do you think he paid Rusty to protect any illegal activities going on in his business?"

"It's possible. I'm keeping my eye on him but without proof we don't have much."

Jeremy and Adeline hadn't recorded that transaction. Witnessing it might be enough if they came up with more evidence.

"There's more." Knox steepled his fingers together. "I've had both Oscar and Evan under surveillance. That woman Claudia saw with Oscar? Her name is Holly Bridgeport."

"Holly..." Tess's nemesis from high school?

Knox lowered his hands. "She's seeing Evan, too."

Seeing him? Both men were married and having an affair with the same woman. Jeremy whistled. Except, he wouldn't call it an affair. A business relationship? An illegal relationship?

"I haven't confirmed it yet, but I think she's working for Evan."

"As an escort?"

"In a word."

"Tess's high school nemesis became a prostitute?" Jeremy grunted with a brief laugh. "I'd have never seen that coming. How'd she end up doing that?"

"She was taken from her childhood home because her parents had addiction and abuse problems. Drinking. Prescription drugs. Dad knocked mom around and got himself arrested. Mom fell apart and checked into rehab. When that didn't work, Holly was taken in by the state and adopted by a family when she was fourteen."

That could be tough on a girl that age. How sad. She'd grown up with low self-esteem and then went to work as a prostitute. Had Tess known any of that? Jeremy doubted so, but she'd also kept her drinking from him for a long time.

"If she works for Evan, Oscar must be using his escort service." Knox hadn't confirmed it but clearly that's what Oscar was doing.

"Yes."

Jeremy had a good enough reason to fire him. Oscar wasn't the man he thought he was. He presented an ethical picture, but that was only a picture. He couldn't have men who paid for sex working for him. Aside from inappropriate behavior, his actions could detract from his performance at work and also could scar Jeremy's reputation. That could cost him some business. But could he give Oscar a chance to clean up his act?

What if there had been more going on between Oscar and Tess? Had she learned of his scandalous behavior and threatened to tell his wife? Maybe focusing only on Livia *was* a mistake. And maybe Jeremy didn't know his own wife as well as he'd thought.

"Maybe you're looking in the wrong direction here." Knox mirrored his thoughts. "Livia could have died in her accident. She might not have caused Tess's. What if Oscar has a motive instead?"

"It is worth checking out," Jeremy had to admit.

"Yes. Let's not drop the Livia angle, though. Oscar and Tess might have had their time together before you married her, and she might have wanted to rekindle an old romance and met him for lunch that day, but maybe Oscar told the truth. He refused her and she left upset. She went for drinks and got in an accident on the way home."

"Tess still could have found out about Holly."

"Most assuredly."

Jeremy thought of Livia and all the havoc she'd wreaked on this town. That woman could still be alive. But Oscar had to be investigated, as well.

No matter what he found, nothing would bring Tess back. Jeremy wished she hadn't died the way she had, drinking and driving. He wished she hadn't died at all. Would she want him to do this, to look into her accident? If Livia killed her, yes.

He saw Knox watching him and sensed his sympathy. Tess died suddenly in a tragic accident and left Jeremy with a young child, shattering his happiness and ideal family unit. He needed closure. He also needed vengeance, perhaps that more than anything. So maybe he didn't need sympathy. Maybe he'd passed beyond grieving and now only needed to put Tess to rest.

Adeline came to mind. Kissing her. The light in her eyes whenever she spent time with Jamie. The heat when she looked at him. She diffused his desire to avenge Tess. Tess's disease had always bothered him, and now he could see that it had dimmed his love for her. Having a family had been more important. Having that family ripped apart had been—and still was—the most difficult part of his loss.

"When my son, Cody, was kidnapped," Knox said, "I thought Livia was responsible."

Jeremy hadn't known that. Livia hadn't kidnapped his son. Someone else had. Everyone blamed Livia for wrongdoings. She made an easy target. But she also held the top card when it came to crime. She may not be to blame for everything, but she was responsible for many crimes.

"Until somebody shows me her dead body, I won't

stop looking for evidence that she killed Tess. I'll look at other suspects, but she's still on my list." Along with Oscar.

Knox nodded twice. "What does Adeline think?"

"She withholds judgment, but I have a good investigator in her."

Jeremy hadn't liked her opposition to his theory that Livia was somehow responsible for Tess's death, but she'd cover every angle. If there was any evidence to be found, she'd find it, one way or another.

Later that day and after dropping Jamie off at her mother's, Adeline met Jeremy at his office, and then they'd driven to see Holly Bridgeport. All the way to the woman's pricey apartment, she kept hashing over her conversation with her mother. She had asked a lot of questions about Jeremy and especially Jamie. She'd picked up on Adeline's feelings for Jeremy. She'd already known she had them for Jamie. Her mother had been the only person alive who had known what hell she'd gone through giving up her son. Adeline had carried her child with her always. She never forgot him.

"You're awfully quiet," Jeremy said from across the car.

Flustered, she glanced at him and then returned her gaze to the apartment building. She and Jeremy had decided to wait for Holly to leave so they could intercept her without risking her refusing to answer the door.

"I'm okay."

"What's on your mind?"

Should she tell him? She wouldn't talk about how she'd suffered after giving up Jamie, not yet, anyway.

"My mother got curious about us," she said.

"Curious? How?"

"When she found out I'm staying with you, she had a lot of questions." Adeline smiled to lighten what carried much more weight in her. "She was just being my mom."

After several seconds, he asked, "What did you tell her?"

"That I was staying with you through the investigation." She left out a lot that her mother had ascertained.

Jeremy remained silent for a few seconds. "What about Jamie?"

Again, she wondered how much to tell him. Maybe he needed to hear some of it. "She thinks we'd make a fine family." She'd heard his friend say something similar. That had thrown her off balance for a while—and also touched her more than she liked.

"You're already his mother."

He surprised her by saying that. "Do you think of me that way? As Jamie's mother?"

"You are. You're his biological mother."

"Yes, but Tess was his mother." She realized she held her breath as she waited for his reaction to that.

"For only a year. Jamie doesn't remember her."

Adeline turned away for a moment, not wishing for this talk to go any further. "You're doing well as a single father. Jamie is a well-balanced little boy."

Jeremy smiled, all his love coming out in his eyes, which she saw briefly before he faced forward. "He is. He's my life."

"You're his."

His smile faded but didn't vanish completely. "I'm afraid what having only a father will do to him."

Adeline had to be honest. Like Jeremy, she wanted what was best for their son. No matter how much she yearned to jump into an instant family and have her son in her life every day, she had to put his well-being first.

"I'd worry about the same," she said, "but you have to do what feels right for both of you."

Jeremy nodded a few times, his agreement whole and passionate. "I try not to project too far into the future, thinking about how long Jamie will be without a mother figure. I need Tess's accident resolved. I need *Tess* resolved. I can't make any decisions until then. Jamie is the most important to me, but what's best for him is also what's best for me."

Confirming what she'd already asserted didn't soften the sting. Despite her inner efforts to remain aloof, to protect her heart from certain crushing if she opened her love to Jamie and even Jeremy, pieces pushed through, pieces of emotion that bound her to her son and his father.

Looking toward the apartment building, she spotted Holly.

"There she is." Thank the stars.

Holly Bridgeport stepped out of her apartment building. A tall, willowy blonde, Holly gave the impression of someone confident and beautiful. That made Adeline wonder what had happened to make her so insecure.

"Did Knox tell you anything about her background?" she asked as they walked to meet the woman.

"She had a rough childhood."

Yes, she had some pretty heavy baggage.

She and Jeremy approached the woman, who saw them, and her steps slowed.

"Holly?" Adeline said.

Holly stopped walking, looking wary. "Yes?"

"I'm Adeline Winters and this is Jeremy Kincaid."

She gestured her hand toward Jeremy and then dropped both at her sides.

"Yes, I know you," she said to Jeremy. "I was sorry to hear about Tess."

Was she? Adeline had to wonder.

"Thanks. That's actually why we're here. Adeline is a private investigator. I've hired her to look into Tess's accident."

Holly's brow creased the smooth, alabaster skin above her pretty blue eyes. "You think someone may have deliberately caused her accident?"

"I have my suspicions."

"Who? Why do you want to talk to me?"

Adeline picked up on some nervous tension. "We know you're seeing Oscar Biggs. How long has that been going on?"

Her nervous tension intensified. "What does Oscar have to do with Tess's car accident?"

"Maybe nothing," Adeline said. "We're just covering every lead right now. He and Tess had a relationship years ago and she met him the day of her accident."

"He did?"

"She wanted to pick up where they left off and he rejected her. How long have you been seeing Oscar?"

"How do you know I'm seeing him?"

"You were seen leaving a hotel together one morning," Jeremy said.

Holly lifted her chin. "I've been seeing Oscar for a while. Several years. Until recently, that is. He said his wife found out about us."

"You work for Evan Sigurdsson, isn't that right?" Jeremy asked.

"Why are you asking me all these questions? What does any of that have to do with Tess?"

"We're trying to eliminate Oscar as a suspect," Adeline said, leaving out the fact that they also considered her and possibly Evan as suspects. Jeremy wanted to eliminate them so Adeline would focus more on Livia, she was sure.

"Oscar wouldn't have hurt Tess. He had a secret sex life but he wouldn't have hurt anyone. He liked having an escort handy. He started coming to me when Tess broke things off with him. He was upset and needed a steady companion. It didn't start out sexual. He mainly took me to dinner or movies, that sort of thing. His wife is busy with their kids and isn't interested in romance anymore. She's quiet and a routine kind of person. Oscar needs more excitement in his women. He would never divorce his wife for the kids' sake. He's an important man with a demanding job. He needs more than what he has with his wife."

"Do you work for Evan?" Jeremy asked the question again.

"I'm not a prostitute, if that's what you're trying to find out. I'm a professional escort."

She had to be in denial or trying to avoid the risk of arrest. "So, you're not also seeing Evan?"

Holly put her hand on her hip and took a sexy but defiant stance. "Evan and I have a special relationship. I help him run his business and we sometimes hang out together on a personal level."

"Are you sleeping with him?" Adeline asked.

"Are you going to tell his wife?"

"I'll take that as a yes."

Holly narrowed her eyes at Adeline, and she got an

idea of what Tess must have felt like when this woman looked at her like that. "I don't sleep with all the men, only the ones I really like. I liked Oscar. I still do. Some of the other girls are different. They take the clients that expect sex. Evan respects me. He thinks I'm good at business." The way she gave her head a little shake told Adeline the woman had worked hard to convince herself of that claim. Evan probably thought she was good at the sexual side of his business.

"When is the last time you talked with Tess?" Jeremy asked.

Holly's animosity eased and her eyes lowered as though guilt had overridden her. At last she lifted her head. "Tess and I had our differences. We didn't get along in high school, and she wasn't glad to see me when I moved back to Shadow Creek. But I would have never tried to run her into a pole and kill her. In fact, we were becoming friends just before she died." She became distant then, as though thinking about a blossoming friendship. But guilt still controlled her demeanor.

"Tess never told me you two were talking," Jeremy said.

Holly turned to Jeremy. "She started drinking again. That's what we did together. We went out and had a few drinks every now and then. She didn't want you to know."

Jeremy made no comment.

"The day of her accident I met her at a pub. She told me she wanted to start things back up with him and he refused."

Adeline wondered if that had made Holly feel triumphant. For once she'd gotten one up on the beautiful and talented Tess.

"Did you like hearing that?" Adeline asked.

"No." She seemed ashamed now. "I admit, I've envied Tess ever since high school. Everyone liked her. She was so smart and good at sports and…beautiful." She turned to Jeremy. "And she married you, a wealthy and handsome man. She had everything I wished I could have."

"So you enjoyed seeing her at her lowest?" Adeline asked the question in another way.

"I'm not proud of that, but yes. Thing is, after all the time I spent with her in pubs, we became good friends. We ended up confiding in each other."

"Did she talk about me?" Jeremy asked.

Holly seemed to hesitate. But then she remained forthright. "Yes. She said she didn't think you loved her anymore. She was pretty upset about that."

"Why did she think I didn't love her?"

"She thought you knew she started drinking again." Holly looked regretful.

Jeremy lowered his head, the news seeming difficult for him to hear. Tess must have still loved him. She must have needed to feel loved and that's what had driven her to Oscar—that and the alcohol clouding her judgment. If she hadn't started drinking again, she and Jeremy would still be together and in love.

"She was such a real person. Warmhearted. I started to really like her," Holly said.

"That's not hard to do. Tess was a friendly, good person," Jeremy said with a smile that pricked Adeline. Would he ever smile like that for her?

"Even when she drank." Holly smiled briefly before she sobered. "She told me she couldn't control it. And it ended up killing her. I'm torn most of the time because

I go from feeling like I helped kill her to glad I had the chance to get to know her."

Adeline could see Holly was being genuine. "It's good you got to know her."

"Did you leave the pub together?" Jeremy asked.

Holly shook her head. "I left before her. She said she was going to leave soon but she must have stayed another couple of hours, given the time of her accident."

"Did you ever see her with Livia Colton?" Jeremy asked.

Adeline almost wished he wouldn't ask about Livia. She just felt the odds Livia was responsible were low. Yes, Tess had taken Oscar from her, but would she kill Tess over it? From everything she knew about Livia, yes, she would, but the crash expert had convinced her the accident wasn't a form of murder.

"With her? No."

"Did she ever mention Livia to you?"

Holly shook her head. "No. Never. Why?"

"Thanks, Holly." She cut the conversation short. "That's all we need for now."

"Thank you." Jeremy walked with Adeline back toward the car. "Do you think she's hiding anything?" Jeremy asked. "She seemed so guilt-ridden."

"Yes. I think she was honest with what she told us."

"You don't think I should have asked about Livia, do you?"

She stopped at the car. "The crash expert doesn't even think Tess was murdered." She didn't tell him she'd called the bank that ran the ATM across from where Tess had driven into the pole and asked them for video footage of the night of Tess's accident and was waiting for the call to tell her it was ready for her to pick up.

She'd wait until after she had that before she made her final determination.

"What do you think?" Jeremy asked.

"I don't know yet."

"Do you think there's at least a possibility Livia killed her?"

"Of course. I just don't think there's a significant possibility." She glanced over to see his annoyance had flared. He cared so much about Tess, and the loss of her needed healing. He thought he could overcome that by holding someone accountable. What would he do if no one but Tess was?

Jeremy understood Adeline worked with clues and facts and that most of the facts pointed to Tess dying as a result of her drunk driving. He was just glad she hadn't given up searching for clues. He had to give her credit for that.

Oscar's wife said he had rented an apartment and she hadn't seen him since she asked him to leave. He'd told her he had an affair with Holly. Jeremy and Adeline didn't enlighten her that Holly was an escort. Now they rode the elevator up to Oscar's apartment, Adeline next to him all sexy in her vest and pants with a smart white shirt underneath. At the floor number, they stepped into the hall. As they reached Oscar's apartment, the door opened and Evan walked out, talking to Oscar, who held the door.

"What are you doing here?" Evan all but hissed.

"We're here to talk to Oscar. What are you doing here?" Jeremy asked.

"I don't have to talk to you." Evan swatted his hand in disgust and walked down the hall.

Jeremy faced Oscar, feeling accusatory. "You and Evan are *friends*?"

"We were friends when he worked for you." Oscar held the door open and stepped aside to allow them inside. Jeremy was a little surprised by the welcome and easy confession.

"I'm sorry I haven't been in to work," Oscar said. "I've had some trouble at home." He didn't say what kind of trouble but his tone hinted Jeremy shouldn't have to be told.

"That's not why we're here. My assistant told me you weren't in the office." Jeremy moved farther into the apartment as Oscar went to lean a hand on one of the kitchen stools.

Light from a patio door brightened the open space and a television played the news at low volume. Jeremy didn't see anything unusual that might hint to what Evan had come to Oscar about today.

"You and Evan are close?" Adeline asked.

"Close?" Oscar looked from her to Jeremy and then back at her. "I just told you we were friends."

He seemed hesitant. Maybe he and Evan were much closer than he let on.

"Why was he just here?" Jeremy asked.

"He gave me the name of a good lawyer and we talked, not that it's any of your business."

He spoke to the owner of the company that employed him rather harshly. Granted, Jeremy may have pushed boundaries by asking him personal questions. He wasn't the private investigator here. He was an employer and Oscar was an employee. And Oscar didn't have to talk to Adeline at all. The fact that he did so willingly worked in his favor.

"Did Tess know you were using an escort service?" Adeline asked.

"Tess?" Oscar looked confused. "What does she have to do with that? I'm not using an escort service."

Why did he lie?

"We know you've been with Holly Bridgeport and that she works for Evan's escort service," Jeremy said.

"I don't pay her." Oscar's tone turned offensive. Again, why did he feel the need to lie?

"Evan gives her to you free of charge?" Adeline asked. "According to Holly, you do pay her. She admitted she's an escort and she sleeps with the men she likes. She likes you."

"You've spoken with Holly?" Oscar continued to sound offensive as he turned to Jeremy. "You've caused me enough trouble with my wife, don't you think? Why are you interfering in my personal affairs? I had nothing to do with Tess's accident."

Was he also lying about that?

"Did she know you were seeing Holly?" Adeline asked.

"I didn't start seeing Holly until after Tess broke things off with me."

He corroborated what Holly had told them. Jeremy didn't need to know more. Oscar might be innocent... except for his taste in prostitutes and friendship with a man who sexually harassed women. He might not have had anything to do with Tess's accident, but his ethics left Jeremy with much uncertainty.

"I find it difficult to believe you're friends with Evan after I fired him," Jeremy said. "And then I discover you use an escort service. I always thought you were a forthright man. Now I'm not sure I can trust you."

"I am forthright. If I wasn't, I wouldn't have come to you and told you about Tess meeting me the day of her accident."

"Maybe you did that to make yourself look innocent," Adeline said. "And forthright."

After holding her gaze for several seconds, his defensiveness fading to an unreadable mask, Oscar turned to Jeremy. "Do I still have a job?"

Jeremy wouldn't get into those issues now. He had to talk to his HR director first.

"We'll talk when you're back in the office. When will that be?"

"Tomorrow. I just needed some time to find a place to stay."

Jeremy believed everything Oscar told them so far. "We saw Evan meet with a Rusty Nicholson and give him money. Do you know why he'd pay a deputy?"

"Rusty?" Oscar asked.

"Yes. He's the same man who responded to Tess's accident and questioned witnesses. He didn't seem very willing to look very hard into any possibilities of foul play."

"He lives on the same street as Evan. He does woodworking on the side and did a built-in entertainment center for him. He mentioned he met him and paid him."

"He does have a nice house. How can he afford that?" Adeline asked.

"His wife can."

That seemed reasonable enough. Still, odd for someone to meet at a café and pay cash.

"Evan seemed angry with him."

"I'm telling you what Evan told me."

Had Evan lied? Maybe Nicholson hadn't built an entertainment center. And the amount of money Evan had given him seemed like a lot more than that job would cost. Could Evan have killed Tess in retaliation for Jeremy firing him? It seemed unlikely. Again, Jeremy came back to Livia. She was the only person capable of doing something like that.

Jeremy and Adeline left the apartment, Oscar staying in the open doorway to watch them a bit before they got on the elevator and rode it to the main floor.

"He's missing a compelling motive," Adeline said.

Jeremy didn't comment. Oscar might not have a reason to want Tess dead, but he very well could know more than he'd let on so far.

Chapter 10

After Jeremy went to work the next day, Adeline dropped Jamie off at her mother's and went to Evan Sigurdsson's office. That morning, she and Jamie had still been in their pj's and had just finished cereal, all three of them at the table. They'd talked about horseback riding at Bluewood Ranch and possibly making plans to go again. Jamie wanted a pony of his own and Jeremy said he'd look into boarding one at the ranch.

Adeline had never felt so much a part of a unit before. She and her mother made a loving family together, but it was just the two of them. Adeline wanted children of her own and a father who'd contribute his share and stick around. She felt so good getting a taste of it with Jeremy. But after he left, she felt as though she played a role, spending the morning with him and Jamie and then seeing him off to work. Now, upon reflection, it didn't seem real.

Adeline entered Evan's office, a small space in a well-maintained and relatively new earth-toned brick strip mall. A reception area with a small, mahogany desk opened to a cozy, dimly lit seating area in soft oranges and greens. Well-lit paintings depicted couples in various, scantily clad embraces.

A tall, thin, dark-haired woman in a sleeveless black dress appeared from a doorway. "Can I help you?"

"I'm here to talk with Evan. Is he in?"

"May I tell him who's wishing to meet him?" She spoke and held herself like a woman far above everyone around her. She had elegance and loads of self-esteem, not the kind of woman Evan likely hired for his escort service…unless the woman acted her part and hid a weighty insecurity.

"Adeline Winters. I'm a private investigator. I need to ask him a few questions."

"Oh. One moment." The refined woman went back through the door and a few minutes later, Evan appeared.

"What are you doing here?" He didn't seem happy to see her. He must know why she'd come.

She stepped closer and stopped before his scowling face. "We saw you at the café with Rusty Nicholson."

"I saw you with Jeremy Kincaid. So what?"

"You gave the officer some money?"

"For an entertainment center he built for me," Evan shot back, appearing insulted.

Was he truly insulted or had he become defensive? "It seemed like a lot of money."

"It was a big piece." Evan sneered. "What did you think I gave him money for? A bribe? Like I'd meet a deputy in public and pay him off. You think I'm stupid?"

Either that or exceedingly clever. Paying a deputy in public covered his story that he'd paid for carpentry work.

"What were you arguing about?" she asked.

"Were you there spying on me?"

"No, we were watching Deputy Nicholson. We think he might be working for Livia Colton." She put that out for him to see how he'd react, and if he'd reveal anything useful.

His defensiveness eased and he said with force, "Livia is dead."

"No body. She might have survived the accident and the river."

Evan grunted derisively. "You're just like Jeremy, always reaching. He actually thinks his wife was murdered?"

"How well do you know Deputy Nicholson?" She'd stick to the reason she'd come there today. Best she didn't follow his lead and end up agreeing with him.

"He's my neighbor. He can be annoying at times but he's a good woodworker. He isn't dirty, so you're wasting your time fishing around for leads. He never worked with Livia." He turned to go back to the doorway. "Now, if you'll excuse me. I'm busy today."

Adeline didn't question him about his escort service. He wouldn't admit to anything anyway, and nothing he did in his line of business would help her solve Tess's case. She'd go pick up Jamie and later they'd meet Jeremy at his office as they'd planned. They were going out for dinner tonight. She couldn't wait. Although she'd keep it to herself, she looked forward to an evening with her son and Jeremy, like a family.

Jamie squealed when he saw Adeline enter her mother's house. No longer having to work two jobs, her mother lived in a comfortable, newly constructed ranch house. Adeline had helped her get into it and fill it with furniture. She'd also bought her a new car. She loved taking care of her mother. Evangeline Winters had worked enough in her life.

Her mother hugged her upon entry. "Hi, sweetie. Jamie has been a darling. He sure is a chatterbox. Told me all about the movie he watched last night and the breakfast he made with you yesterday. He wanted pancakes but you made him eat cereal. He sure is getting attached."

She wasn't so sure that was a good thing. "He is a special kid."

Her mother dyed her hair blond now that she'd turned gray and had the same blue eyes as Adeline. She'd kept her figure, too. Good skin gave Adeline promise that she'd age as well approaching fifty. Her mother smelled the way she always did, a subtle scent that wasn't too perfumed.

"Adda!" Jamie came running into the entry and Adeline crouched to receive his hug.

"Hi, honey. Did you have fun with Evangeline?"

"Yeah. We baked cookies."

"Oh. There goes the healthy breakfast."

Jamie laughed.

"Can you stay a bit?" her mother asked.

"Yes. We have a little time. Why?"

"I went shopping for new bathroom decor."

Her mother wanted to show off her latest hobby— decorating. Now that she had some extra cash she could do that sort of thing.

After admiring the new, brighter main bathroom, Adeline stayed for about thirty minutes talking with her mother before she checked the time. "Come on. We have some errands to run before we go meet your dad. We're going out for dinner."

"I want fries."

"How many cookies did you eat?" Adeline looked at her mother, who looked guilty and mouthed *three*.

That explained the energy.

"Go get your stuff, Jamie."

At Adeline's request, Jamie bounded off to do as told.

"When do I get to meet your mystery man?" The twinkle in her mother's eyes said she wanted her daughter to find love and be happy. She wanted her daughter to find a man not like her father. She must think Jeremy held promise.

"He's not a mystery man. You know of him."

"Yes, but I don't *know* him." Her mother eyed her expectantly.

She'd never been shy about letting her daughter know when she felt slighted, even in a nonserious way. But she only knew that Adeline had given him and Tess a son.

"I'm investigating Tess's accident. We've been over this. He's not my boyfriend."

"Yes, but he asked you to live with him. That suggests he's interested in more than an investigation."

Adeline would have liked to think so, too, but doing so would be foolish, at least this soon. "He's still grieving, Mom. I don't want anything to do with him if he's not ready to move on." And he wasn't.

Her mother sobered and reached over to touch Adeline's cheek. "How many times do I have to tell you not to let that man who sponged off you ruin your chance at happiness?"

"You don't have to tell me at all, Mom. I just have to be sure the next time I let a man get that close to me.

I'm not sure about Jeremy." Secretly, she wished she was, though. Secretly, she wanted nothing more than to be a part of her son's life. "I can't make him want me."

"That's just it. He does want you. Maybe he can't admit it to himself, but he does. He wouldn't have asked you to live with him otherwise."

That all rang true, but her mother didn't understand why she had to keep her distance. Well, maybe she did, and that's what she tried to tell Adeline. She should let go. Take a chance on Jeremy.

The idea tantalized her for a few seconds.

"Jeremy has his own money, Adeline. It won't be the same with him. He's like that way. Successful. A doer. He doesn't need anyone to take care of him."

"I wouldn't have minded taking care of my boyfriend if he contributed in some way, if he didn't purposefully take from me. It's not about money. It's about respect and trust."

"And you don't trust Jeremy, but you also don't know him well enough."

She knew him pretty well on a friendly basis, just not intimately. Big difference.

Jamie came back into the entry with his tiny backpack.

"I'm rescued," Adeline said, smiling and leaning in to hug her mother again. "I love you."

"I love you, too. Give Jeremy a chance."

"I'll think about it." She moved back and reached for Jamie's hand. "Come on, little man."

"'Kay!"

Outside, she walked with Jamie to the car. Just a few steps from the porch, a shot rang out and she felt sharp, powerful pressure pierce her chest. She registered falling, her head hitting the concrete sidewalk and losing Jamie's hand. Then all went black.

Overwhelmed with worry, Jeremy rushed into the emergency waiting room and spotted Knox with a woman that had to be Adeline's mother. Knox had called him on his way to the hospital. Evangeline Winters had phoned 9-1-1 to report her daughter had been shot. Knox arrived on the scene within minutes along with paramedics and police and had called Jeremy. Adeline had been taken by ambulance there. Jeremy had raced here as fast as he could.

Knox turned as Jeremy neared, Evangeline doing the same. She was an older version of Adeline and so far had retained a rather youthful look.

"How is she?" Jeremy asked, not recalling ever feeling so frantic before.

"She's in surgery," Knox said.

"Is she going to be all right?" She had to be. What if she died?

Evangeline's blue eyes were red and puffy from crying, intensifying his anxiety. The wispy cut fell to the top of her shoulders and chest; her blond hair was a little messy. She must be going through torment, with her only daughter clinging to life.

"We don't know yet," Evangeline said on a fresh wave of tears.

If Jeremy hadn't been so backlogged at work, he'd have gone with her. He hadn't wanted her to go alone but she did know how to use her gun and she was a professional detective. He had to make himself be less overly protective. Besides, Adeline seeing Evan at his office was too public. He wouldn't have shot her there. If Evan was dangerous. He harassed women and had an arrogant personality lurking beneath all his false charm. Although the charm Jeremy had seen while he worked for him didn't seem to be present anymore. Evan likely reserved it for the women he preyed upon and the friends he had.

"What happened?" Jeremy asked.

"Adeline picked Jamie up and on her way out, Evangeline heard a gunshot." Knox took over for the distraught Evangeline. "She went outside and found Adeline lying on the ground." Knox paused, which gave Jeremy a sinking feeling.

"Jamie…?" In the midst of the emergency, Knox had only told him Adeline had been shot and to meet him at the hospital. A fresh wave of fear coursed through him.

"Evangeline saw a man put him into a black Suburban and drive away. She didn't get a complete plate number, only the first three characters."

Jeremy stumbled backward a step, reeling. Someone took his boy? Who? He'd kill the man!

"Jamie was kidnapped?" Someone had shot Adeline to take him.

"I have every available law enforcement officer out looking for him right now," Knox said. "My son was kidnapped, too. I know what you're feeling right now."

While that came as some comfort, Jeremy couldn't stand by and do nothing. Where was his son? Was he all right? How was he being treated? He stopped himself from imagining the worst.

"There's nothing you can do that isn't already being done," Knox said as though he'd heard his thoughts. "Adeline needs you. You should be here with her. I'll keep you informed on any changes in progress in the search. You have your cell phone?"

Jeremy nodded.

"I'll make sure calls to your home phone are forwarded in case the kidnapper tries to contact you. I'll also set up tracking and recording. Give me a key and the code to your security system."

Jeremy gave him his house key and told him the code.

The urge to leave and chase across every inch of the town looking for Jamie eased, leaving only sickening apprehension and a sense of extreme helplessness. Not knowing where his son was or how he was doing would be tortuous.

Adeline.

She'd been shot and was in surgery. "Where was she shot?" What if she didn't make it?

"Right side, just below the rib cage."

Jeremy's breath whooshed out of him and he backed up to sit down. Rubbing his hand down his face, he feared Adeline wouldn't survive a shot like that. This was all his fault. If he hadn't asked her to help him investigate Tess's death, she wouldn't be in the hospital right now. Part of the reason he'd asked her was selfish. He'd wanted to see her again, but he hadn't thought things through enough.

Evangeline sat on the chair beside him, wiping her tears and regaining her composure. "Adeline told me about you. I said I wanted to meet her mystery man. I didn't count on it being in the emergency waiting room."

"Mystery man?"

"That's what I called you. Adeline isn't very talkative about the men in her life. Ever since she had to get that restraining order on her ex-boyfriend, she's kept to herself. She dated here and there but never brought any of them home to meet me. She wasn't serious enough with them. They didn't last. I have a feeling it will take quite a while for her to trust a man enough to let him meet me."

"Yeah, I've picked up on that with her." Jeremy smiled, bittersweet.

"She probably will never tell you this, but she loves Jamie. She's loved him since the day he was born. That happens with mothers. The moment they see and hold their newborn, a special bond forms."

Adeline had indicated as much.

"I'm afraid she'll end up like me, loving a man she can never have and doesn't want anyway because they could never grow up enough."

Who was she talking about? Adeline's feelings for her ex-boyfriend?

"She might tell people she didn't love that man, but she did. She loved the man he could have become. I loved her father that way." Evangeline sighed. "No one came along after him who captured my heart the same way. I'd rather be alone than with someone I don't truly love."

"I doubt Adeline will end up like that. She's honest with herself about how she feels. She's also successful. She doesn't need anyone to take care of her. She's found her own way. She'll find a man she trusts." He tried not to think of that man as himself. He held back.

"Will that man be you?" she asked.

"Your daughter is an amazing woman. I wouldn't lead her to believe I'm worthy unless I believed it myself."

Knox stood nearby, a silent witness up until then. His mouth turned up ruefully at Jeremy's declaration. "I know the feeling."

Knox was married now. Had he felt unworthy because he was Livia's son? Jeremy's situation was different. He had a son who lost his mother. No decision would come lightly, none that would change Jamie's life. A new woman would be a big change.

That new woman was in an operating room with a bullet wound.

"Mrs. Winters?"

Feeling a jolt snap him to attention, Jeremy stood with Evangeline. A doctor approached. They'd find out how Adeline was doing.

"She made it through surgery. The bullet grazed her liver, but most of the damage was to her muscle tissue. She must have moved just before the bullet struck. Either that, or the shooter's aim was off. The angle of the bullet sent it through her side." The doctor indicated by drawing an invisible line on his white coat from a point below his rib bone to his flank. "If the caliber of bullet would have been any bigger, I don't think she would have survived the ambulance ride. There would have been a lot more damage to her abdominal cavity. She lost a lot of blood and when she fell she hit her head. We had to stitch her up there, as well."

"Is she going to be all right?" Evangeline asked.

"I'm concerned that the bullet grazed her liver. We're going to keep a close eye on her tonight."

Jeremy ran his hand over his face again. He couldn't bear to lose her. And Jamie. The blood left his head thinking of that. What was happening to his son right now? Was he scared? Did he want his daddy to come and get him? That thought killed him inside.

"You can go see her in about an hour. We need to move her to her recovery room, but she's just gotten out of surgery."

When the doctor left, Evangeline dropped down onto a chair, looking relieved but still stressed.

"Why would someone try to kill Adeline?" Knox asked Jeremy, keeping his tone low.

"Why would anyone kidnap Jamie?" Why try to kill Adeline and abduct a three-year-old boy? Ransom? "Somebody was threatened by Adeline. They took her out in order to capture Jamie."

"Whoever it is, they must not like her looking into Tess's accident."

Jeremy had known something was wrong with Tess's accident all along. "This has all the earmarks of Livia."

"I'm starting to believe you. I think Adeline will, too, after this."

If she survived.

Livia might have enlisted one of her henchmen to help her. She'd want everyone to assume she was dead, so having someone else carry out a ransom scheme made sense. Adeline and Jeremy had nosed into Tess's accident too much; now Livia had upped the stakes. She'd use this situation to her advantage to get some money, which would help her escape into obscurity.

Jeremy's neck began to ache and he realized he'd fallen asleep in a chair with his head back. He lifted his head with a wince. Adeline still lay in the same position with her eyes closed. The nurses had come in several times during the night to check on her. Jeremy watched her sleep, long eyelashes brushing soft, smooth skin. Her blond hair fanned out across the pillow, silky and shiny despite her condition.

The last time he'd seen her in a hospital, she'd held Jamie in her arms. He'd never forget the look on her face. He'd seen exactly what her mother had described. That look had haunted him over the last three years. Thoughts had interfered with the way he regarded Tess sometimes.

Jamie.

Where was he? Although he'd only slept for maybe an hour, Jeremy couldn't believe he'd slept at all. Knox had called once in the middle of the night to report none of Evangeline's neighbors had seen anything.

Rubbing his neck, he checked the time. Almost five in the morning. The hospital room was dark, with the blinds closed and only one small light on above the sink. Lights from the equipment hooked up to Adeline provided more dim light. He could see through the cracks in the blinds that the sun hadn't come up yet.

He rubbed the back of his neck.

"Is Jamie with my mother?"

At the sound of Adeline's voice, Jeremy sat upright and leaned toward her. She must have gone unconscious before Jamie had been taken.

"You're awake." Relief came in a giant wave. She made it. "How do you feel?"

"Like someone ice skated over my side. What happened?"

"You don't remember?" It wasn't uncommon for people not to remember how they acquired traumatic injuries.

"I remember leaving my mother's with Jamie." Her brow scrunched as though she tried to remember more.

"You were shot."

She stared at him. "I remember a black Suburban. And a man with a gun. I didn't recognize him."

Jeremy reached over and put his hand on hers. "Are you sure?" She could help save Jamie if she could remember.

She moved her head on the pillow, shaking it no and then touching the bandage on the side of her head.

"You hit your head when you fell. The bullet grazed your liver. The doctor was concerned about that and the amount of blood you lost." He'd wait until the doctor checked her out before he said she'd be all right.

"Where's my mother? Did she take Jamie home?"

"She was here until about midnight and went home to try and get some rest." He had difficulty voicing what had happened to Jamie. Saying it out loud made it too real.

"Jamie?" She struggled to sit up.

Jeremy stood and moved the bed to a more upright position. Adeline grimaced in pain as her gunshot wound must have protested.

"Try not to move just yet. You had surgery." He took her hand and held it, lowering his head as he searched for a way to tell her.

After closing his eyes briefly, he met her frightened look. "Jamie was kidnapped."

She sucked in a horrified breath. "No!" Now she struggled to sit again, only this time trying to get off the bed, tugging at lines connected to her, and then crying out in pain.

Jeremy pushed her shoulders so she lay back down. "Don't move, Adeline. We think you were shot to stop you from investigating Tess's accident. We also think Jamie was taken to be held for ransom."

"Who would do that?"

He let her come to her own conclusion.

"Livia?"

"Knox agrees she could have hired someone to shoot you and take Jamie."

"Jamie was with me when the Suburban almost ran me off the road. He would have killed us both." She paused to catch her breath after a wince that revealed her pain.

"Do you need the nurse?" he asked.

She rolled her head from side to side. "Why would Livia try to have me and Jamie killed and then kidnap Jamie after that failed?"

"She could have changed her plans. Ransoming Jamie gets her money to escape and stay hidden. And remember, something like this has happened before. One of Livia's employees kidnapped Knox's son, Cody, when she didn't pay him for helping her escape. He did it to force her to pay, but Livia didn't care about her grandson and killed the poor employee herself. Livia is all about money."

"You expect a ransom demand?"

"Yes." Except the amount of time passing did unnerve him. What if he was wrong? What if Jamie was already dead? He couldn't think that way. He would have shot both Adeline and Jamie if he didn't intend to kidnap Jamie and hold him for ransom.

Adeline turned her head and looked toward the window. The sun shone today, the sky a pretty blue.

"I should have been more watchful," she said. "No one should have taken him from me."

"It's not your fault." She couldn't blame herself for that.

"I should have kept him safe." Tears bloomed in her eyes. "I was armed. I could have protected him. I was so happy to see him. I didn't even see the Suburban until it was too late."

"Adeline." Jeremy put his hand on the side of her

face, making her look at him. "It isn't your fault Jamie was taken. I know you love him and would do anything to keep him safe."

She blinked when he said the word "love."

"Knox has an entire team searching for him. You need to concentrate on healing." Leaning down, he pressed a kiss to her mouth. Then he rose up just a bit and looked her in her eyes. "We will find our son."

Just then Evangeline stepped into the room. "Did I come at a bad time?" She smiled big as she entered, holding a vase of colorful flowers. Going to the other side of the bed, she leaned and kissed her daughter's cheek. "I'm so happy to see you awake. You gave me such a scare."

"*You* were scared…"

Jeremy imagined going unconscious after realizing you'd just been shot would be awful.

Evangeline put the flowers on the windowsill. "This room needed some cheering up."

"They're beautiful, Mom."

"Just like my daughter. Now." She clasped her hands in front of her. "I'll go find the doctor and tell him you're awake."

"They'll be in soon enough," Adeline said. "Stay."

"You two need a moment."

When she left, Jeremy shared an awkward moment with Adeline. He'd called Jamie *their* son. When he'd said the word, he'd felt it all the way to his soul.

Chapter 11

A witness came through and claimed to have seen a black Suburban drive by their house. The man had just gotten home from work. He saw a man driving and a young boy with his hands flattened against the backseat window. While that had torn Jeremy's heart out, he had new hope in finding him. Knox took him along to the witness's house, where Knox questioned him on the front porch.

"I saw him drive down the street. He may have turned left at the stop sign. I can't be sure," the witness had said.

Jeremy and Knox went door to door while the sheriff's deputies searched the entire neighborhood for any sign of a Suburban—or Jamie. Jeremy had to hand it to them. They carried out the search with thorough professionalism.

After leaving the tenth or eleventh door, Jeremy began to lose his flicker of hope. But then Knox's phone rang and he went a little still and said, "We're on our way." As he walked fast to his car, he said to Jeremy, "Someone else spotted the Suburban. Get in."

Jeremy did, and Knox sped a few blocks away to the edge of town and a small, two-story farmhouse; a light at the end of the driveway lit the way and an outdoor porch light welcomed them up the creaky steps. A tall, lanky man with short brown hair and green eyes opened the door, his wife beside him. She was much shorter with her red hair up in a ponytail. The man put his arm around her and she looked up at him with love. The two had lots of land but probably not much money.

"You Sheriff Colton?" the man asked Jeremy.

Jeremy thumbed over toward Knox. "He is."

"We've heard a boy went missing."

"My son, Jamie," Jeremy said.

The man nodded and the woman looked sympathetic.

"My neighbor stopped by and said deputies were searching a few blocks from here," the farmer said.

"That's right. Dispatch said you saw a black Suburban?" Knox said.

"Yeah. I was finishing up in the barn when I saw it drive by. He was driving fast and there was a boy in the back. He sort of moved across the back seat like he saw me and wanted to get my attention. He put his hand on the window, pounding it a few times. You know how kids can be. I thought he was just foolin' around."

It pained Jeremy intensely to hear that. Jamie hadn't been fooling around. He'd been trying to get the farmer's attention all right, but for help.

"Did you see where the Suburban went?"

The farmer pointed down the street. "That way."

"That way" was a long stretch of highway leading out of town. Jeremy's heart plummeted with dread.

"I'm sorry, mister," the farmer said to Jeremy. "I wish

I'd have heard about the missing boy sooner, especially that he'd been taken in a black Suburban."

"We have two boys ourselves," his wife said. "I can't imagine how horrible it would be to lose one of them."

Jeremy wouldn't comment on how horrible it was that he'd lost Jamie. He refused to succumb to feeling bad. He had to find Jamie. How he felt didn't matter. Only Jamie mattered.

"There's more farmhouses a few miles down," the man said. "Three before it's a whole lot of nothin' for several more."

"Thanks. We'll check it out." Knox led Jeremy back to the car.

It was starting to get late but Knox drove to the first farmhouse. A grouchy older woman answered and said she'd been inside watching television all day and hadn't been outside. The second didn't answer the door and Knox radioed to his team to send someone over in the morning. They peeked into windows but the interior was dark and no sounds came from inside.

"Can we break in?" What if Jamie was inside?

"Not without reasonable cause. If you want your son's kidnapper to get away with what he's done. Breaking in without that or a warrant won't help you."

Of course, Jeremy knew that. He just wanted his son back. Now.

Knox drove to the third and last house before tens of miles of nothing but trees and grassland led to the next county. Knox had already notified other sheriffs in the entire state. An Amber Alert had been sent and so far no one had called in with any viable tips.

This house had lights on. He and Knox went to the door. A man in his forties and wearing overalls and a weary face answered. Kids hollered in the background and a woman yelled for them to quiet down. The smell of hamburgers filled the small space of the ranch house.

"Sheriff," the man said.

"Hello, Mr. Smith. How's the family?"

"Misbehaving and late for bed, as usual. How's your missus?"

"Very well, thanks. We're here looking for a missing boy who was last seen in a black Suburban with a man driving."

"He ain't here." The man chuckled at his bad joke.

"Have you seen a black Suburban?"

"No, sir. I spent the day moving cattle, nowhere near any roads." He turned and called to his wife and kids. "Any of you see a black Suburban today?"

"No," the two kids called back.

"I spent the day cleaning up after these kids," the wife said. "Sorry."

Another dead end. If Jamie's kidnapper had taken him out of Shadow Creek, they were long gone by now. Jeremy sat in agonizing silence as Knox drove back toward town.

He watched the landscape change from open fields to trees, darkness swallowing all but the road.

"We'll find him," Knox said.

Jeremy wasn't so sure anymore. It had been more than twenty-four hours. He tried not to give in to despair, but his son was missing. Jamie. His sweet, smart, adorable son. What would he do without him?

"We will," Knox repeated.

Jeremy glanced at him and then returned his gaze to the passing landscape. Spotting a dirt road he hadn't seen on the way to the third house, he pointed.

"Where does that go?"

"It's a forest service road. There's a campground a few miles up. We can check it out. Leave nothing left to guessing, no rock unturned."

Jeremy heard Knox's indulgent tone. He doubted the road would yield much other than a ride up a dark dirt road. But Knox was right. Leave no rock unturned. He'd feel better not letting the slightest possibility go to assumption.

Headlights lit the way, casting an eerie half circle ahead on the road and above on the canopy of trees. The tires rolled over gravel and spit up dust in the taillights. They reached the campground where the road ended. There were a few campers.

Knox drove through the loops until he drove back onto the dirt road. Jeremy experienced another drop inside. They'd get no leads tonight.

He stared out the window, thinking of Jamie, fighting his imagination of what he was doing right now, what he was feeling. Was he hungry? Tired and scared?

Something reflected off the headlights, something off the road.

"Stop," he said to Knox.

Knox stopped the car. "What did you see?"

"Back up."

Knox did, slowly.

Jeremy saw something in the woods. "Stop."

The car stopped. There wasn't a road there, but Jeremy saw evidence that vehicles had driven through there on occasion and wondered if he'd find a secluded campsite in the trees. Getting out of the car, he followed the worn path just wide enough for a car to make it through.

About twenty feet in, he found a black Suburban in a clearing, a rock-bordered fire pit nearby.

Knox appeared beside him with a flashlight and uttered a single swear word not fit for church.

"Yeah," Jeremy said. "Let's check inside."

"Don't touch anything," Knox said. "And be careful where you step." He shined the flashlight on the ground as they made their way to the vehicle.

Jeremy avoided the tire tracks made by the Suburban and noticed another set of tracks overlapping those. At the Suburban, he looked inside along with Knox, who aimed the flashlight. The car was clean. Nothing littered the interior and there was no sign of Jamie at all. He hadn't expected to find anything. Besides, the second set of tire tracks might be more important.

Knox began searching around the Suburban. "The second tracks lead here." Knox aimed the flashlight at the fresh set.

Jeremy went to stand next to him. "There was another car." The kidnapper had used the Suburban to tail Adeline and kidnap Jamie. He'd parked his own car there.

"I'll get a team here. We'll get those tracks analyzed."

Jeremy looked through the dark spaces between the trees, turning in a circle. "If only the woods had eyes."

Lying in the hospital bed, Adeline fidgeted, as she had for the last several hours. She wanted to get out of there. Twice, the nurse had come in to keep her from getting out of the bed. The last time she'd threatened to sedate her. She didn't want that. She didn't like drugs of any kind, not even over-the-counter pain medication.

Jeremy had been gone all night, searching for Jamie with Knox. Had they had any luck? She wished he'd call. Her mother had stopped by this morning on her way to work. She'd come by again over lunch and after she got off. Adeline hoped she wouldn't be in the hospital much longer. The doctor wanted to make sure she was safe from the risk of infection.

She flipped through channels on the television as she'd done repeatedly through the night. Nothing captured her interest or distracted her from Jamie's kidnapping. Dropping the remote onto the bed, she tossed the covers off her and would have once again tried to leave when she spotted Jeremy coming through the doorway.

He came right to her, leaned down and kissed her. "Where do you think you're going?"

Flustered that he'd kissed her, as though they'd done that a million times, she leaned back against the reclined bed.

Jeremy covered her back up. "I'm sorry I didn't call. We found the Suburban."

He had all her attention now, and not the physical kind.

"Prints were wiped clean, but they found a blond hair in the back seat that will be tested to confirm it's Jamie's. They will keep searching for evidence."

Adeline covered her mouth with a wave of apprehension and worry for Jamie.

"We found a second set of tire tracks at the scene. Investigators will run some tests and ask an expert what kind of car made them."

That sounded like a huge lead.

"That's good but it's been almost forty-eight hours since Jamie was taken," Jeremy said.

Adeline lowered her head, knowing too well what that meant. "We haven't received a ransom demand."

Jeremy took her hand. "No."

"What if it isn't a ransom? What if…?" She couldn't bring herself to say it. What would she do if something terrible happened to Jamie? She'd feel responsible. He was with her when he was taken.

"Don't, Adeline."

How did he know what she thought? "I should have checked for suspicious people. I usually do. I didn't that time and now Jamie is missing."

"You're not the one who kidnapped him."

"How can you be so forgiving?"

"Because I know how much you love him."

How did he know that? "W-what?"

"Your mother told me, but I didn't need her to. I've been denying the fact that you're Jamie's mother, especially now." He pinched the bridge of his nose momentarily. "I kept forcing myself to think of you as the surrogate and egg donor, that Tess was Jamie's mother. Even when Tess was alive that was hard for me. You are his mother now, Adeline."

He seemed pained to admit all that. The reason scared her. Even knowing how much she loved her son, he still needed time to get over losing Tess. Maybe he and his wife had had conflicts, but they had loved each other enough to marry and have a child. Jeremy was the kind of man who valued integrity. Faithfulness. He was a family man through and through. While that made her fall for him even more, she could not allow her heart to get any more involved with him. She had to protect herself. She'd already been hurt once. She never wanted to feel that way again. Jeremy refused to give up on the investigation into Tess's accident. He couldn't let go. That made him too risky for her.

"Who could have done this?" Jeremy asked. "Someone planned to take a Suburban and park it at a hidden campsite. He likely parked it at different locations to avoid detection. He drove his own car there and drove the Suburban. Police ran the plates. It's stolen."

"Oscar?"

"He was at work the day of the kidnapping."

"I had just left Evan," she said. "He wouldn't have had time or a reason. He was annoyed I came to ask him questions but that's nothing to incite him to murder and kidnapping." Jeremy had fired him but that was so long ago. He'd have retaliated already. Besides, he ran a seemingly successful escort service now. He'd made something new of his life. She'd expect him to not like Jeremy but he'd have to have more of a reason to kill and kidnap.

"I'm telling you. This is Livia."

Adeline nodded. She'd begun to believe him now. If Livia killed Tess, she'd used or attempted to use the same tactic on her and Jamie, having them nearly driven off the road. When that failed, she grew bolder. She could have paid someone to drive the Suburban, to shoot her and take Jamie.

"You believe me now?" Jeremy asked.

"Yes. I've always believed you had a good reason to suspect Livia. I only need the proof. We don't have any proof, but we do have circumstantial evidence."

He half smiled and Adeline watched as heat was injected into the expression. Satisfaction that she finally agreed with him about Livia fueled his response and caused one in her, too.

"When do I get out of here?" she asked to douse the chemistry.

"When you're well enough. You were shot."

"Your concern is touching." She kept her tone teasing and softened it with a smile similar to the one he'd bestowed on her.

He moved closer. "You must be getting better."

Her breath stopped for a second while a delicious zing flashed.

He closed the distance between their lips and kissed her softly.

When he lifted away, she said, "Then get me out of here."

Warm, swirling desire mushroomed, soothing the ever-present fear for Jamie. Although brief, the moment somehow made the waiting more bearable. They would get through this together.

Jeremy moved back. As he did, his phone rang. He checked caller ID. Adeline saw that the number was restricted. He answered.

"Yes?" A moment later, Jeremy flashed a look to Adeline. "Where is he? Did you take him?"

Adeline sat straight up on the hospital bed. He must be talking to Jamie's kidnapper.

"Why did you take Jamie? For money?" Jeremy asked, and then said, "We need proof of life." He stepped across the room and then turned, agitated. "That's not good enough." His head tipped back as he must be listening to the caller. "How do I know you're going to bring him? That you'll give him back to us?"

Jeremy lowered the phone and stared at her. The caller must have disconnected. She felt his anger brewing, and the helplessness to put it to good use.

"Five hundred thousand. Rabbit Trail Park," he said. "Nine p.m. the night after tomorrow."

"They won't give proof of life?"

Gravely, and with more anger, he shook his head.

"What are we going to do?"

"Pay the ransom and kill whoever took him. That's what I'm going to do."

His resolve was chilling. He'd kill Livia if she had anything to do with this.

"We have to wait two days. Why is he giving us so much time?" Jeremy asked.

"Maybe he knows getting that kind of cash takes time. Will Jamie be there?" The caller had refused Jeremy's demand for proof of life. What if he'd already harmed Jamie...or worse?

Anything could go wrong at the drop site. The kidnapper had given them plenty of time to get the cash.

The doctor came into the room. Lean and gray haired with glasses, he walked to the computer to read her file. "How are you feeling today?"

"Ready to go home."

Jeremy moved away to allow the doctor to go to Adeline. The doctor checked her wound.

"How's your pain level?" the doctor asked.

"Manageable." She hurt but she could hurt at home as much as she could in the hospital.

"You're tougher than you look." He finished checking her out. "No sign of infection. I think we can let you go." He pointed his finger at her. "But you need to rest. I'll send you home with some physical therapy instructions. Work slowly back up to your original speed."

"I'll do anything as long as I don't have to stay here."

The doctor smiled. "We'll start the discharge process."

When the doctor left, Adeline went back to the terrible facts. "As soon as we leave, let's try and find Jamie."

"Adeline, no. You heard the doctor. You have to rest. You won't be able to move well for a while anyway. Besides, Knox has a whole team behind this, helping."

"The kidnapper won't let us talk to Jamie. What if he's being treated badly?" She couldn't bring herself to think of him worse than injured.

"It's a fear tactic."

She hoped that's all it was.

Chapter 12

Two days later, Adeline's movement was much better and she insisted on accompanying Jeremy to the drop site. He only agreed after she promised to stay in the car. Looking back as he walked, he saw her still there and held his hand up as a way of reassuring her. She raised her hand in response, the sleeve of her white blouse sagging down. She'd worn one of her PI outfits again, silky slacks cupping her rear end a bit too appealingly for him and the vest dipping low in front, just below the top button of the blouse. He glanced around for signs of Knox and the team but they kept themselves hidden. Jeremy would stay in contact with Knox.

He walked to a bench. At this time of night, the park was deserted and this area didn't have much lighting. Moving in a circle, he searched for Jamie and his kidnapper. It was too dark to see very far. He waited fifteen minutes before his cell rang.

"Jeremy." The voice sounded altered.

"There's a bus stop straight ahead from the park bench. Take a bus to Ashland and get off at Main and

Second. Come alone. It's all right if the boy's mother joins you but no one else."

"You want me to go to the next town over?"

"Do as I say or your son dies." The kidnapper disconnected.

The kidnapper knew Adeline was Jamie's mother. Whoever had the boy must know Jeremy pretty well.

He called Knox. "He has me getting on a bus to Ashland and getting off at Main and Second."

"We'll get set up there."

"He knows Adeline is Jamie's mother."

"He said that?"

"Yes. He said the boy's mother can join me."

"It's someone you know, then."

"That's what I thought." Jeremy looked ahead from the bench and spotted the bus along the street that bordered the park there.

He jogged back to the car to get Adeline. She'd never forgive him if he didn't take her with him.

She'd gotten out of the car when she saw him approach. He could see her looking for Jamie. He explained what the kidnapper had instructed. Carrying the duffel bag, he walked with her back to the bench and the bus stop. The bus had just arrived. The kidnapper must have known it would arrive just in time.

He let Adeline on first and sat beside her, putting the bag down in front of him.

"Is the kidnapper leading us on a wild-goose chase or is he trying to cover his tracks?" she asked.

"Covering his tracks. Making sure we don't bring the sheriff or any of his deputies." He noticed the dark circles under her eyes. "You should have stayed home."

She looked at him and seemed to hesitate over his use

of "home." He said the word as though his house was their home. Maybe living with her had begun to make him feel that way.

Her eyes traveled over his suit. "Are you armed?"

"Yes." He'd put a gun in his waistband.

She turned her head and looked at him as though surprised. "You own one?"

"I keep it locked up in a safe. Licensed and legal." With Jamie in the house, he couldn't be too cautious.

"You didn't tell me."

He grinned. "You didn't think you were the only one who could handle a gun?"

"It's not that I don't think you can… I just…"

"I've owned one ever since Jamie was born."

With her soft smile and twinkling eyes, he felt her admiration. She liked that he took extra steps to protect his son. As a detective who carried her own weapon, she understood when the need warranted doing so.

"Was it really one of your cases that made you get one?" he asked.

"My mother always had one. I bought one when I moved out on my own. I took lessons back then."

She'd learned her independence, or had been taught. She was different from Tess in many ways. Tess had decided not to work after she had Jamie. She'd worked as an accountant before that. He wouldn't go so far as to say she was dependent, but she was much needier than Adeline, her emotions more sensitive. Jeremy respected Adeline's ambition. She needed no one. She'd made her own way. While he'd had similar thoughts before, this time he felt something deeper for her. Respect had grown into a personal admiration, one with definite sexual undercurrents. He was growing more and more attracted to her.

The bus stopped at Main and Second. Jeremy picked up the bag and led Adeline to the exit. With a chill in the air, he put his arm around her and went into the well-lit, covered waiting area. A man left a pub across the street, letting out the sounds of country music and boisterous voices. A breeze swirled around the plastic walls of the shelter. Patches of stars glimmered beyond gathering clouds.

Adeline huddled closer with the chilly breeze. He wasn't sure if warmth kept her by his side or if she shared the pleasant tingles he experienced. She felt good right next to him.

Minutes passed and he grew more and more aware of her. She seemed to experience the same as she turned her head up to look at him. When he looked at her, his lips came into position just above hers. Holding her gaze, he did what instinct drove him to do. He pressed a soft, light kiss on her mouth, and it felt comforting in such a perilous time. His cell phone interrupted.

He answered.

"Walk east down Main Street to the library. Wait on the front steps."

The caller disconnected.

"We're supposed to go to the library," he said to Adeline.

"Will Jamie be there?"

"Let's go find out."

Jeremy kept his arm around Adeline as they walked, feeling her slip her arm around his waist. He caught her nervous glance up. She sought comfort. He was nervous, too. He just wanted his son back.

He spotted the library ahead. No sign of Jamie. He shared another nervous look with Adeline. Reaching the library steps, he stopped with Adeline, looking for a place to get out of the wind. He expected to wait several minutes again, but his phone rang.

"There's a construction site across the street," the kidnapper said in his disguised voice. "Put the money in the front, southwest corner."

"Where is my son?"

"You'll get him when I have all the money."

"Show him to me." Jeremy looked around and saw no movement. The construction site was dark, except for the spheres of light coming from the top of two poles.

"You have five minutes to deliver the money. If it's not there, I'll kill Jamie."

"How did you know Adeline was Jamie's mother?" Jeremy wanted to keep the man talking for as long as possible, try to get as much information out of him as he could.

"Bring the money or the kid dies." The caller disconnected.

Jeremy let out a frustrated breath. Had Knox traced the call? He wished he had mental telepathy so he could know who had his son. He'd track that monster down and wring the life out of him. What kind of man kidnapped children?

"Let's drop the money," Adeline said.

She must have realized the kidnapper had threatened Jamie's life.

"Be ready." He walked into the street.

"Oh, I'm ready. I've been ready since we got the call."

Together they crossed the street and walked along the construction fence to an open area where vehicles could pass. Someone had either left the makeshift gate open or the kidnapper had.

When he drew nearer the shell of concrete, he took out his gun and turned the safety off. Beside him, Adeline did the same. The structure had spaces for windows and a front entrance but no ceilings, only steel beams running across each floor. The building was large enough to be some kind of department store. At the entrance, light from outside faded.

He stepped into the building. While he aimed to the right, Adeline aimed to the left. No one and nothing stirred. Only the breeze rustling light debris broke the silence.

"We're just supposed to leave the bag?" Adeline whispered.

Jeremy didn't want to do that. If they left the money, what would become of Jamie?

"Let's leave it but stay until someone comes to get it," he said.

"Okay." Jeremy walked to the southwest corner and dropped the bag.

They stepped back toward the entrance and waited. A text dinged on his phone shortly thereafter.

Leave, the message read.

Not without my son, Jeremy responded.

The sound of feet shuffling over concrete alerted him just before gunfire erupted. Adeline screeched and leaped through the opening. They each took cover. Bullets hit the concrete on the other side. At last they subsided, the shooter probably having run out of bullets.

Jeremy peeked inside the building. A darkly dressed person ran away, carrying the duffel bag. Small of frame, the figure didn't look big enough to be a man.

"Livia!" Jeremy called.

The figure looked back and aimed a gun. She must have had two. She fired and Jeremy ducked in time. Then he pushed away from the wall and ran after the woman.

"Stop!" he shouted. "Where is my son?"

He ran as fast as he could to the back of the building where the woman had gone. At what would likely someday be the shipping dock, he took cover along with Adeline on the other side of the opening. The woman fired at them again.

Jeremy aimed his gun out the opening. The woman had gotten into a white sedan. He aimed for the rear tire and fired. Missing, he jumped down from the dock and ran after the car. What if Jamie was inside?

Obviously the shooter had no intention of giving them Jamie in exchange for the money, so why bring him along? Jeremy kept running long after the car disappeared from sight, too far away to catch a plate number. Not until he was out of breath did he slow and stop, leaning over.

Footsteps from behind signified Adeline on her way. He saw her running, blond hair floating, and her slender, sexy legs graceful and strong. He straightened as she stopped beside him, breathing as hard as him and wincing and holding her side.

"Why are you running?" Was she crazy? She could injure herself more severely.

"I called Knox," she said between gulps of air that came with more wincing. "He's…going…to send…his people after her." She inhaled several more breaths before slowing her frantic need for air.

"You noticed Jamie's kidnapper is a female?" he asked, beginning to catch his own breath. He yanked her shirt out from her pants and lifted it to check her bandage. There was no fresh blood leaking through so maybe she hadn't done any further damage.

"Yes."

"It has to be Livia. She could have sent a woman." He dropped her shirt. "Don't overexert yourself like that again."

"I don't think so." She shook her head as her breathing began to normalize. "And I won't."

Damn, why did she have to refute him on that every time? He thought he'd gotten through to her. But then he saw she held her hand palm up and a woman's necklace dangled from her fingers.

He took it from her, holding it up to see a pendant with the letter *E* engraved there.

"I found it on the ground near where she got into the car. It must have broken off."

"How can we be sure it belongs to the kidnapper?" The necklace could have fallen from anyone at any time before they'd arrived.

"I saw something fall as she got into the car," Adeline said. "It's hers."

How had she seen that? "You have good vision."

"I always look for details that could be easily missed. I couldn't see what had fallen, I just saw that something had."

"All right, but we still can't be sure Livia isn't behind all of this. A man shot you, remember." A woman hadn't shot her. More than one person could be involved. More than one person *had* to be involved.

He watched her ponder that a moment. "I'm not saying she didn't have anything to do with it."

"Right. You just don't have any evidence."

* * *

After a long, hot bath, Adeline dried herself and got into a nightgown. She then donned a robe and left her room to go downstairs. In the family room, Jeremy leaned over the back of a chair. The tub had eased her aches after sprinting the way she had, but hadn't eased her mind. She felt his agony.

"Any calls?"

He pushed off the chair, eyes drawn. He'd removed his suit jacket and loosened his tie. "No. Knox called, but all he confirmed is Evan did have a new entertainment center in his house."

So he hadn't paid off the deputy, who was clean—unless he was crooked and did carpentry.

She walked across the family room. Jeremy had turned the television on at a low volume but wasn't watching anything. Adeline didn't have to wonder why. Most kidnappings where the ransom was paid and the child was not given back didn't end well. The Lindbergh case was one of the most famous examples of that. Adeline knew of several more. She felt sick that Jamie might end up the same way, that he could be killed.

"Jamie's nanny's name was Emily," Jeremy said. "I didn't think of this before, but she took her firing very badly. She was also arrested for shoplifting before I hired her. She was only arrested once, but maybe she has stealing in her blood. She also would have motive to get even with me."

He could be on to something. Evan's name began with an *E*, too, but he probably wouldn't wear a necklace with his initial. And the person getting into the car had had a lighter frame than a man.

"Do you know where she lives?" Adeline saw that

the sun had broken over the horizon. They hadn't slept at all last night.

"Yes."

When Adeline had taken Jeremy's case, she hadn't anticipated it would explode into a child kidnapping. "Let's go talk to her, then."

"After you get some rest."

"You need rest, too." She saw flowers on the front entry table. "What are those?" She walked over to them.

"I wasn't going to show them to you until you slept." He followed her to the flowers. "They were on the front step when we arrived home. They must have been delivered just after we left to make the drop."

Adeline lifted a card from its holder and took it from the small envelope. Handwritten in block letters was, YOU DIDN'T THINK I'D MAKE IT THAT EASY, DID YOU?

She turned to Jeremy. "Do you recognize the writing?"

"No. It looks deliberately disguised. Also, whoever delivered them must have bought them at a flower shop and dropped them off themselves." Most florists closed early in town. "We'll talk to the neighbors but I doubt any of them saw anything. The houses are spaced too far apart and it was late."

Adeline thought a moment because something didn't add up. "Someone dropped these off after we left?"

"They weren't here when we left."

The kidnapper seemed to know where she and Jeremy were at all times as they'd followed the drop instructions, or at the very least, at the construction site. Could she have dropped the flowers off and then driven to the construction site? "Is it possible the kidnapper isn't working alone?"

"Sure. Livia could have arranged to have Tess killed and then realized she could make some money on a ransom. If Emily hooked up with her, she'd have found an ally."

All theory and possibilities, but Adeline wasn't convinced. "If Emily is working with someone, then it's someone close to her. Livia doesn't have enough of a reason to kidnap Jamie and hold him for ransom, especially leaving a note like this." She held the small card up.

If Livia survived the accident and swam out of the river, she'd have more to worry about than revenge and an elaborate plan for kidnapping. She'd be busy running from the law again. Granted, she needed money, but why Jeremy, and why kidnap Jamie? To Adeline, Livia's grudge against Tess seemed weak. There had to be other people she could prey on, people she resented far more than Jeremy. Besides, what had Jeremy ever done to Livia to make her think of using him for her gain?

"No matter how wronged Livia feels against someone, if she sees an opportunity, she'll take it," Jeremy said. "She doesn't need motive. She only needs an opportunity. I'm vulnerable. I lost my wife and now I'm a single dad. I also happen to have a lot of money."

"Opportunity," Adeline said. "Okay, but surely she knows of other people she can use. You aren't her only option. So, why you? Why Jamie?"

"Not everyone is rich like me," he said. "That would narrow down her options."

"You suspect Livia because she had a reason to despise Tess, but other than her nefarious character, I don't see enough to suspect her."

"If Livia survived that accident, she's desperate. Desperate people do desperate things."

Adeline nodded, folding her arms. "Desperation is valid, but this seems more personal than Livia selecting you for money. This seems like whoever took Jamie wants to see you suffer."

After a while, Jeremy finally relented. "I agree."

She went to the bookshelf along a side wall of the family room where an electronic frame switched through several photos. Most included Jamie. His adorable, smiling face and bright blue eyes told of a happy boy. The pictures of Tess haunted her. She felt at odds falling for her husband, especially knowing how much Tess had loved him. Although now Adeline questioned that love. If Tess had approached Oscar with a proposal to start up their affair again, could she have possibly loved Jeremy as much as she'd claimed? Alcohol could have certainly clouded her judgment, but even then, wouldn't true love steer her in the right direction?

Jeremy reached to the photo frame and pressed a button to stop its cycling. Adeline didn't realize he'd followed her across the room until then. He'd moved closer and she felt his warmth. She also sensed his absorption with one photo. Jamie must have been about two. He sat at a picnic table with a cake before him, what looked like half his piece covering his face around his mouth. He smiled big.

"That was the first time he was really happy."

After Tess died.

"He had all his friends over. I set up an inflatable bounce house in the backyard and gave him his first tricycle for his present."

Adeline stared at Jamie's playful face and felt a surge

of love. She'd helped to create such an angel. Now that angel was in the hands of someone evil and they might not ever get him back. He could be killed. He could be dead already.

Unable to suppress the sting of tears, she turned to Jeremy for comfort. "Oh, Jeremy."

Jeremy took her into his arms. His hands rubbed her back, slow, sensual and firm. Then he pressed a kiss on her head. She felt his warm breath on her hair and scalp. With her arms under his and hands on his back, she snuggled closer, resting the side of her head on his chest.

"We'll find him," he said.

She heard his doubt and worry. Jeremy would fight for his son. He wouldn't give up. But the reality of their situation delivered a heavy load.

He kissed her head again, and then kissed her forehead. Adeline leaned back a little, bringing her cheek against his. The soothing warmth of his nearness calmed her. In his arms like this, tension eased. The temptation to stay wrapped in this refuge enticed her.

He seemed drugged by the same potion as he slid his head down and pressed his lips to her neck. The gesture could have been for a friend. He moved so naturally and instinctually needed solace as much as her.

"Let's get some rest." He offered his hand, holding it out to her and waiting with patience.

He helped control the spiraling impulse to let him ravage her. She gave him her hand and he didn't let go as he led her upstairs. In his bedroom, she saw all the masculine touches that fit the man who slept there. A pedestal table nestled between two blocky wing chairs. Narrow, five-foot chocolate-brown bookcases flanked a king-size bed with a leather upholstered headboard.

Pendant lighting over the pedestal table provided the only illumination, unintentionally romantic.

Jeremy went to the dresser and put down his phone before facing her. She met his eyes for a long stare, electric undercurrents testing what might follow. Maybe they both needed a break from the stress, an escape. No more thinking, projecting. Just feel this, whatever they generated together. Use it to get through the waiting.

Without looking away, he further loosened and removed his tie, draping the bright blue piece on the dresser. Then he continued to meet her eyes.

Adeline understood what he waited for and untied her robe, letting it slip off her shoulders and then dropping it onto one of the chairs. Then she met his gaze again.

Eyes darkening with rising passion, Jeremy unbuttoned his dress shirt, exposing rippling muscles. Heat intensified as he shrugged the garment off his broad shoulders and tossed it to the floor.

She walked to him. Reaching up, she ran her hand from the shorter strands of his hair on the side to the longer ones on top. Their warmth and smooth texture added kindling to the fire.

She couldn't look away from his face, which conveyed such naked desire. Like the photo of Jamie, she wished she could capture him like this so she could have it forever. Why couldn't she?

Picking up his cell phone, she opened the camera.

"What are you doing?"

"Just let me." She put his face in the center of the camera's lens. "You have to send me this." She waited for his eyes to melt back into their smoldering state before snapping the picture of him looking at her like that.

Adeline set the camera back on the dresser and then

reached for the fastener of his slacks. He stepped out of them and then removed his underwear. She lifted her nightgown off and stood only in her underwear.

He stepped closer and kissed her, soft and tentative, asking. She kissed him back, feeling his hard chest and arm muscles.

Breaking away from her lips, he went to the bed and sat against the leather upholstered headboard. Adeline crawled on her knees to straddle his thighs. Sitting on his lap, she took his face between her hands. Watching his eyes close as she leaned down, she touched her lips to his. He angled his head and took command of the kiss, pressing harder and tasting her tenderly with his tongue. With his hands on her butt, he pulled her higher up his thighs. Then he took her mouth for a deeper, hungrier taste.

Cupping the back of his head in her hand, she trailed her other hand over his shoulder, down to his flexed biceps, where she squeezed and felt heat course through her. Lost in growing sensation, she kissed his lips and moved against his hard ridge.

"What about protection?"

"I'm on the Pill." She moaned as he trailed his tongue down her neck between soft kisses. She let her head fall back as he tasted her breasts. Then he nipped the curve of her chin with his lips as his hands took over what his mouth had left. He held her breasts, testing their weight, feeling their softness and driving Adeline wild.

Wrapping his arm around her waist, he leaned forward, making her fall back against his strong arm. Her breasts jutted toward him, urging him to have more of her. He put his mouth over one and his tongue repeatedly grazed her nipple. Her lips parted in a silent moan.

She moved her hips against his hardness again, needing him inside her now.

He buried his fingers into her hair and pulled her head back. Looking up at his raging passion, she parted her lips as his crushed down on hers.

His hands roved over her bare back and butt. Then he slid one hand between their bodies, going down, down, until he reached the part of her that yearned for him. He penetrated her with his finger. She had to stop kissing him against the shudder that gripped her.

When his face came back into focus, she put her hands on his shoulders and positioned herself over his erection. He held her by the waist and guided her down. She listened to his ragged sigh and watched him close his eyes and lean his head back against the headboard as her weight pushed him deep inside her. She kissed the strong cords of his neck and held still, savoring the feel of their joining.

His biceps bunched as he dug his hand into her long, tangled hair and tilted her face back. Hot dark eyes drilled into hers with passion. Adeline began to slowly rock her hips. The sweet grind drove her to press harder and add a circular roll to her movement. Jeremy groaned and lifted his hips to meet her. He took her lower lip between his teeth, holding it but not biting. She licked his upper lip and he kissed her with animal urgency. Adeline lifted her hands to the top of the headboard and continued to grind herself on him. Spirals of sensation built to a crescendo until she shattered.

Afterward, she lowered her hands and wrapped her arms around his neck, holding him close, kissing him sweetly while she tried to catch her breath. Jeremy rolled her to his side, then laid her flat on the mattress. Spreading her legs wider with his knees, he reentered her with a hard thrust. Adeline grunted, amazed that he could make her ready for a second orgasm. He withdrew and pressed inside again, sending mind-numbing sensation swirling through her, radiating outward, and much more intense than the first time.

He began to pump his hips faster, building the sensation to unbearable heights. She heard her own cry of ecstasy as he went deep and pulled back with each slippery stroke. She felt his stomach rub hers, listened to his breathless pants, smelled his musky scent. She came apart along with his fiery eruption.

Jeremy collapsed on top of her. She folded her arms around him and rubbed his back, content to stay in the aftermath of something she had yet to comprehend.

Chapter 13

Jeremy began to wake to something soft and warm pressed along his side. His arm had fallen asleep where a woman's head lay. Her soft hair tickled his chest. Waking up further, his mind cleared. This wasn't just a woman next to him. Adeline. They'd slept together. The potency hit him. Every sensation and desire, the passion. He'd connected with her, looking at those photos of Jamie, and resulting temptation in a vulnerable moment led to disaster.

He felt as though he'd betrayed his son. And his wife…

Easing his arm from beneath her, he stood from the bed and went into the bathroom. Closing the door, he turned the water on and leaned over the sink. How could he have done that? Looking at himself in the mirror, he met his own brown eyes and saw the disappointment he felt.

He wasn't sure about starting anything with Adeline—with any woman. That wasn't fair to Adeline any more than it was to Jamie or Tess. To make matters worse, while Jamie was being held captive, he'd allowed carnal needs to take over. Upon reflection, he could see how he'd lost control, but now he'd have to deal with consequences.

He may have entertained some fanciful notions about Adeline being Jamie's biological mother, but he hadn't intended to start up anything. He'd thought having her around for a while would be good for Jamie, with the added bonus that she'd donated her eggs and served as his and Tess's surrogate. Everybody benefited for a few weeks. Had he spent too much time convincing himself of that?

How would he go about handling this? Everything in him recoiled when he considered going with whatever had begun, with making love with Adeline. Not when he thought of her and the amazing chemistry they shared. Just what the future would bring. That, and guilt. He intended to resolve all his questions and suspicions surrounding Tess's death.

He still felt…what did he feel? Responsibility? Moral obligation?

Yes, and more. When he and Tess talked about having a child, they'd agreed both of them had to be sure they'd raise him or her as their own. Tess had had major reservations about having a baby that wasn't hers. A certain amount of selfishness yearned for one of her own. Tess couldn't have kids. That had always bothered her. Although she had never said so, she was jealous of Adeline. He'd seen how she watched her sometimes. Adeline often put her hand on her growing belly. She also let Tess feel the baby move or kick. Tess had been in awe every time but, afterward, Jeremy would see her eyes sadden and she'd either look away or watch Adeline in that envious way. But her desire to be a mother overruled any insecurity she may have felt.

Tess had wanted Jamie with all her heart. The fact he wasn't theirs biologically might have bothered Tess but she loved Jamie.

"Everything okay?"

He straightened from the sink, realizing he'd turned on the water and had been just standing there. Adeline eyed him warily.

"Troubling thoughts?" she asked with a bit of bite to her tone.

"No..." He couldn't be dishonest with her. "I...last night kind of threw me."

She folded her arms, growing more and more distant. "It threw me, too."

"I'm not sure the timing was right."

"Because Jamie is still missing?"

"We have no choice other than to wait for another call." He didn't want to delve into more. He walked out of the bathroom to get some clothes. "Let's just take it a day at a time, okay?" Today he'd take some time away from thoughts of what had happened.

"That's all I get? Not even a 'good morning'?" She followed him. "Just, 'Last night threw me—can we take it a day at a time'?"

He dropped the jeans he would have brought into the bathroom for after his shower back into the drawer. Adeline stood with one hand on her hip—a very sexy hip, one he had run his hands over many times. She exuded a need for him to go to her and reassure her, but he couldn't even reassure himself right now. He began to feel cornered. What did she expect from him?

"I just need some time to process," he said. "Do you have an issue with that?"

She stood there several seconds, eyes exuding emotional turmoil that likely resembled that in his gaze, but for some reason she refused acceptance.

"Were you ready for that?" he asked.

She averted her eyes briefly and then finally said, "No. I'm not even sure I can trust you."

"Me?" Why did she feel she couldn't trust him? Even if ultimately they didn't end up in a relationship, he wouldn't do anything to hurt her. He wasn't discounting a relationship. He still felt beholden to Tess. And with Adeline being Jamie's biological mother, he felt…strange…awkward. He couldn't explain why.

She turned, her nightgown flowing out. "I'll let you take your shower."

"Adeline."

Stopping, she looked back, expression blank now. She'd erected a swift wall as though she'd practiced it many times.

"Why don't you trust me?"

"Let's just take it a day at a time," she answered, and then left.

After handing over the note to Knox for evidence, Adeline agreed with Jeremy to ignore the sheriff's advice to leave the investigation up to him and his team. He would go talk to Emily Stanton, but Adeline could not wait any longer.

The ride to see Emily was tense, the silence weighty and speaking volumes. Adeline didn't care. She still fumed over Jeremy's easy dismissal. Typical man. She hadn't decided if he'd descended to the ranks of her ex-boyfriend. Probably not, since she didn't think she'd have to get a restraining order to get rid of him, and he made his own money. His selfishness might be right in the ball park, however. He placed Jamie as a top priority—which he should. She didn't dock him points for that, but he elevated Tess out of guilt. Moving on entailed coming to terms with Tess's death and he hadn't done that yet. If he knew he wasn't ready for last night, then he shouldn't have allowed anything to happen.

While she tried to put the blame on him, deep down she knew she couldn't, not all of it. She'd succumbed to their chemistry equally. If she examined her feelings enough, she'd acknowledge her past failures had tainted her quite a bit. Her ex-boyfriend wasn't the first, either. Before him, she'd gone through several relationships that hadn't progressed. All of the men had one thing in common—none of them were mature enough to commit.

Had she found another man like them in Jeremy? Why did she gravitate to them? What about them drew her?

Except… Jeremy was nothing like any of those men. He was successful, sure of himself and a grieving widower. He didn't depend on anyone. Maybe that was her downfall, her mistake. She'd been attracted to those other men because they'd seemed to care; they had warm hearts, but what she failed to consider was their inability to take care of themselves. That intensified her reaction to what she could only call Jeremy's rejection. Who *liked* rejection, anyway?

In retrospect, she'd never experienced it before. She'd always been the one to end a bad relationship. If she were completely honest with herself, she'd acknowledge that maybe she chose badly because she had no fatherly role model. No man in her life taught her what a *good* man should be like. She'd only had her mother.

Now that she'd had time to analyze everything, she regretted allowing herself to react the way she had. She wouldn't allow that to happen again. Given the uncontrollable passion that had led to their making love, she couldn't be certain she could prevent a repeat encounter. But she could control her reaction afterward. If this was only a fling, then she'd look back on her time with Jeremy and Jamie with fond memories. She had a choice on how she reacted and she chose not to lament over what-ifs and losses.

And why was she hashing over all of that now? She should be thinking of Jamie.

"Everything okay?"

She turned when Jeremy spoke and then looking ahead through the windshield, she saw he'd parked along the street in front of Emily Stanton's house.

Without responding, she opened the door and got out.

Time to go to work. Time to be a detective, the only thing in her life that gave her structure, surety and a sense of purpose. Another epiphany. She'd found her calling in life professionally. No problem. But when it came to men, that was another matter completely.

She went to the front door and rang the bell, a few seconds before Jeremy appeared beside her. In jeans and a white Oxford shirt with no jacket on this unseasonably warm, sunny Texas day, he called to her femininity far too much.

"I'll take that as a no."

Ignoring him, she rang the bell again. Feeling him eye her, she rang the bell once more and then leaned to peer through the narrow side window. No one seemed to be home.

Without saying anything she walked to the driveway and then to the side of the house. In the back, she tested the garage door and found it unlocked. As she went inside, she found the inner door also had been left unlocked. Someone was either forgetful or distracted.

As she began to turn the knob, Jeremy clamped his hand on her wrist.

"Let me go first," he said, close to her ear.

"Just because we had sex doesn't mean you need to protect me." Knowing she'd responded rashly, she amended, "I'm the detective. You hired me for this." She met his eyes from across her shoulder.

He released her.

She took out her gun and entered the house. Nothing stirred. In the silence, their footsteps resonated through the kitchen and living room. Emily lived on a small ranch house. The garage door was off the kitchen. Items cluttered the counters and dishes filled the sink. The light above the round table had been left on. Around the alcove of the kitchen, the living room wasn't in much better shape. A throw was strewn on the floor. Drinking glasses and plates had been left forgotten.

A mantel full of haphazardly arranged framed photos drew Adeline. She hadn't seen a picture of Emily until now. Emily smiled from a picture of herself with what must be her mother. She had the same build as the woman she'd seen getting into the vehicle the night of the drop. Plus, she wore the same jacket.

"That's her," Adeline said. "Look at the jacket."

"Yeah. It looks the same."

Jeremy moved on to the three bedrooms and bathroom

down a single, straight hallway. A guest room was the neatest and most untouched. In the master bedroom, a ten-by-fourteen room with a small walk-in closet and a half bath, clothes lay in a pile on the floor and covered a wicker chair. Emily wasn't much of a housekeeper. Adeline went through the lower dresser and he went through a taller one, finding nothing of significance to Jamie's kidnapping.

"No computer," she said.

"No desk," Jeremy said.

"If she doesn't have a laptop, she must use her phone for everything." Adeline stepped over more clothes on the floor of the walk-in closet.

He went to the doorway and leaned against the door frame. Top shelves held more crumpled shirts and pants, but on the far right corner he spotted two boxes. Adeline must have seen them, too. Crouching, she lifted the first and put it down, opening the lid; sifting through tax documents, she then put that box aside. The second box held bank statements and used duplicate checkbooks. She looked at the most recent bank statements.

"Anything unusual?" Jeremy asked from behind her.

She glanced back and took in his folded arms and posture against the doorframe, as though the sight of him magnetized her.

"Typical expenditures. Grocery store. Superstore. Gas. Consistent deposits."

"No one's paying her to kidnap Jamie," Jeremy said.

"If she is being paid, she didn't deposit it into her account."

"Smart? Or just no time?"

"Exactly." Adeline stood and followed him out of the

bedroom and through the house. Back through the garage door, she headed toward the street.

He followed, seeing her stiff gait and having registered her equally stony face. He wasn't good at talking about emotions, but he owed her something. Or maybe not *owed*. She needed him to talk to her.

"I'm sorry about this morning," he said. "I should have talked to you then."

"It's okay. I understand." Her aloofness made its way into her tone.

"I don't think you do. For Jamie's sake, I need to be sure if I get involved with someone, and I'm not. It's not that I don't feel anything for you. I do." He glanced down her sexy body and then realized he'd done so automatically. Together, they triggered uncontrollable chemistry. "I don't think falling into a passionate affair would be healthy for him right now and I don't want to hide anything from him."

She stopped walking and turned to him. "We're good, Jeremy. I don't trust you anyway. I don't trust any man who has unfinished personal business in his past."

Fair enough. While he disliked her lack of trust in him, he did have unfinished business where Tess was concerned.

"I think you're reaching for a way to come to terms with Tess's death," Adeline added.

"Reaching?" All he wanted was definitive answers surrounding her accident so he could put her death behind him and move on.

"Do you feel guilty about anything?" she asked.

"Why would I feel guilty?" Had her skepticism over

whether Livia had anything to do with Tess's accident made her say that?

He watched her contemplate him awhile. "I don't know. Maybe you never completely trusted Tess as a recovering alcoholic and you feel bad for not doing something to help her after you discovered she had fallen back into her addiction."

Why did that feel so accurate? He felt a jab right through his chest, as though what she said seemed so reasonable. Of course he wished he would have done more, and sometimes wondered if he hadn't cared, at least not enough. He hadn't considered that he'd need to vindicate Tess in some way, and that his quest to pin her death on Livia might give him that.

"Let's stick to finding Jamie." He started walking toward the car again.

She came into step beside him. "I must be right, then."

"You keep discounting the possibility that Livia could be responsible somehow."

"What if Livia is dead, Jeremy?"

He refused to argue with her. She hadn't believed from the beginning. She might have agreed with him on some occasions but she still wasn't completely convinced.

"Even if she did kill Tess, if she is dead, will you move on? Will it be enough?" she asked, stopping at the car.

He wasn't ready to give in to her assertion that he felt guilty just yet. "All I wanted to say is, I'm sorry for not talking to you about last night. I don't want to hurt you." And especially Jamie. He had to tread carefully with her.

According to what Adeline had found out, after Jeremy had fired Emily, she'd taken a job as a janitor for a microchip manufacturing company. She and Jeremy had met with Knox and together devised a plan to move the kidnapping investigation forward. Knox would continue to push his team in the search for Jamie and she and Jeremy would question Emily. She might feel less threatened if someone not wearing a law enforcement uniform approached her.

Her boss was a short, balding man with a clear self-image problem. They'd introduced themselves and asked about Emily and he'd gone on a long diatribe over her betrayal.

"Nobody walks out on me like that," he'd said, as though he'd seek revenge when—or if—he ever saw the woman again. "I gave her a chance after she'd been fired from her last job and this is the way she thanks me." He mentioned he'd heard Emily had called him a midget once. For a manager he sure was immature. He'd also sized Adeline up as though threatened by her, as though all women threatened his manliness or his ability to maintain control of everything and everyone.

"You say she called in sick?" Adeline asked. Emily had done so on the day Jamie was taken.

"Yes. She left me a message early. I haven't seen her since. I can't wait to fire her."

Emily had to know she no longer had a job, but then, if she received ransom money she must have believed she wouldn't have to.

"Was she friends with anyone here?"

"She and my administrative assistant sometimes went to lunch together. They talked a lot during work. Too much, if you ask me."

He didn't seem very nice to work for. "Can we have a word with her?"

"Sure." He pointed outside his office door. "She sits in that cubicle."

Adeline thanked him and went to the cubicle, where a thin woman, with long, dark, silk hair, typed on her keyboard. She looked over and up as they appeared in the opening.

"Can I help you?" she asked.

"I'm Adeline Winters and this is Jeremy Kincaid. We're here to talk to you about Emily Stanton."

"You two are cops?" She swiveled on her chair with a smile, seemingly intrigued to be involved in a police questioning.

"I'm a private investigator. We're trying to locate Emily. When is the last time you saw or spoke with her?"

The woman sobered, concern for her friend taking over. "The day before she called in sick. Nobody here has seen or heard from her since."

"Were the two of you close?"

"I wouldn't say 'close.' We were coworkers. We didn't do anything outside of work together."

"Did she have other friends? Did she ever mention them to you? What about family?"

"Emily didn't have any family. Her mom died when she was young and she didn't know her dad. She talked about her neighbor. I don't know if she had any other friends."

"Did she ever say anything you thought was unusual?" Adeline asked.

The woman thought a moment. "No. 'Course, she didn't work here long. She used to be a nanny. The guy fired her. She said he was a real jerk. He's got lots of money and held his kid up on a pedestal."

Amused, Adeline glanced at Jeremy. Clearly Emily

hadn't mentioned who she'd worked for as a nanny. This woman didn't recognize Jeremy's name.

"Why did he fire her?" Jeremy asked, playing along.

"Emily said he accused her of taking his wife's jewelry but she didn't. His wife died and he was obsessed with the loss."

Interesting that Emily had lied about why she was fired and yet appeared to have told the truth about Jeremy's obsession.

"Emily hasn't contacted you since the day before she called in sick?" Jeremy asked.

The woman shook her head. "We're friends but I haven't known her very long. Is she missing or something?"

"Thanks for talking to us today," Adeline said and then turned to walk away, steering Jeremy to join her.

They reached the vehicle and Jeremy drove the short distance to Emily's house. After knocking and ringing the bell and checking windows once again, they walked over to the neighbor's house. The woman lived in a similar ranch home. The woman who answered the door was a five-five, curvy blonde; she wore a wedding band and Adeline could hear children playing off what she could see of a small living room.

"Yes?" the woman said in the open doorway.

Adeline did a quick introduction and saw no recognition on the woman's face. "We're looking for Emily Stanton, your neighbor. Have you seen her?"

"Really? Why are you looking for her?" the woman asked warily.

Adeline would try to avoid answering that question. She'd just said she was a private investigator. "Has she been home in the last few days? When is the last time you saw her?"

"Yesterday. She came home during the day and then left again. I haven't seen her since, but that's no surprise. Why are you looking for her?" she asked again.

"Did she say where she was going?" Jeremy asked.

"Not really. She was going to run some errands and then meet a friend. She needed a night out, I guess."

"How well do you know her?" Adeline asked.

The woman hesitated.

"Are you friends?" Adeline pushed her.

"Are you going to tell me why you're looking for her?"

"She's missing," Adeline relented. "We're part of a team trying to find her."

"Missing...wow. Since yesterday?" She glanced over at Jeremy. "Who reported her missing?"

"If you could answer our questions?" Adeline said. "We can't discuss the reason why we're looking for her."

"Oh." The woman looked apprehensively from Adeline to Jeremy. "Well, then, maybe I should only talk to the police."

"We are working with the sheriff's office. If you like, we can have Sheriff Colton give you a call to confirm that," Jeremy said.

The woman's eyes lowered and averted as though she was contrite. "No, that won't be necessary. Do you think I was the last person to see her?"

"Possibly," Adeline said. "Would you say you two are friends?"

"Yes. We go over to each other's houses for drinks every once in a while. Do each other favors. Talk."

The shriek of a young girl's voice carried out from one of the bedrooms.

"Sorry." The woman smiled. "My daughter." She stepped out onto the porch and closed the door behind her.

Adeline moved back a step to make more room for her. "How long have you known Emily?" Jeremy stood far enough away that he didn't have to move.

"Oh, gosh. Five years?" She seemed uncertain, as though she hadn't counted the years and only then had thought of it.

"Did she ever mention anything unusual to you?" Adeline asked. "Anything she may have been planning?"

"No. What do you mean 'unusual'?" The woman tucked her fingers into the pocket of tight blue jeans.

"After she was fired from her nanny job, did she tell you about that?" Jeremy asked.

"Oh, yeah. She was really upset about that. She was worried about losing her house. Luckily I knew of a job opening and she started about a month later."

"She never mentioned seeking revenge on the man who fired her?" Adeline asked.

"No. I can't imagine Emily doing anything like that. She's kind of a quiet person. We respect each other's privacy. She keeps to herself...except when we get together. She gets talkative then and we have a fun time. She's really good with kids, too."

"Did she ever tell you she was arrested for shoplifting?"

The woman opened her mouth. "Oh. No. Was she? Wait a minute...has she done something? Why are you looking for her?" She kept asking that.

"Can we get your name?" Adeline asked.

"Julie Smith," she answered hesitantly.

"Thanks for talking to us today, Julie." Adeline used her token phrase and again steered Jeremy away from the house.

"Well," Adeline said. "Emily has been home since Jamie was kidnapped a few days ago."

"Knox will put eyes on her house."

Adeline didn't think that would do much good. Emily's neighbor would warn her they'd stopped by with questions.

Back at Jeremy's house, Adeline grabbed a little something to eat and would have gone up to her room. Plaguing worry stopped her. They'd received no call from the kidnapper today. She wouldn't be able to sleep. Why had the kidnapper done that? He—or she—seemed to be taunting them, or Jeremy. Drawing out the agony. If Emily sought revenge, she'd get it with Jeremy's suffering.

So much didn't add up, though. Why had that man broken into Jeremy's house, and why had he shot her? Why try to kill her and then kidnap Jamie? The more Adeline thought, the more the idea of Livia changing her plans didn't seem likely. Did the kidnapper merely intend to eliminate a threat in order to carry out his plan to take Jeremy's son? What was the kidnapper's purpose in all of this? What was Emily's relationship with the man?

Jeremy would have liked to link Livia to the entire series of crimes. Adeline still didn't discount the possibility; she only doubted the likelihood. But the man who shot her could be linked with Emily, and the man could have shot her to get her out of the way, to prevent her from stopping his and Emily's plan.

Jeremy sat on the sofa in the family room, staring at his cell phone on the coffee table. The television played an action hero movie. The room suited him, masculine, very functional with lots of electronics and theater-style sofa and chairs. The bar was dark. Tess had told her she'd wanted one in her house. That was long before Adeline had learned she had a drinking problem.

Adeline sat on one of the chairs and reclined a little. Maybe this would help her relax enough to go to sleep.

She rolled her head to look over at Jeremy. He'd looked up from the phone and now stared at her. She caught his gaze going from her chest to her face. She had on her nightgown, a modest, knee-length, white sleeveless nightie she'd bought for comfort.

He still had on his jeans but had changed into a superhero T-shirt. She liked the shirt…a little too much. The material clung to his chest and biceps. His sleepy eyes held weariness and the same stress that kept her awake, but more. Underlying the gravity, an embedded desire percolated.

"What if he's…" She couldn't say the word.

"We aren't going to think that way," he said. "I have thought that way, but I don't want to."

She met his eyes for a time. Then he stretched out his arm along the sofa and said, "Come here."

He probably didn't mean to lure her sexually. He'd share comfort with her, something she needed.

Adeline went to the sofa and sat beside him, leaning her head on his shoulder as he curved his arm around her shoulders.

"We just have to wait."

"For what?" she wanted to ask. "What if no call comes?" Why would the kidnapper call again?

"We can't lose faith a call will come." He kissed her head.

She could tell he spoke with more bravado than he felt. If he lost Jamie on top of losing Tess, he'd be devastated. He'd never be the same man. Adeline hadn't been a part of Jamie's life up until now. She'd feel the loss, too, but probably not as much as him.

Optimism didn't come easily. The kidnapper had already made one ransom demand and hadn't returned Jamie. She felt terrible dread churn in her stomach and reached for Jeremy's hand, which rested on his left thigh.

He entwined their fingers. "He wouldn't have sent those flowers if Jamie was already dead."

He did have a good point there. Why would any kidnapper do that if not to deliberately torment loved ones? Whoever had taken Jamie intended for Jeremy to suffer.

"Okay," she said, clinging to that.

He rubbed her arm. "You're as concerned as I am."

"He's my son." The fact held different meanings for them both.

"In the short time you've spent with him, you've gotten very close," he said.

"I felt close to him as soon as I held him in my arms," she answered without raising her head.

He didn't say anything for a while. And when he did, he surprised her.

"Adeline?" He kissed her head again. The gesture was becoming something of a trademark, a nonsexual but loving and friendly kiss of comfort.

"Yes?"

"No matter what happens between us, you can see Jamie whenever you want."

She lifted her head to see his eyes and met sincerity.

"Someday I'd like to tell him you're his biological mother," he said.

She drew her head back farther. Was that his vulnerability talking? "Do you mean it?"

"Yes."

"You're sure?"

"Yes. I can't say when… I'm not…"

Not ready. She would rather not get into that again. "I understand. Thank you. That would mean a lot to me." While that would mean a lot to her, deeper down, she felt slighted that she wouldn't be in Jamie's life every day. Jeremy had too much to overcome before that could be even a possibility.

A small smile lifted the corners of his mouth, softening her partial regret.

Once he had Jamie back, would he keep his word? Adeline rested her head on his shoulder again.

She'd go back to investigating Tess's accident. That would end with some kind of resolution and she'd return home, to her normal life, lonely and working long hours. Funny, how she hadn't thought of it that way before now. Her life gave her happiness. She saw her mother a lot. She had a nice house, and she had made great strides professionally in a short period of time. Plus, she loved what she did. She loved solving cases. Probably the single most gratifying element entailed bringing criminals or otherwise not-so-nice people to justice and giving those they hurt back their lives.

She avoided men and rarely went out with her friends. More than just not trusting men or holding the bar far higher for them to earn her trust, she'd welcomed those long working hours. Thrived. Her accomplishments exhilarated her. But maybe she'd allowed herself to carry that too far.

Of course, she'd made a promise to herself never to be hurt the way she had been with her last boyfriend, to never be that naive again. One heartbreak had done that. When she'd first met him, he'd painted a charming, intelligent picture of himself. She'd had visions of them both excelling in their careers, having nice things and plenty of money for trips. Maybe have kids someday. All that had shattered the day he'd shown his temper.

Still, she'd fallen in love with the man from college. He'd shown glimpses of that person when they lived together. Between fights over when he would either go to law school or get a job, they'd actually had some pleasant times.

She'd trusted him. When he'd betrayed that trust by misleading her, by filling her head with declarations of ambition that had all been lies, he'd broken her. The man she thought she knew in college was not the one she lived with. He'd used her, thinking he could have an easy life.

Jeremy would never use her for that, but she couldn't trust his invitation to see Jamie after they parted ways. What would he do when he met a woman he decided to marry? She wouldn't be able to see Jamie then, would she? She couldn't imagine another woman would feel comfortable with that. To compound matters, could Adeline's heart handle visiting Jamie only on occasion?

No.

She moved back from Jeremy, scooting over on the sofa.

"Are you going to bed?"

"In a bit." She needed to say this the right way. "It's really sweet of you to offer that I see Jamie after I leave.

Thank you for that. But I don't think it's a good idea to tell Jamie about me."

His brow lowered. "Why not?"

"Think about it, Jeremy. I can't keep floating in and out of your lives after you get married again. That would be just…awkward. So it's best if…if Jamie doesn't know about me at all."

He stared at her, glanced across the room, and then looked at her again. "We can talk about that later."

She didn't see the point but didn't comment. Instead, she stood and headed for her room, wondering what had gone through his mind as he looked away. Had he not considered the consequences further into the future? Once she'd made him think about it, what had he thought? Had he imagined himself with another woman? No one? Her…?

Adeline refused to speculate.

Chapter 14

Late the next afternoon, Jeremy worked from home in case the kidnapper called. Knox had a team set up off-site to monitor any calls and had coached Jeremy and Adeline on what to say when the next call came. Jeremy couldn't concentrate. Worry over Jamie tortured him. He also couldn't understand Adeline's refusal to see Jamie. Well, he could. They'd had sex and if he did marry someone else, that would be awkward. But what she didn't know was that Jeremy had no intention of re-marrying. He couldn't think of himself with anyone… other than Adeline. And that caused problems, the same as before. Mass confusion over how he felt.

Brought on by guilt?

He stood from his desk and left his office. Going downstairs, he saw Adeline looking out the back patio window. Today, clouds had gathered and threatened a cold rain. Wind swayed the trees in the backyard. Soon darkness would fall again for another night of sleep-less waiting.

She'd said she felt close to Jamie since he was born,

but Jeremy wondered if much of that stemmed from her imagination. He didn't doubt she felt close to his son, but she hadn't spent every day with him. Giving him up must have been difficult on her, and caused fantasies. A mother bonded with her baby after birth but what happened after they separated? Not that it mattered now. Jeremy wanted her to be able to see Jamie. He'd never stop her from doing so.

"We should go out for dinner or something. I can bring my cell. That's the number the kidnapper used to call me."

Adeline turned with alertness. "Your cell? That means they knew your number."

"Emily knew my number."

Slowly she nodded in disappointment.

"Knox called earlier," he said. "Emily's bank transactions have been minimal but she had a cash withdrawal of three hundred dollars yesterday. She went to her bank, which she appears to do on a regular basis. That's all we've got on her movements. She hasn't gone home, either."

Adeline turned back to the view of his backyard just as his cell phone rang. She pivoted as he retrieved the phone from his front pocket.

He read the display and answered.

"Bring another five hundred thousand to the same location at nine tomorrow night." The voice sounded the same as last time, disguised.

"Why are you doing this?" Jeremy asked. "I gave you five hundred thousand already. Why aren't you giving me my son back?"

"Did you receive the flowers?"

"Yes."

"Then you know why. Bring five hundred thousand dollars to the same location as before. Nine tomorrow night."

What kind of person would kidnap a young boy and purposefully demand two ransom drops just for the sake of causing suffering? How long would this go on and would he ever see his son again? He had to have a strong arm right now. He had to show this animal he wouldn't let fear turn him into a coward.

"No," Jeremy said at last.

After a notable pause, the caller said, "No?"

"I want proof of life. No proof of life, no money."

"I'll kill your son."

Jeremy hardened himself against crumbling and giving the kidnapper whatever he asked without condition in order to save Jamie. But saving Jamie included pushing back a little; Knox had warned him of that. "I demand proof of life. You give me proof and I'll deliver you the money."

Another silence passed, this one longer. "I'll call you in fifteen minutes."

Jeremy closed his eyes and let his head fall back. Disconnecting, he said to Adeline, "He—or she—will call back in fifteen minutes."

Adeline covered her mouth briefly with a glad squeak. "That means he's still alive!"

He hoped. The kidnapper could just be toying with them, or buying time to come up with a way to avoid providing proof of life.

Jeremy phoned Knox. "He called again. Another drop tomorrow at nine." He gave Knox the cell number.

"I'll see if the team traced the call, run the number and meet you at your house."

Disconnecting, Jeremy met Adeline's eyes. The hope and relief he'd seen when the kidnapper had agreed to show them Jamie still lived had vanished. They still didn't have Jamie.

Fifteen minutes came and went. Adeline paced one end of the family room to the other and Jeremy still held his cell phone.

The doorbell rang, signifying Knox had arrived. Closer to the door, Adeline let him in.

"Anything?" Knox asked as he entered in a denim shirt and pants with a jacket.

Jeremy shook his head as Adeline closed the door, first checking outside as she usually did. She never lost awareness of her surroundings.

In the living room, Knox turned, blue eyes bright. "The call came from the same general location as the first ransom demand."

"He's got to have Jamie somewhere in that vicinity," Adeline said.

"Not if he's going to a certain location just to make the calls," Jeremy said.

"That's right," Knox said. "I don't think we're dealing with anyone unfamiliar with technology. He's planned as much as he could."

"Or she," Adeline said. "The caller uses voice alteration. Emily could be the one calling."

"Yes," Knox agreed. "I suppose I have a difficult time wrapping my head around a woman kidnapping an innocent kid."

Unless it was Livia. "So do I," Jeremy said. "I have a hard time with someone being capable of kidnapping anyone else, especially my son."

"We'll follow the same protocol as last time. We'll—"

Jeremy's cell rang and Knox stopped talking.

He recognized the kidnapper's number. It was different than the one used for the first ransom demand, which indicated the use of a disposable phone. He answered, giving Knox and Adeline a single nod.

"Daddy?"

Jeremy breathed his relief out in one hard breath when he heard his son's voice. "Jamie. Are you all right?"

Adeline put her hand to her mouth and tears moistened her eyes, although she didn't outright cry.

"I want to go home," Jamie said. "Where are you? Why haven't you come to get me yet?"

"I'll come and get you as soon as I know where you are, okay?"

"Why don't you know? That man brought me here after Adda fell down."

Jamie didn't realize Adeline had been shot. "Have they hurt you?" Jeremy had precious little time to gather as much information as possible. But first he had to know Jamie was all right.

"No."

"You're okay? You're eating well?"

"They let me eat pizza and hot dogs and watch TV. Daddy, come get me. I miss you."

"I miss you, too. I'll come and get you as soon as possible. Do you know who you're staying with? Do you know their names?"

"She said she was—"

Jeremy heard the phone being taken from Jamie.

"I'd say that was more than generous of me," the kidnapper said, voice once again disguised. "Nine tomorrow night." Then the line went dead.

He hung up. "First Jamie said a man brought him

wherever he is and then he said *she* when I asked who he was staying with," he said to Adeline, whose eyes had grown big with adrenaline.

"Emily is working with someone. A man," Adeline said. "Jeremy, I really don't think this is related to Tess's accident."

"I don't, either." Not anymore. He looked at Knox. "The kidnapper used his phone to let Jamie talk. He or she must be using a device, like maybe a voice altering megaphone or something."

Knox nodded.

"Emily?" Adeline said. "Working with whoever shot me."

"Maybe whoever shot you is the one behind all of this." Jeremy rubbed his chin. Two people had it out for him. Who could they be?

The next day, Claudia Colton had called and asked to meet Adeline and Jeremy at a pizzeria at five. Adeline sat with Jeremy at a booth in the small, quaint restaurant. In this older brick building, the wood floors had been renovated and historic photos of Shadow Creek covered the walls. White linen tablecloths with lit candles and centerpieces brightened the dim but romantic space. The smell of pizza warmed the cozy space.

Nervous for nine o'clock to come, Adeline couldn't appreciate the ambiance. She hadn't said much and sat with Jeremy, with only the bustle of waitstaff and other diners with less tension than they currently faced to distract her. The couple at the table nearest theirs smiled and ogled each other and the man took the woman's hand. A group of three men laughed boisterously. The lightness and joy felt surreal with the second ransom demand looming.

They didn't have to wait long before Claudia appeared in the front entry of the restaurant. Her long, blond hair floated in a slight breeze as she approached with a smile of greeting.

"Hi," she said, taking a seat next to Adeline, bringing wafts of fresh, cool evening air in with her. "Knox sent me here. He's still back at the park."

Adeline shared a perplexed look with Jeremy and then turned to Claudia for further explanation.

"I like to take walks and sometimes I go to the park," Claudia said. "I went for one earlier today and saw Emily Stanton on foot at the park. Knox showed me pictures of her when I stopped by to see him one day. When I saw Emily, she seemed to turn from a minivan that was in the parking lot. I couldn't tell if she had just turned from talking with the driver of the minivan or if she was just heading across the parking lot. The minivan drove away." Claudia signaled for the waitress.

"Wait," Jeremy said. "You *saw* Emily?"

"Yes."

"Are you sure?"

"Yes. I saw her. What kind of pizza do you like?"

The waitress had started toward them.

Jeremy shrugged as though not caring. "Anything."

When the waitress arrived, Claudia ordered two different kinds of pizza.

"Why would Emily be at the park?" Adeline asked. "Going for a stroll before a ransom drop?" That seemed unlikely and too strange to be a coincidence. Had she returned to the original drop site? Maybe she went looking for her necklace.

"I think she met someone there," Claudia said. "The driver I saw seemed to have just left a parking space and headed for the exit. I followed Emily and tried to catch up with her. She kept looking around, though, and saw me. As soon as she did, she bolted. I chased her through the parking lot, but she was too far away. She got into her car and sped off. Knox confirmed the plates coincided with her vehicle. He put a team on her right away. So far no one has located her. Wherever she's hiding, she's out of sight."

Maybe Claudia only thought Emily had met someone in the parking lot when she'd seen the vehicle drive away. Maybe whoever drove the minivan was the person she worked with in kidnapping Jamie.

Jeremy rubbed his hand over his mouth as though agitated. "Wherever she's hiding is where Jamie is."

Adeline fingered the napkin roll. If only they had a crystal ball to show them where.

"Emily could have gone to the park to look for her necklace," she said. "She may have rehearsed her ransom drop instructions, gone to the bench, then taken the bus to the construction site."

Jeremy nodded. "That makes sense."

Claudia sipped from a glass of water the waitress delivered.

Adeline felt too nauseated to put anything in her mouth. She wished Claudia hadn't ordered the pizza.

"Why did Knox send you here?" Jeremy asked.

"He didn't want you to worry about anything else other than the drop later. He's got it covered. They're looking for anyone who might have seen Emily and the minivan."

"There aren't any cameras in or around the park," Adeline said. "I checked."

"Did you see who was driving the minivan?" Jeremy asked Claudia.

Claudia nodded. "Not clearly, but as soon as I saw her I thought she resembled Livia. She had on a beanie and big-collared jacket."

"Livia." Jeremy's tone sounded deadpan.

"I can't be sure. It was dark. Her face was illuminated by the dash lights. She had the same shape of face."

Despite Claudia's conservative hedging, Adeline could see Jeremy take the sighting to heart. He was convinced Claudia had seen Livia driving that minivan. But why would she meet with Emily? How likely would it be for Livia to cause Tess's accident *and* be involved in Jamie's kidnapping? Not likely at all.

The pizza arrived. Adeline sat back.

Claudia put a slice onto her plate. "What's the plan for later? Are you ready?"

"Jeremy and I will go to the drop location. We anticipate more instructions like last time. I'm sure the kidnappers won't risk police waiting for them there."

Lifting her finger as though a thought had come, Claudia said, "Knox asked me to tell you detectives found a cuff link in the Suburban and it had the initials *ES*. They tracked the owners of the stolen vehicle. They said the cuff link didn't belong to them. The initials didn't match the owner's name, either. So it must belong to the thief."

"A cuff link?" Adeline queried. "The person at the last drop was a woman." She knew that for a fact.

"We always thought there were two at work here," Jeremy said.

"Why a necklace and cuff link with the same initials?" Claudia asked.

Emily Stanton. Evan Sigurdsson. Could Evan be involved? His character certainly fit the profile. And he hated Jeremy. Still, would he go to such lengths? Adeline lifted her glass of water and sipped, thinking. She eyed the pizza, which smelled good. "It's like they were planted. Emily lost her necklace and then we find a cuff link with the same initials. Too coincidental." More thoughts came to her as she pictured Emily discovering her necklace might have been left somewhere along the ransom route. "Maybe that's why Emily went back to the park. When she realized she lost her necklace, did she retrace her steps to look for it?"

"And when she couldn't find it, she planted the cuff link," Jeremy said.

"To throw detectives off," Claudia finished.

"The Suburban was in the sheriff's custody," Adeline pointed out.

"Where she or whoever she is working with could have paid someone off to get them in the SUV," Jeremy said.

Adeline nodded. "Okay. Where did she get a cuff link with her initials?"

"She could have had it made," Jeremy said.

"I'll get Knox to check local jewelers that do engravings," Claudia offered. She'd become a big help in the investigation.

Adeline checked the time on her cell. Still three hours to go.

"We should eat something."

Looking up, she saw Jeremy had noticed her inability to dive into the pizza. He must be suffering the same lack of hunger. She hadn't eaten since breakfast, and that had consisted of a glass of juice with half an English muffin.

He reached for one of the pizzas, put a slice onto her plate and then put one onto his. "Root beer is also good."

Claudia paused in her chewing to observe them.

The waitress came to check on them and he ordered two root beers. Claudia already had her soda.

The sodas arrived and Adeline lifted hers when Jeremy lifted his. They each sipped theirs; she enjoyed how he held her gaze with his, his dark eyes messaging inspirational strength. They had each other during this terrible time. She felt her eyes smile and her insides tickled when his answered.

She wasn't sure whether the root beer could be accredited for her returned appetite or not, but she picked up the slice of pizza and took a delicious bite. Claudia still hadn't resumed her feasting.

Adeline saw her still watching them.

"Are you two dating?" Claudia asked.

"No," Adeline answered quickly.

Claudia wasn't fooled. Her sly look gave her away. "Then you should."

Outside, Jeremy stood with Adeline, watching Claudia get into a cab. Going back home seemed too tortuous of a prospect. As the cab drove off, he looked across the street at the ice cream parlor he and Jamie frequented.

"Let's go have dessert." He started to cross the street and then waited for Adeline to catch up to him.

"Ice cream?"

"We'll have Jamie's favorite kind."

Inside the bright shop with small round tables and a glass-encased freezer full of colorful bins of ice cream,

Jeremy stepped up to the counter and ordered two spaghetti ice cream plates. The server thought nothing of the choice but Adeline eyed him in question.

He watched with her as the young man, barely out of high school with his hair in a ponytail and a nose piercing, used a potato ricer to squeeze vanilla ice cream onto two small plates. When he finished, he topped them with strawberry sauce, then sprinkled them with white chocolate shavings.

Jeremy handed Adeline her plate, seeing her smile in delight.

"Jamie's favorite, huh?"

"It tastes great, too." He took her to a two-seater by the front window.

She used a spoon to scoop a bite. After swallowing, she said, "Not bad. Reminds me of when I was a kid. Strawberry and chocolate sundaes were my favorite."

"Jamie loves strawberries."

Her soft smile faded and she averted her head, looking away from him, as though some thought had dampened her mood. What could that be? Jamie's kidnapping? Or did she regret not being there the first time Jamie had ordered the spaghetti ice cream?

At last she faced him again. "I've been thinking a lot about what you said before—about seeing Jamie after the investigation is over and Jamie is found."

"All you have to do is let me know when you want to see him. No matter where we are or who is in our lives, there's no reason for you not to spend time with him."

"I don't want him to know I'm his biological mother, Jeremy."

"You'd have me let him believe Tess is?"

Wasn't that what he'd have done if Tess had lived? Perhaps he and Tess would have decided to tell Jamie the truth at some point. That didn't matter to Adeline. She not only intended to protect her own heart; she'd protect Jamie's, as well.

"I'd be your friend and nothing more," she said. "If an occasion presents itself that I might see Jamie, then so be it."

"I just want you to know I wouldn't prevent you from seeing him."

She contemplated him. Did he think seeing her would be good for Jamie? Jamie had taken a liking to her. She could be a positive influence, especially since she had such an intimate link to him. But Jeremy hadn't considered the consequences for her…and probably not even for himself. He might claim to have no desire for serious relationships, but he had to have feelings for her. Their sexual chemistry generated too much heat. She'd started to think he blocked himself off to the feelings.

"Why?" she finally asked.

He stared at her, lowering a now empty spoon. "Because I can see what he means to you."

When she didn't respond, he said, "After Tess died, he cried a lot. I tried everything I could to get him past his grief. He was so young, he didn't fully grasp what happened, but he knew she wasn't there anymore. It took a long time but he finally stopped crying so much. Seeing him with you…he's even better now than ever. That makes my bond with him stronger. I'm afraid I'll lose that if you disappear. Why would I not support you being part of his life?"

His version did not include being in a relationship

with him, though. He was off-limits to any woman as long as he wasn't over Tess.

"Just because the investigation ends doesn't mean we have to stop seeing each other," he added. "I mean… as friends."

"Yes, it does, Jeremy. And you know why."

His head cocked as though he didn't follow her. "No, I don't. What's wrong with seeing Jamie? We wouldn't mislead him. He likes you."

Since he did such a good job deluding himself, she'd speak frankly. "I can't invest in a man who won't commit. That's why I don't trust you, Jeremy. All I want to do is have sex with you and fantasize about being with you more permanently. While you may not have the same fantasies, I'm pretty sure you'd like more sex. How do you think visiting Jamie will go with that between us?"

"I'm only thinking of Jamie."

That couldn't be truer. He *only* thought of his son. "You're part of that equation. You're Jamie's father and I'm his biological mother. We're physically attracted to each other but you aren't in a place to commit. Being with you would be a gamble. I've already gambled and lost. I won't lose again." She stood, leaving her ice cream unfinished. "And I think of Jamie, too. If things between us end badly, that could harm him."

He caught up to her outside. "Hey, wait." He took a hold of her arm and tugged her around to face him. "What are you saying? Do you want to be with me as more than my PI?"

What did she want? Did she want more from him as a man or did she only want Jamie? She might want more if he didn't have such baggage.

"No." If she could distance herself enough, she'd love

nothing more than to spend time with Jamie—even after Jeremy stopped needing her professional services.

"If we can be friends, I would like to see Jamie."

If they could be friends...just friends.

Nine o'clock finally came. Adeline and Jeremy arrived at the construction site, and as expected, no one was there. They waited until ten, after which Jeremy received a call.

"Go to the campsite where you found the Suburban," the caller said.

"Will my son be there?" He saw Adeline standing with her hands clenched before her.

"Leave the money and then wait for further instructions."

"How long will that be?"

"As long as it takes."

"I'm not leaving any money unless you give me my son." As last time, Adeline's face tightened with tension.

"You'll leave the money, or your son dies."

The kidnapper had threatened that many times, but would they go through with it? "I gave you money last time and you didn't give me my son."

"I have no intention of killing Jamie, but I will if you don't follow my instructions."

Jeremy couldn't risk otherwise. "I'll bring the money. Why the campsite?"

The caller disconnected.

"Jeremy, what if Jamie isn't there?" Adeline ran with him out to the vehicle.

Jeremy finished dialing Knox as he got inside. He couldn't answer her. He feared as much.

He told Knox the next instructions and raced to the

highway that would take them to the drop site. Moments later, the headlights shone on the nearly imperceptible lane. Jeremy turned and drove through the darkness, parking where the campsite opened up.

He got out with Adeline. No one was there.

His phone rang again.

"Yes?"

"Leave the money and go."

"Give me my son!"

"You'll receive more instructions on where to pick him up. Leave the money."

He couldn't trust a kidnapper.

"I have no intention of harming Jamie. As long as you do what I tell you, you'll have him back in the same condition as the day you last saw him," the kidnapper said.

The caring in the words seemed more appropriate coming from a female. Was he talking to Emily? He didn't ask, not wanting to frighten her. Frightened, she might run and he might never see Jamie again.

"Leave the money and go. You'll get no further instructions until I know you've gone," the kidnapper said. "Don't pull what you did last time. I won't warn you twice."

Jeremy turned to Adeline. He couldn't make this decision on his own. If they left the money, what then? He had no guarantee the kidnapper wouldn't kill Jamie.

At last she nodded.

Their only chance to get Jamie back was if they left the money. Jeremy dropped the bag.

"All right. We'll leave the money and go," Jeremy said. "But if you don't give me my son back, I won't stop hunting you. And when I find you, I'll kill you."

"You will never find me." With that, the caller hung up, leaving Jeremy sickened.

The kidnapper seemed so certain. Did he or she claim to be willing to return Jamie unharmed but have no intention of doing so?

"How did they know we were here?" Adeline asked.

The caller had contacted them right when they'd stopped. Jeremy searched through the darkness, looking everywhere the headlights reached. After a few seconds, he saw them reflecting on something about fifty yards away.

"There's someone out there," he said.

Adeline drew her pistol. As soon as she did, Jeremy heard running. Footfalls crunched through the understory. A whishing and snapping sound came; the runner must have brushed a branch. He ran toward the sound, Adeline on his heels. The vehicle headlights provided illumination for a short distance before the trees swallowed them in darkness. Jeremy had a small flashlight on his key chain and had the way forward lit enough to avoid colliding with anything.

"Ahead to the right," Adeline whispered loud enough for him to hear.

He shone the light in that direction and caught sight of someone running, small of frame like Emily. He ran faster, leaving Adeline a little behind. He reached a clearing and stopped, checking to make sure Adeline did the same. She did, standing behind him and peering out to see the clearing and an old cabin in marginal disrepair. Light in the biggest front window indicated someone could be there.

He searched for Emily and didn't see her, but he heard an engine starting.

Running into the clearing, he almost made it to the cabin when a midsize hatchback appeared from the other side of the cabin and raced down a nearly overgrown dirt driveway.

Taking out his cell, he called Knox. Watching the taillights disappear into the trees, he listened to one ring before Knox answered.

"She's heading toward the highway. There's a cabin near the campsite. It should be the next driveway down from there."

"We're almost there," Knox said.

"We're going to check out the cabin. It looks like Emily was here. Lights are still on."

"Roger. I'll let you know when we have her."

Disconnecting, he saw that Adeline had already reached the cabin door. With her pistol drawn, she pushed open the door, which had been left unlocked. If Emily had walked to the campsite to watch them drop the money, she might have left the cabin door open.

He walked to the door. A lamp on a side table next to a worn, leaf-green sofa lit the small living room and part of a smaller kitchen. Two doors opened off the living room, one to a bathroom and the other to a bedroom.

A dirty plate on the table indicated someone had recently had dinner. There was no television, only a fireplace. A few flames flickered over cooling embers. She must have been here awhile.

Adeline had moved on from the living room to the bedroom. Jeremy followed her. She searched the room, presumably for signs that Jamie had been here. He hadn't seen any. The dishes in the kitchen sink and on the table suggested only one person had stayed there.

His cell rang, bringing Adeline turning as he answered. It was Knox.

"We got her."

Chapter 15

Knox arranged for them to watch Emily Stanton's interrogation in an adjacent room, through one-way glass. They'd first met with detectives to go over all they knew so far and to help the one Knox had assigned to lead the questioning.

Adeline moved closer to the window. Emily sat with her hands folded on the table, her wrists cuffed. She seemed so at peace…even innocent, with her head slightly bowed. In black slacks and a black-and-white printed knit shirt, she looked businesslike. Her shoulder-length blond hair was clipped back, with a few strands falling loose as though her arrest had harried her.

A detective entered the room and she looked up as he moved around the table and took the chair opposite from her. He introduced himself and informed her he'd be asking her some questions.

Emily nodded, hazel eyes that leaned more to the gray side flashing up almost timidly. Her nervousness showed so obviously that Adeline had to wonder how someone like her could pull off a kidnapping. Then she reminded herself that she wasn't working alone. A man had shot Adeline and taken Jamie, not this woman.

Adeline contained her eagerness for her to reveal the man and Jamie's whereabouts.

"Were you involved in any way with the kidnapping of Jamie Kincaid?" the detective asked.

"No," Emily answered firmly.

The door to the observation room opened and Knox entered. Adeline returned her attention to the interrogation room as his tall frame came to stand beside her. Jeremy stood to her left.

"Who were you working with?" the detective asked.

Emily didn't respond. Her lips pursed slightly and her eyes seemed wider than normal.

"This will go a lot easier on you if you answer all my questions."

"I don't know who kidnapped him." Emily's hands clenched and released. She flattened them on the table and tapped her right hand three times, a nervous reaction. Adeline doubted she had any awareness of what she'd done.

The detective stared at her awhile. Then he picked up a pen on top of a five-by-six notepad and tapped the top a few times.

"Are you aware that we found a stolen Suburban seen at the location where Jamie Kincaid was kidnapped?" he asked.

"I'm aware you found a Suburban." She put her hands down onto the table.

"Are you aware that we found it at the same location where you specified the second ransom drop?"

"Me? What ransom?" Emily feigned ignorance and

her attempt didn't succeed. Adeline could tell she lied. She could also tell the detective had noticed, as well.

"Did you plant a cuff link in the stolen Suburban?" he asked. "How did you get them in there?"

Again, Emily didn't answer. Would she demand to talk to an attorney? Did she know she had that option?

"Did you know we found a cuff link in the Suburban?"

She shook her head. "No."

That much was probably true. Police likely wouldn't reveal that detail. But she had to know they were in the Suburban. Did she arrange to plant a cuff link? Adeline glanced at Knox and then Jeremy, whose gazes remained on the interrogation room.

"It had *ES* engraved on it," the detective said. "Those are your initials."

Emily scoffed. "I don't wear cuff links."

"No, men wear cuff links, don't they?" The detective expertly led her toward the information he sought.

Emily didn't respond.

"What were you doing in the woods in that location?" the detective asked.

"I was staying in a cabin nearby." She looked smug but only for a second or two. Her nervousness, her fear, took over her demeanor again.

"Why were you watching Jeremy Kincaid and Adeline Winters?"

"Who is Adeline Winters?"

"She's a private investigator Mr. Kincaid hired. Why were you in the woods?" The detective didn't miss a beat, staying on target with the question he needed answered.

Emily hesitated. "I was taking a walk."

The detective leaned back against the chair, propped his elbows on the armrests and entwined his fingers, looking relaxed as he contemplated her.

"Why did you go to the cabin?"

"I needed to get away."

"Ms. Stanton, I think you're lying about why you were in the woods. Mr. Kincaid and Ms. Winters both saw you watching them. Don't you think it's too coincidental that you were there after they were instructed to leave money at the campsite?"

"I didn't have anything to do with Jamie's kidnapping."

"Ms. Winters saw you drop a necklace at the first drop site. How do you explain that?"

"I can't. What necklace? And what drop site?" Emily seemed to be getting the hang of countering the detective's inquiries. Afraid or not, she'd do and say whatever necessary to avoid prosecution.

Adeline looked over at Jeremy, whose brow had crowded as he intently listened, no doubt feeling as discouraged as her.

The detective stood and went to the door, knocking. The door opened and another detective handed him a clear plastic evidence bag. The first detective returned to the table and his chair, sitting and putting his ankle on his knee, again looking relaxed.

He put the bag down onto the table. "Is this your necklace?"

Emily glanced down at the bag and then began tapping the table with her hand again. "No."

"That's interesting because one of our detectives asked your mother and she said it was yours."

"When did you talk to my mother?"

Adeline looked over at Knox.

"I asked a detective to go over there," he said.

"Just this evening, probably just before you left for the construction site," the detective said.

Emily stared at the necklace and Adeline felt her thinking the sheriff might actually have enough to throw her in jail. After several seconds, she raised her eyes. "I didn't kidnap Jamie."

"Then who did?"

Emily didn't respond.

"If you help us, we might be able to go easier on your sentence."

In the stone-cold silence that followed, Adeline didn't think Emily would cooperate.

But then she at last said, "I was blackmailed."

"Who blackmailed you?"

"I was arrested for shoplifting a long time ago. He caught me shoplifting recently and threatened to expose me if I didn't help him."

"Who?"

Emily tapped her hand twice more and then went still, staring at the detective in indecision.

"We can't help you if you don't tell us."

"You have the initials," she said.

"So you did plant the cuff link in the Suburban."

"Yes."

"How?"

She hesitated. "A friend helped me."

"Who?"

"I cannot tell you that."

"If he is clean of anything other than helping you plant the cuff link, we will grant him immunity," the detective said.

"Deputy Rusty Nicholson."

Adeline glanced at Jeremy and then Knox with that revelation. The deputy was not as clean as he appeared.

"You lost your necklace and feared being caught, so you left another clue to throw us off," the detective asked.

"Not to throw you off, but to lead you to the real criminal. I'm no criminal. So I shoplift on occasion. I would never hurt anyone, especially a kid. I was Jamie's nanny. I was attached to him. I cared about him. I still do."

The emotion in Emily's voice convinced Adeline she told the truth.

"This person who blackmailed you," the detective said in his leading tone, "did he catch you shoplifting?"

"He got me on video with his cell phone."

The detective nodded. "What's his name?"

Jeremy and Emily said at the same time, "Evan Sigurdsson."

Knox's sharp turn of head indicated he hadn't put that piece of the puzzle together yet. Adeline had. And now it made perfect sense.

"He threatened to give the video to the sheriff if I didn't help him. He made me make all the phone calls and pick up the ransom money. He also made me take care of Jamie. He took care of the actual kidnapping and he was the one who shot the woman you call Adeline Winters."

"Where is Evan now?"

"I don't know. Home, probably."

"Where are you keeping Jamie?" the detective asked.

Adeline flattened her hand on the glass. Jeremy took her other hand in his and squeezed gently.

"My neighbor's house. Julie Smith. I think Evan felt

safe with Jamie there, not attracting attention to where he lived. That was his plan, to pin everything on me if he had to. He'd come by every once in a while to make sure I did what he said. And he also kept telling me he had cameras in Julie's house and in mine. I never did find any, but I didn't take the chance that he was bluffing."

Shocked, Adeline recalled going to Emily's neighbor's house. Jamie had been there. She'd heard sounds from a bedroom. He must have been there with the woman's child. She'd come out onto the porch to talk to them. Had she feared detection?

"She helped you in the kidnapping?" the detective asked.

"No. I told her Jamie's parents were out of town and I needed someone to watch him when I couldn't. He was with me whenever I felt it was safe, whenever Evan wouldn't be there."

"What about the Amber Alert?"

"She must not have seen it."

"What about the woman in the minivan you met in the park?"

Emily's face contorted in mild confusion. "What woman? I met no one at the park."

She appeared to be telling the truth. Had the woman in the minivan been Livia or someone not connected to the kidnapping at all?

"Why did Evan kidnap Jamie?" the detective asked.

"I don't need to hear any more of this." Jeremy let go of her hand and went to the door.

"Jeremy, you shouldn't go there alone," Knox said.

He turned at the door. "I'm going to get my son. Evan did this for revenge over the way I fired him."

"I'll get a team assembled. Don't go there alone. You don't know what you're walking into."

Adeline would help Jeremy evaluate the situation when they arrived. She didn't want to wait, either. She trailed him out the door.

He took her hand again, hurrying for the exit. "Let's go get our son."

At Julie's house, Jeremy pounded on the door. He pounded again when no one answered right away.

The door opened and the woman they'd spoken with before stood there. "You're back? Have you found Emily?"

"Yes." Jeremy pushed the door open and forced the woman out of the way.

"Hey," she protested. "What are you doing?"

"Jamie?" Jeremy called, heart slamming with urgency. He heard Adeline talking to the woman.

"We're here to pick up Jamie," she said.

"Emily said his parents would be back from vacation today," the woman countered.

"Jeremy is his father," Adeline snapped back.

Jeremy headed for the hallway and shouted, "Jamie?"

"But... Emily said she worked with his mother."

"She lied."

Reaching the first door, Jeremy saw a bathroom and moved on. Down the hall, he saw Jamie's adorable blond head appear out of a bedroom door. A light was still on in the room, which told Jeremy he must have still been up despite the hour.

His face lit up into a broad smile. "Daddy!" His little legs, clad in dark blue pj's, ran toward him.

Jeremy crouched, gladness choking him as he felt his

son's body crash into him. Wrapping his arms around him, he closed his eyes and let out an uncontrollable groan of joy. He pressed a kiss to Jamie's head, smelling his kid scent. He smelled clean.

In the hall he saw a little girl about the same age as Jamie step out of her room, looking sad with her hands clasped in front of her.

Leaning back, but keeping his arms around his son, Jeremy inspected his boy. "Are you all right?"

Jamie bobbed in a few jerky nods. "Chrissy has a train set! And a bunch of construction trucks!"

"Construction trucks? Oh, yeah?" At least Emily's neighbor had kept him amply entertained. "Sounds like you've been having some fun."

"Yeah." Jamie's animation abated. "Where were you?"

"I've been looking for you," Jeremy said. "I didn't know where you were until now." He gobbled up the sight of Jamie, seeing he had dark circles under his eyes. "They've been letting you stay up late, haven't they?"

Jamie looked bashful, as though he'd been caught doing something wrong. He wouldn't tell him there was nothing he could do that Jeremy would call wrong, not for a long, long time. He was just so happy and thrilled to see him again, to have him back in his arms.

"Come on, buddy. Let's go home."

Jeremy stood and offered his hand, but Jamie had caught sight of Adeline in the living room next to Julie.

"Mommy!" Jamie yelled, and ran toward Adeline.

Adeline looked stunned as Jamie neared, but she knelt in time to receive the same crashing hug as Jamie had bestowed him. She held him tight to her, closing her eyes

briefly and turning her head in for a kiss and sniff of the
boy's head. She'd smelled him as Jeremy had.

Jeremy chuckled low, unable to stop himself and not
having any desire to.

"Jamie." She leaned back and took the boy's face between her hands. "It's so nice to have you back. How
are you feeling?"

"Good." With Jamie's back to Jeremy he had to
picture him beaming at Adeline, but he knew his son
enough to know he was smiling right now.

Adeline smoothed his hair, maternal instinct likely
making her wonder if he'd been cleaned.

"Can we go home and have pancakes?" Jamie asked.

"Yes." Adeline smiled. "Then we'll get you cleaned
up and tuck you into your warm, cozy bed."

"I miss my room. Chrissy's room is fun but I miss
mine."

Adeline stood. "Your room is fun, too."

Chrissy appeared beside Jeremy, looking forlornly at
Jamie. "You have to go home now?" she asked.

Jamie turned his head to her. "Yeah. We can play
again." He looked up at his dad. "Can't we, Daddy?"

"We'll see. Right now we need to bring you home.
You've been here too long."

"They've become quite good friends," Julie said. "My
daughter is a bit of a tomboy, which Jamie latched on to."

Adeline took Jamie's hand without acknowledging
the woman. "Let's go home."

Jamie skipped along beside her to the door.

Jeremy saw the woman standing in discomfort as
she looked on.

"I didn't know," she said.

He paused before leaving. "Thank you for taking good care of my son."

Her tension visibly eased. "He was a delight to have. You have a wonderful son."

While that warmed him and he appreciated her observation, he'd let the police handle her from here. The only thing he cared about right now was Jamie.

Hearing sirens, he felt reassured she wouldn't be going anywhere until she answered a lot of questions.

After taking Jamie to the hospital to have him checked just in case, Jeremy drove him and Adeline home. Jamie fell asleep on the way. Adeline sat on her left hip in the front passenger seat and watched him all the way there. Rather than wake him up, Jeremy carried him up to his bedroom. He was already in pj's. Adeline pulled the covers back and Jeremy eased him down, drawing the soft covers up to his chin. He pressed a gentle kiss to his cheek and straightened.

Adeline stood beside him near the foot of the double bed. Having Jamie back felt so good she didn't want to leave him. She suspected Jeremy felt the same, since he hadn't moved away from the bed and watched Jamie with the same rapt attention.

Not caring how she appeared or if she overstepped boundaries, Adeline crawled onto the bed and curled up next to Jamie. She just could not leave him alone tonight. Careful not to wake him, she moved as close as she could without touching him, content to be near his warm little body and have the back of his sweet blond-haired head in sight.

Jeremy moved around to the other side of the bed, behind her, and she felt him lie next to her. She closed her eyes to pure heaven when he draped his arm over her waist and his hand rested with hers.

"I can't leave him, either," he said close to her ear.

"He doesn't seem to have suffered," she said quietly.

"No, but he missed home."

"We'll take care of that. I just hope this doesn't affect him later in life."

"We'll make sure it doesn't." He rubbed her hand and propped his head on his other, watching Jamie sleep as she did.

"Emily and her neighbor seem to have taken care of him."

"Other than feed him junk food and let him stay up late, yes."

"And play with Julie's daughter." He could have been treated worse. Adeline would be thankful he wasn't.

She nestled her head on the pillow. Jeremy continued to caress her hand with his thumb. Closing her eyes, she breathed in Jamie's smell that mingled with Jeremy's much manlier one.

"Why do you think he called you *Mommy*?"

Adeline popped open her eyes. She hadn't forgotten that. When she heard Jamie call her that, her entire body had reacted, stunned at first, then with a powerful wave of pure love.

"I don't know," she answered truthfully.

"I heard you talk," Jamie said. He opened his blue eyes and smiled and laughed. "You said I was your son."

"When did you hear that?" Jeremy asked.

"When Adda was packing." He looked at her. "You were going to leave."

"Where were you?" she asked.

"In the hall," Jamie said.

"What were you doing sneaking up on us like that?" Jeremy asked.

"I didn't sneak. I heard you fighting."

"We weren't fighting," Jeremy said.

No, they'd argued over Adeline leaving.

"You were fighting about something and I didn't go in the room," Jamie said, eyes closing sleepily.

He'd gone back to his room—after he heard Adeline say he was her son.

"Go to sleep, Jamie," Adeline said. He seemed all right with his discovery, but had he struggled up until now? At such a young age, he might not fully grasp what it all meant.

"Adda?"

"Yes?"

"Don't leave."

She absorbed the sight of his sweet face, his tired eyes finding hers and then closing against the weight of exhaustion.

"You can keep calling me Mommy if you want," she said instead of responding to his sweet request.

The next morning, Adeline woke before Jamie and Jeremy. She eased from the bed, climbing off the end to avoid rousing either. She left the room and walked down the hall to her bedroom, seeing a cloudy day through the windows on the way. It must be about noon.

Feeling rumpled and grimy after a long day in the same clothes and having slept in them as well, she walked into her bedroom and then into the bathroom for a shower. She undressed while the water warmed and steam gathered.

Stepping under the spacious, rainfall-style showerhead, she basked in the warm spray . The glass door slid open, startling her and ending the bliss. Another kind of bliss stirred when she saw Jeremy stepping into the shower with her. Water rained down on them both, wetting his dark hair and slickening his skin. He moved close behind her.

"What are you doing?"

He ran his hands up and down her arms, slow and sensual. "I don't know."

She could tell him he wasn't playing fair. He knew how she felt about this, about staying with him with the ever present threat of feeling more and more for both him and Jamie.

"Jeremy…"

With eyes closed, he put his face beside hers. "I don't want the magic to end. Let's just shower together. I promise it won't go beyond that."

How could he promise that? They hadn't planned on having sex and that had happened anyway.

His warm, wet body and gentle kiss on her cheek made her abandon any more protests. Magic, indeed.

He soaped a sea sponge and began to slowly scrub her, starting with her arms; he was extra careful around her healing gunshot wound. He moved on to her back and Adeline fell back into wonderland. He spend the longest on her front, going from her breasts to her stomach, trailing the soapy sponge with his other hand.

Did he give that area special attention because he remembered when she carried Jamie? The sentiment became infinitely more poignant now that they had Jamie back home, safe.

When he finished with her, she faced him and rinsed, enjoying his engrossed attention. Then she took the sea sponge from him, rinsed that, and then added more soap. She started with his chest because that had captivated her first. Then she soaped his arms, going over the muscles and then sliding on to his back. Her breasts pressed against him as she reached around to cleanse him all the way down his butt.

Running out of breath too quickly, she stepped back and handed him the sponge. He would have to do the rest, lest her self-control fail her as had happened before.

"I'll get dressed and get Jamie ready for pancakes."

He grinned and let her get out of the shower without any more temptation. "Looking forward to it."

Every second with Jamie today would be that way, something to cherish and remember forever. They were so grateful to have him again. Everyday routine was no longer routine but something special.

By the time she dressed in jeans and a thin, long-sleeved blue-and-green sweater, Jamie had gotten out of bed. She caught him about to leave his room.

"Shower time, Jamie."

"Aw. Do I have to?"

"Yes."

"The babysitter didn't make me."

"Well, she should have." Adeline didn't like imagining how he must have been left on his own much more than he should have.

She managed to get him in the shower and picked out some jeans and a blue sweater. He chattered with her nonstop while she helped him get dressed. Chrissy liked playing dress-up and he didn't like that much, but she had lots of Play-Doh and other toys.

She took him downstairs, where Jeremy had already prepared their lunch-hour breakfast. Pancakes steamed

from plates at the table. A bowl of strawberries beck-
oned, along with whipped cream.

"One last meal of too much sugar and fat and then
it's healthy time for you, buddy," Jeremy said, putting a
glass of milk down in front of Jamie.

Adeline sat to Jamie's right and Jeremy took the one
to his left, a cartoon playing a little loud. She couldn't
keep from bursting on the inside over how good this felt,
to be part of a family.

Halfway through the meal, Jeremy's cell phone rang.
He took it to another room so Jamie wouldn't hear, Adeline following. He doubted he'd listen, as engrossed in
the cartoon as he was. In the living room where he could
still see Jamie, he pressed the speaker button.

"How is your first day with Jamie back?" Knox asked.

"We're eating chocolate chip pancakes with strawberries and whipped cream."

"Syrup, too," Adeline said.

Knox chuckled briefly before growing more somber.
"We've questioned Julie Smith and those close to Emily.
Everyone corroborated both their stories. Julie didn't
know anything. Emily is working with us in exchange
for a lighter sentence. Bad news is, we haven't found
Sigurdsson. We think he's fled the county."

"No surprise there," Jeremy said.

"I'm concerned he'll try to go after you."

"We did thwart his plans to collect a second ransom,"
Jeremy said. "But if he so much as sets one foot on
my property or anywhere near Jamie or Adeline again,
I'll…" He stopped and glanced at Jamie, who continued
to devour his pancakes.

"Yeah. It's what I'd want to do. I just called to warn

you. And ask that you be careful. Protect your own, but don't cross the line."

"I will." As he said that, he looked right at Adeline.

"We'll be searching for him, Jeremy."

Chapter 16

A few days later, Adeline received a call from the bank regarding the ATM that was close to the location of Tess's accident. She hadn't yet heard from the other businesses she'd contacted, asking to have a look at their surveillance video from that night. The bank manager had finally located it and had it available for her. Tess might have run some errands before she met Oscar that day. Adeline hadn't told Jeremy yet because he might not respond well to her checking for evidence to support the idea that Tess had not been murdered.

She brought Jamie with her to the bank. The manager met them in the lobby. A five-foot-seven-ish man with a bald strip from his forehead to just above his neck, he exhibited more exuberance than appropriate. Adeline had the impression he must put on that face every day when inside he felt the opposite, like not smiling at all.

"Mr. Harris?" she said.

"Yes. Right this way, Ms. Winters." He turned and led her to a conference room, where someone had set up a projector.

In the open space before that, a small playroom had been set up with books for kids.

She helped Jamie put his backpack on a chair there and told him to wait for her. She unzipped the center compartment so he could retrieve his drawing book and colored pencils. When he was all set, she went into the conference room and looked at the screen, which Mr. Harris had turned on and started the video.

"I'll fast-forward through the customers using the ATM," he said.

She watched several people go up to the machine, do their business and leave, all fast. Then Mr. Harris slowed the video. Adeline could see the road in the background. Light from a convenience store across the street put passing vehicles in more detail. A couple walked along the sidewalk that passed by the bank where the ATM had been installed.

Seconds after they passed, Adeline saw Tess's car approach. She swerved in and out of the center line. Adeline searched for a dent on the side of Tess's car but the image was grainy.

"Can we zoom in on any of this?"

The car veered too far to the right as though Tess had overcorrected and crashed into the pole.

Adeline jerked her head, not wanting to see Tess's crash. When she looked back at the video, though, she couldn't see the car. The camera hadn't captured it hitting the pole. She could only see the taillights.

"I'm afraid not."

The bank manager stopped the video. Tess had died as a result of an accident. No one had driven her off the road. No one had deliberately caused the dent in the side of the car. Going to Jeremy with this would be difficult. He needed closure for Tess's death. He wanted Livia to pay.

But she needed irrefutable proof before she presented him with her findings. For that she'd have to have the video analyzed by another expert.

"Can I have the video?" she asked Mr. Harris.

"I made you a copy."

"Good. Thanks." She almost asked Jamie to put his things away when she saw the couple stop and turn when the car crashed.

She recognized Oscar right away, and the woman with him looked a lot like Holly Bridgeport.

Seeing Jeremy later that day caused Adeline an attack of conscience. Had she made the right decision, not telling him about what she saw at the bank and that she had contacted an FBI agent who had agreed to have the video analyzed? Would he be angry when she told him everything later? Yes, especially if she had proof that Tess hadn't been murdered.

Now she had to come up with a way to leave the house without him so she could go talk to Oscar. He'd witnessed Tess's accident and hadn't revealed that to anyone, in particular, the sheriff's department. She'd called his office and was told he'd gone home for the day. Jeremy had decided not to fire him.

"I ordered a cake for Jamie," she said. "I need to go and pick it up."

"We'll go with you."

Adeline glanced over at Jamie, who had the family room floor cluttered with toys and was deep into play. "I'll go. I want it to be a surprise."

"You're throwing him a welcome home party?"

"Why not? I still feel like celebrating." That was true. She didn't have to lie about that.

Jeremy looked at his son with an amused smile. "Okay, but be careful."

Evan was still on the loose.

"Always." She stepped to him and leaned in for a quick kiss, not knowing why she'd done so. The action was partly natural and maybe partly out of awareness that she had another reason for leaving and was keeping that secret.

His eyes flared with warmth and question, which she ignored. Giving him a coy smile, she left him with Jamie.

A few minutes later she arrived at Oscar's building. He told the doorman to let her in and up to his apartment. A short elevator ride and a few doors down the hall and she reached Oscar's home.

"Adeline." Oscar had his apartment door open. "What brings you by?"

"Tess's accident." Entering, she faced him in the foyer. This wouldn't take long.

He looked confused.

"I obtained video footage of her accident from a nearby ATM," she said. "I'm sure I don't have to tell you what I saw."

His mouth pinched in dismay and he sat down. After a moment, he raised his eyes.

"I kept that to myself because I didn't want my wife to know I was with Holly," he said.

"I gathered that much. But your wife knows about your affair. Why didn't you come forward after that?"

"To be frank, I didn't see the point. I expected Jeremy to fire me. I still do. Now that he has his son back, he'll be able to attend to business here. That includes dealing with me."

"You haven't been honest with him. You made him believe you were a forthright man with integrity. He was disappointed to discover you were the opposite."

"I am forthright and I do have integrity."

Adeline would let Jeremy be the judge of that. "Did you know Evan kidnapped Jamie?"

"No," he answered adamantly. "I saw the story on the news and there has been a lot of talk around the office."

"Have you been in contact with him at all since Emily Stanton has been arrested?"

"No. He wouldn't be that stupid."

Evan wouldn't try to call anyone. He wouldn't go to anyone for help. In all likelihood, he had a contingency plan. If anything went wrong, he'd know what to do.

"I think I'd be wise to end our friendship," Oscar said. "I knew Evan had licentious tastes, but I never guessed he'd go so far as kidnapping for ransom." He sounded convincing but Adeline couldn't be sure without evidence.

"Will that include your relationship with Holly?"

"She has nothing to do with Jamie's kidnapping, but yes, I do see a need to change my ways."

Adeline would let that go. "Did you see anyone else on the road the night Tess died?"

Oscar shook his head. "It was rather late. There weren't many out and about at that hour."

"Why were you there at the time of Tess's accident? It's coincidental, don't you think?"

"Yes. I couldn't believe it myself until Holly told me she'd walked to meet me from the bar where she'd met Tess for drinks. We went to the hotel. A few hours later,

I walked her back to her place. That's when we saw the accident and I realized Tess had been killed."

"What did you do after you saw the accident?"

"I ran to the driver. As soon as I reached her, I recognized Tess and could see she was dead. Holly called for help."

"And you told the sheriff none of this."

He lowered his head briefly, a sign of contrition. "No. We left before anyone arrived."

"Are you certain she was dead?"

"I checked for breathing and a pulse. And her head…"

It had been obvious Tess was dead and there was no resuscitating her.

"Does Jeremy know you're here?" he asked.

He must have asked because Jeremy wasn't with her. "Did you see anything else that might stand out?" she asked instead of answering. "Any other cars that may have driven her off the road?"

"No. Like I said, there was no one."

She nodded. Having no more questions, she said, "Thanks for seeing me," and turned to go.

"Would you like me not to tell him?" he asked to her retreating back.

Stopping, she turned to look at him. He meant Jeremy. "I'll tell him myself." Just not today. She sure hoped that analysis came back soon. "He's convinced Livia killed Tess and I don't think she did."

"But you thought I might have?"

"No. I think Tess died in a car accident of her own doing." Seeing his eyes calm, she turned to go. "Thank you again."

On her way home, she received the call.

"You've got the results already?"

"It didn't take long. All the techs had to do is enhance the video. The driver's side was dented before the accident. I'll email you the report."

There was her proof. She almost felt guilty. This was the outcome she'd expected all along. Jeremy wouldn't like it.

"Thanks." She disconnected. All the way to the bakery she debated over how to break the news to Jeremy.

After quickly picking up the cake and some balloons, she raced for Jeremy's house.

Her phone rang again. This time it was Jeremy.

"Where are you?"

She didn't want to tell him over the phone. He was too sensitive about Tess's death. "I had another stop to make. I'm on my way."

"What other stop? What's taking you so long?"

"I'll explain when I get home."

"Yes, home. I like the sound of that."

Did he? She heard the lengthy silence on the other end and sensed his regret in saying what he had.

"I'll see you shortly," she said, and disconnected.

Jeremy checked the time when Adeline finally made it home. She'd been gone well over an hour. It didn't take that long to pick up a cake. Where had she gone?

He met her at the garage door, seeing how she avoided eye contact. His stomach did a flop of dread, something he hadn't felt since high school, when he'd discovered his girlfriend had started seeing one of the football players.

He took the cake from her. "What was your other stop?"

Jamie came running into the kitchen. "Is it chocolate?"

"Lots and lots of chocolate." Adeline smiled and passed Jeremy as she headed for the kitchen.

Jeremy had no choice other than to follow with the cake that Jamie had a particular interest in. He set it on the table as she tied the balloons to a chair.

Jamie sat on that chair, tipping his head back to look up at the colorful bulbs floating above him.

"It's not my birthday," he said.

"We're celebrating you coming home. You were gone way too long." Adeline bent to plant a kiss on his cheek, eliciting a short giggle from him.

"It's dessert before dinner tonight." Adeline found a knife and plates and busied herself slicing three pieces.

Jeremy thought she seemed to use the task to hide the true purpose of her outing. Where had she gone?

Later that night, after his son had fallen asleep, he turned the light off in Jamie's room and turned to Adeline, fully intending to demand answers. Her soft expression stopped him. She loved Jamie so much, as much as he did. Nothing stronger could link him to a woman. No other woman could share that with him.

"We created that," she said.

Yes, they had, a miracle of life. All his reservations about her fell away. Only love surrounded him now.

She rose up onto her toes and kissed him. "Thank you for that."

For Jamie. Her son. Their son.

Without a word, she walked down the hall, passing her bedroom, and went into his.

In the doorway, he stopped. She faced him and as he'd done the last time, she began to undress, starting with her vest. She tossed it to the floor with playful animation. Adorable. The mother of his child. He leaned on the door frame to watch.

She smiled when he didn't move to take off any of his clothes, then unfastened her belt, slid it from its loops and tossed it on top of the vest.

He pushed off the door frame and went to her, lifting his Henley up over his head. She took in his upper torso, much as she had before, admiring his form, his muscles. She put her hands on him and the rest would be history. As soon as she touched him, he couldn't stop.

Touching her face, his warm palm against her cheek, he moved his thumb over her lower lip, full and warm. Sliding his hand to the base of her head, he kissed her. She opened to him and he devoured her. He trailed his lips down her neck.

She unbuttoned his jeans. He unfastened her pinstriped pants. Stepping back, she pushed them down and stepped out of them.

Seeing she wore skimpy lace underwear, really just strings and a patch over her crotch, he wondered if she'd planned this night all along. He removed his jeans, down to his underwear now. She still wore the blouse, which fell to just above her panty line. He found the sight of her like that infinitely sexy.

When she released the first button of her blouse, he stopped her. "Just the bra. Leave that on."

She removed her bra without taking off the blouse, pushing the straps down her arms and then unclasping the front to slip it off underneath. Then she stood there for him, letting him look at her for as long as he liked.

He must have spent an entire two minutes doing that. Then he pulled her against him.

"Why are you doing this?" he asked.

"I want to make love with my son's father," she said. "Even if we don't end up together, or friends after this, I want one night with you like this, with nothing standing between us."

He could deliver on that. Sliding her underwear down her thighs, he waited for her to kick the scanty thing aside.

Steering her backward, he pressed her against the wall next to the dresser. She wrapped her legs around him. He moved against her, letting her feel how hard she'd made him. She tipped her head back to catch her breath and he kissed her throat.

Moving his hand under her blouse, he caressed her breasts and fondled her nipples. He kissed her with the softness of feathers, whispering her name.

"Take me to the bed."

"No. This is how I imagined I would have gotten you pregnant."

She lowered her head to level a look at him. "Against the wall?"

He chuckled. "I'm a man."

She smiled brightly and laughed a little.

He didn't wait. He probed for her and sank inside. Then he thrust up and down, making her rise and fall. He kissed her as sensation took over. He had her peaking in a few strokes. Lucky for him, because he couldn't have held out much longer. She did that to him.

She undid him.

Chapter 17

Waking to darkness, Adeline at first thought morning had yet to come. She sat up on the bed, seeing she'd slept all night in Jeremy's room. Memory rushed forth. Sex with him packed a powerful sensory overload. She had to admit to herself that, in part, she'd gone headfirst into making love with him on purpose. As strong as their first intimate endeavor had been, he couldn't remain indifferent for long. Could she crack his hard shell?

She dreaded telling him what she'd learned about Tess's accident and hoped what they shared at least physically would help to soften the blow.

Getting out of bed, she kept her mind on the potency of their lovemaking. She went to the patio door and opened the drapes. A gray drizzle clouded the day. No wonder the room had been so dark. She checked the time. After nine.

She spent longer than usual in the shower and getting dressed. Could she just stay here in this moment when nothing would ruin the aftermath?

In black slacks, gray, black and white checkered

blouse and a vest, she left the bedroom and headed down the hall. She heard Jamie before she reached his room.

Peeking her head in, she saw he still wore his pj's and played with an assortment of construction vehicles, making a motor sound as he rolled a skid-steer loader, its attachments scattered around him. Without bothering him, she left him to his imagination and went downstairs.

Walking into the kitchen, she saw Jeremy fully dressed in a suit. He must have woken much earlier than her and planned on going into work today.

Seeing he held her cell phone, Adeline stopped short. Why had he looked at it? He must have seen her enter the code to unlock it at some point.

The FBI agent had said he'd send her a report.

He turned his head to look at her. She saw hardness in his eyes and the set of his mouth.

Holding up the phone and showing her what he'd opened, she saw her email app. The message he'd just read was from the agent.

"Were you going to tell me about this?" he asked in an even, tight tone.

"Yes. As soon as I received the report."

Facing her, he handed her the phone. She took it.

"Why did you sneak out to pick up a bank ATM video?" he asked.

"I didn't sneak."

"No?" His tone grew harsher. "Where did you go yesterday?"

She could say she went to pick up Jamie's cake but she'd done more than that, and he'd called her, wondering what was taking her so long.

"I asked the bank manager to check any video surveillance he had the night of Tess's accident," she said.

"He called yesterday morning to let me know he had it. I stopped by there to pick it up and…to view the footage."

"You lied when you said you were going to get the cake."

"No. I didn't lie. I did go get the cake."

"But you didn't tell me you picked up the video."

"I know how you feel about Tess's accident, Jeremy. I wanted to be sure before I talked to you about any findings."

His eyes hardened further as his temper rose. "You know how I feel? I don't think so."

"You need closure regarding her death."

"What did you need to be sure about, Adeline? That Tess wasn't murdered? That's what you've thought all along, isn't it?"

"No. I had my suspicions. I just needed proof."

His face gave away his emotion. He felt betrayed. Adeline had betrayed him. Maybe she should have trusted him to react calmly to her news. "I understand why you would be upset. I should have told you about the bank video."

"Have you seen the report?" he asked.

"No." She looked down at her phone and the message from the agent. There was an attachment but in the message he basically confirmed the dent had been there at the time of the accident. She looked up at Jeremy. Through his anger she also saw hurt. She'd done what he'd hired her to do. Her findings just weren't what he'd pushed for all along.

"Oscar and Holly witnessed her accident," Adeline said. He had to know the rest. "I spoke with him. He didn't come forward because he feared his wife discovering his affair. They didn't see anyone try to drive Tess off the road."

"Another thing you didn't tell me. Why the secrets, Adeline?"

Rain pattered against the patio door and other kitchen windows as the wind picked up. Jeremy had turned on some lights or it would be a lot dimmer in the room.

"I shouldn't have. I'm sorry."

He didn't respond, but his eyes conveyed his disappointment. "Why did you go through my phone?" she finally asked.

"I heard your phone go off. You took so long yesterday I felt I had to find out why."

"You could have just asked me."

"I'm asking you now. Why didn't you tell me?"

"I knew you wouldn't like the outcome." An outcome she'd suspected but hadn't been able to prove until now.

"So you avoided having to face me?"

"I delayed facing you until I had all the facts." Didn't he want to know the truth? "Livia wasn't anywhere near Tess when she crashed."

"She could have poisoned her. The coroner might not have done the right tests to reveal that."

When would Livia have had the chance to poison Tess? Tess had come from the bar. Jeremy knew all of that. Granted, witnesses might not recall if she was there or not, but Holly hadn't seen Livia, either. Livia dropping poison into one of Tess's drinks seemed highly improbable, not only logistically, but based on motive, as well. Livia didn't have a strong enough reason to kill Tess. Besides, the coroner had run tests to check for poisoning. Adeline had read the report.

"What kind of poisoning did the coroner miss?" she asked.

He didn't answer because he couldn't. He didn't know, and most likely the coroner had checked every viable possibility.

"Livia didn't kill Tess," Adeline asserted. "Tess died in a car accident because she was too drunk to drive. When are you going to accept that?"

He stepped closer. "When are *you* going to accept that Livia is evil and could have killed her?"

Adeline sighed heavily and moved back. Arguing was pointless. He wanted so badly to pin Tess's death on Livia that he could see no reason.

"Have you talked with Livia?" he asked.

Why would he ask such a thing? She didn't need to ask. "No. Livia is most likely dead, Jeremy."

"Are you sure? Maybe you're protecting her. Maybe she's paid you, too."

She folded her arms with the insult. "Now you're being ridiculous." Why was he going off like this? He couldn't let go of Tess; that's why. The truth stared him in the face right now and he resisted.

"Am I? You were a donor and surrogate for money. What else would you do?"

His accusations stung painfully, but she could see where they came from. He still could not let Tess go. Maybe knowing how she died would someday give him the peace he needed. After he had some time to think it over.

"What kind of woman could give up her own child, anyway? I've always wondered how you could do that so easily. You acted like it was difficult, but was it?"

Adeline felt the blood descend from her face, despite

seeing the anguish in Jeremy's eyes. She could give him a lot of leeway, given his difficulty getting past Tess's death, but she had a limit on how much she'd take. Lowering her arms, she started for the kitchen exit. Tossing over her shoulder, "I'll get my things and be on my way." He no longer needed her anyway.

She fought the sting of tears as she hurried up the stairs.

In her bedroom, she closed and locked the door and took her time packing. All the while hurt welled up in waves, stinging her heart and burning her eyes. She couldn't believe he'd said those things. Even grappling with the truth, did he really have to go that far? No, and she suspected he'd soon regret saying what he had. Jeremy wasn't a callous man. He'd recognize his mistake. Adeline wasn't sure she could forgive him, though.

Hearing an email come through on her phone, she checked the sender. The FBI agent sent her another video clip, this one from a local grocery store. The brief footage showed Tess backing out of a parking space and another car hitting her side. Tess had backed up some more and turned in the opposite direction, speeding away. The time stamp showed she'd gone to the store midafternoon, after she'd met Oscar and before she'd gone to the bar. The crash report had said there had been a few nonperishables in the car.

The agent further explained someone had reported a hit and run. Tess had backed out of the parking space when a car had been oncoming. She forwarded the email to Jeremy with a note that said only, In case you're interested. She also included the report from the agent.

Finished packing, she took her luggage downstairs. She found Jeremy at the front door.

"I'm sorry," he said.

"Too late. I'm leaving." She stopped when he wouldn't move out of the way. Getting involved with him had been a big mistake. She should be glad he'd lost his temper. Now she had ample reason to get away. No man would hurt her again.

"I am sorry. I shouldn't have spoken to you that way."

"But you still meant what you said. You still insist Livia killed Tess, even though all the evidence proves otherwise."

He didn't respond but he didn't disagree.

"I'll put my things in the car and come back to say goodbye to Jamie." She couldn't leave without seeing him one last time.

Jeremy moved out of the way of the door, opening it for her and taking both her suitcases.

She unlocked her car and he loaded the luggage, then tossed her coat on the passenger seat. She marveled at how easily he helped her leave.

She headed back inside. Jamie was still playing in his room. He looked up when she entered.

"Hi, sweetie. I came to say goodbye."

Jamie's eyes drooped in dismay. "Where are you going?"

"It's time for me to go home now. You're safe and your father no longer needs me."

"But…you're my mommy."

"Yes, I am your mommy. Nothing will change that. I'll still come and see you." She hoped Jeremy wouldn't stand in the way of that. He'd told her she could, but she wouldn't trust a thing he said now. She'd rather not take him to court, but she would if she had to.

Looking back, she saw him in the doorway. He nodded a couple of times.

Good. He'd let her see Jamie. She'd make arrangements so that he wouldn't be around when she did. Just like divorced couples.

"If you ever want to talk, tell your dad and he can call me, okay?"

"Okay." Jamie stood and put his tiny arms around her. She held him for a while, again feeling the sting of tears. She hated leaving him at all. She wanted to spend every second of every day with him, or as much as she could. Mornings and evenings and weekends. No gaps in between. But Jeremy would make that impossible.

She kissed his cheek and let him go. "I'll see you soon."

"Okay." Jamie looked crestfallen as she stood.

"I promise," she said. "We'll have a pancake breakfast real soon."

Jamie smiled hugely. "Yeah!"

She faced forward. Jeremy moved out of the way so she could pass. Maybe some morning soon she could come over when Jeremy had to go to work.

A lump formed in her throat as she descended the stairs. She'd go home to her empty house. No more family nights.

When she reached the door, Jeremy said, "I'll call you."

She stopped and looked back. "Don't bother. I'll contact your executive assistant and make arrangements to see Jamie through her." She would not talk to him directly. "I'd rather not have to see or speak to you."

He stood stock-still at that.

Adeline forced herself to turn and leave, closing the

door softly behind her. Each step to her car brought more agony. Jamie's adorable face had permanently implanted itself on her brain. She wouldn't be able to get that out of her head. At least she'd think of him more than Jeremy.

At least…she hoped.

Standing at the back patio window, looking out at the rainy morning, Jeremy tried calling Adeline again. He'd tried a couple of times already. She had good reason not to answer. He should not have let her go without resolving his outburst this morning.

After he calmed down, he regretted everything he'd said. He'd seen her emails after she'd gone. At first, reading what the agent said about Tess backing out of a parking space in front of an oncoming car infuriated him. Not only did it suggest Tess had started drinking before she had gone to the bar, he'd thought Adeline had sent that to dig the knife in deeper. Then he realized he had gotten angry with Adeline and none of this was her fault.

He was angry because he couldn't blame someone for Tess's death, for her being taken from him when they had just started a family. Livia had been a convenient culprit. After Tess had died, he'd struggled with disbelief and grief. It had taken him a while to get to the anger stage. Taking over one hundred percent of Jamie's care had slowed the process. He'd had to learn how to carry on all the responsibilities of both father and mother. He'd also had to keep his business going. All along, though, he couldn't accept that Tess had simply died as the result of a car accident. Sure, she drank, but to die so suddenly and so soon after they brought Jamie home?

Life wasn't fair. Life happened no matter what plans

people made. He couldn't have prepared for losing Tess, even if he'd tried.

Why had he gotten so angry over Tess's accident? Her death?

Guilt.

The word came to him like a train rushing by, plowing through air and sending a gust of wind at him. Adeline had seen it long before he had. He couldn't believe he'd felt guilty then. Now he could. He had missed all the signs Tess had relapsed into drinking again. If he had known, he could have done something, but since he hadn't, she'd wrecked her car and died. He might have been able to prevent that. That was what had him so torn up inside, and why he had lashed out at Adeline. Now that he recognized that, he could finally let her go. Yes, he might have been able to prevent her accident, but he couldn't go back in time. He had to accept she'd died as a result of her drinking.

He and Tess had other problems in their marriage. Her drinking must have awakened those. He'd always worried she'd fall back into her old patterns, but looking back he realized more than that had been at play. He'd wanted all-encompassing love for his family, but her addictive personality influenced more than her alcoholism. A creature of habit, she needed structure and sameness. As an entrepreneur, that would send him to an early grave. They hadn't been a match made in heaven.

He and Adeline, on the other hand...

Where was she?

He couldn't go after her with Jamie. He wouldn't expose his son to that conflict, not when he'd been such an ass and now had to find a way to make it up to Adeline.

His ringing doorbell sent hope firing. Had she come back?

Hurrying to the door, he opened it to Knox and two deputies standing there.

"Adeline called 9-1-1 from her cell phone," Knox said. "Come with me." He nodded his head toward the deputies to his left. "These two will watch over Jamie."

Stunned with a rush of dread, Jeremy had to take a second to gather himself. "Where is she?"

"The dispatcher said the line went dead as soon as she said she needed help. She was able to get a location on her, though. She was at her house."

Jeremy could see by Knox's face that Adeline was no longer there.

Adeline came out of unconsciousness and opened her eyes to darkness. She remembered arriving home and someone had followed her into the garage before she could close the overhead door. She'd recognized Evan and saw he had a gun. She'd tried to draw her own pistol, but Evan had reached her. She'd struggled with him and he'd knocked her gun out of her hand. Rather than shoot her, he'd tried to subdue her, to strike her with his gun. She'd kicked him in his groin, which bought her enough time to make it to the inner garage door. She'd dug out her cell phone and ran into the house, pressing the numbers with one hand and trying to close the garage door with the other.

Evan had put his foot in the door so she couldn't lock him out. She ran through her house. Unfortunately, Evan had caught up to her and tackled her on the living room floor. Her phone had fallen from her hands as she'd frantically called out for help. She didn't know if the dispatcher had heard her and she didn't remember anything else.

Evan must have hit her with his gun. Her head hurt. She lifted her hand to test the area, only to discover he'd bound her with a zip tie. Next, she realized she was in the trunk of a car, which then slowed to a stop.

In the dark she felt around for something, anything, to use as a weapon, but the trunk had been cleaned of any items. Evan had planned to put her in there.

Would he kill her? He'd failed to get the second ransom, therefore failing to make Jeremy suffer as much as he'd intended—and also hadn't gotten the money. Would he take his revenge out on her now?

Only the sound of light rain pattering on the trunk broke the silence. What should she do?

Make sure he gets caught.

She pulled out some of her hair and dropped it in the trunk, as far in the corner as possible so Evan wouldn't find it before the sheriff did…if she didn't make it. She had every intention of making it.

She heard Evan's steps approach the rear of the car. Closing her eyes briefly, she gathered her strength. She wouldn't get out of this alive if she succumbed to fear.

The trunk opened and Evan's impassive face appeared. Rain dripped on him as he aimed his gun.

"Get out."

She braced herself on the edge of the trunk. Evan grabbed her by her zip-tied wrists and dragged her out of the car.

Finding her footing, she shoved Evan. He stumbled a couple of steps back.

"What are you doing?" Rain dampened her hair and clothes. She wasn't wearing a coat.

"Take a walk." He gestured toward the woods.

She looked around, not recognizing the area. Would he kill her and leave her body? She glanced back. He had the gun aimed midtorso. If he shot her this close, she'd be in bad shape.

She started walking, having no choice. After a few steps she saw a cabin ahead—the same cabin where Emily had stayed. Why would he take her there? Did he not know that's where authorities had captured her? The news had reported her arrest but hadn't said where, only that she'd been arrested for the kidnapping of Jamie Kincaid. Evan must have known where Emily had kept Jamie. He must have assumed she'd been arrested either there or at home.

Adeline watched for an opportunity to escape. As she approached the cabin she looked for the best route to run.

At the front door, Evan grabbed her arm and stopped her. He dug into his jacket pocket and produced keys. His aim faltered as he fumbled with them, searching for the one to open the door.

Adeline took her chance. She stomped down hard on his ankle at the same time she swung her arms to knock the gun out of his hand. He hollered in pain but didn't drop the gun.

She ran away from the front porch, her feet sinking into soggy ground, balance unwieldy with her hands tied. She ducked behind a tree and headed for more cover in the woods. Gunfire rang out. She ran so that tree trunks protected her, but heard him running behind her. His footfalls sounded uneven, as though he limped.

Seeing a boulder ahead, she veered to her right, running along the back side and slowing to see if Evan saw her. She heard his unsteady footing approach the boulder. The canopy overhead protected her some from the rain.

She moved to the side of the rock as Evan neared. His running slowed, indicating he'd either lost sight of her or had seen her go behind the boulder.

When he kept going through the woods, she breathed a sigh of relief. Walking softly along the front of the rock, she peered around the edge and watched Evan walking and looking to his left and right and straight ahead. He stopped and began to turn.

Adeline ducked behind the boulder, out of sight.

She heard him walking again and took another peek. He continued to walk away.

Adeline walked the opposite direction, staying quiet and low, with the boulder blocking the line of sight between her and Evan. When she made it far enough to no longer use the boulder, she began running, struggling with her hands bound. She didn't see Evan anymore, but he would give up and retrace his steps to search for her. He might even consider she'd used the boulder.

Back at his car, she looked inside for keys. There were none. She ran to the cabin, hair soaking wet now and dripping water. The front door was locked, but the back was open as before. She entered and closed the door, trying to lock it, but the lock was broken.

She looked for something to use as a weapon. In the kitchen she found a butcher knife. Taking that, she sawed off the zip tie, every second that took feeling like an eternity. The zip tie fell off. She left the cabin, running for the road leading to the highway. She ran until she had to slow to a walk to catch her breath. The hem of her pants were brown with mud. Her skin was chilled through her wet clothes and her teeth chattered.

Then she heard an engine start up. Evan had returned to his car.

She ran into the woods, getting off the road leading to the cabin. When she was deep enough into the trees, she hid behind one of them and watched the road, or what she could see of it.

Catching glimpses of Evan's car passing by, she crouched as low as she could and waited for him to pass. A few minutes later she left her refuge and walked to the road, then toward the highway.

She hadn't been on the road five minutes before she heard a vehicle. The engine sounded the same as Evan's. She jumped over the drainage ditch. The vehicle approached fast, too fast for her to get out of sight. Headlights cast her running form in a shadow in front of her. She dove for the ground, careful to hold the knife up and away from her. Flattened on her stomach, she craned her neck to try to see. Tall grass and tree trunks blocked her view. She heard the car skid to a halt on the dirt road.

He'd seen her.

Adeline ran through the woods toward the road. She shoved branches out of her way. Some scraped her as she raced by. Seeing the road, adrenaline soared. If she could flag down a car...

Evan swerved his car out onto the highway just as she reached the drainage ditch. She stopped as he sped toward her. He had the passenger window down and began firing at her. Ducking, she leaped back into the woods, taking cover behind a trunk. Bullets hit bark. She screamed and crouched down.

Seeing Evan had stopped his car and got out, she had started to turn and run when he ran out of bullets. As he dug into his jacket pocket for more ammo, she stepped out from behind the tree and marched toward him. Raising the knife, she flung it at him as hard as she could.

He looked up just as the knife torpedoed toward him. He only had time to take one step back before the knife sank into the right side of his chest.

Looking stunned, he dropped the gun and put his hand around the handle of the knife. Stumbling, he fell onto his butt and then slumped back. Grimacing, he pulled the knife from his chest. Dropping that, he pressed his hand over the bleeding wound.

Adeline went to the gun and picked it up. Then she stepped on his left hand and reached into his jacket pocket, retrieving the ammo. After removing the empty clip, she inserted the other and aimed for Evan's head.

"Move," she growled. "Give me a reason to blow your brains all over this road."

Jeremy and Knox drove with lights flashing down the highway, windshield wipers issuing a monotonous tap-tap sound. Jeremy had insisted on going with him despite the pushback. They'd checked Evan's house and also Emily's and her neighbor's. Jeremy had the desperate idea to check the cabin. His mind reeled with the threat of losing Adeline. He could lose two women he loved. While he had to fight to control those terrible thoughts, the man in him refused to give up. He'd do anything to keep her from harm. If Evan hurt her in any way, he'd kill him with his bare hands.

As it happened, he wouldn't have to. He spotted Adeline ahead on the highway, pointing a gun at Evan, rainwater dripping from her. Jeremy jumped out of Knox's vehicle before it came to a complete stop.

He ran to her. "Are you all right?" He checked her body for signs of injury, removing his jacket.

"Yes." She lowered the gun.

Jeremy draped his jacket over her shoulders. She clutched it to her, but took a step back when he put his hand on her shoulder.

He didn't try to touch her again.

Evan lay holding his hand to his chest, clearly in pain and fear as he fought for air.

Jeremy went to stand over him. All of his evil scheming had led to this moment. What a waste.

"Why?" Jeremy asked, even though he knew. Was anything worth this—risking death or a prison sentence?

"You," Evan forced the word out. "You…had…to pay." He coughed and struggled for breath.

"I fired you for sexual harassment and you think killing Adeline and kidnapping my son are justifiable?"

Evan stared up at him. If he wasn't stabbed in the chest and in pain, that stare would probably hold a lot more malice, crazed malice. "Your…company…wouldn't be what it is today…" He coughed and caught his breath. "If it weren't for me."

"You?" Jeremy couldn't believe it. "You think you're the one—the only one—responsible for my success?"

"I…built…your first start-up."

"It was my money and my idea. I hired you to manage the finances, which you did."

"Yes…with no thanks from you." He coughed again, this time spitting up blood.

"I compensated you well. It isn't my fault you were unethical. Why should I have to pay for your bad choices?"

Evan coughed more, rolling a little to one side to expel more blood. He needed medical attention fast.

Knox appeared. "I called an ambulance." He knelt beside Evan and helped him apply pressure to his wound. As he did, he read Evan his rights and arrested him for the kidnapping of Jamie Kincaid and kidnapping and attempted murder of Adeline Winters.

Jeremy noticed how Adeline avoided eye contact with him. Now probably wasn't the best time to apologize. Sirens grew louder. Police would need to question her. But he had to at least say something.

"Adeline, about earlier," he said.

She held up her hand. "Please, let's not talk about that now."

"I just wanted to tell you after you left I realized what a jerk I was."

She nodded. "Yeah. You were a jerk."

A fire truck and sheriff's department vehicles arrived along with an ambulance. Adeline was taken aside for questioning and a paramedic asked if she was all right.

Jeremy stayed out of the way, saw Evan being loaded into the ambulance and watched Adeline, seeing how her adrenaline eased the longer she talked. She had never looked as beautiful as she did right now. Now that he'd faced losing her, he realized what he had. She was someone quite special. And he might have botched things up good for himself. He might not have another chance with her. She might not give him one.

Chapter 18

Two weeks later, Adeline sat in her antique office on the second level of a 1912 redbrick building in the oldest part of downtown Shadow Creek, trying to stop thinking about Jamie. And Jeremy, but she missed Jamie terribly. She ached. She'd rented the office space a year and a half after graduating from college, when she'd landed her first big client. Then she'd slowly decorated, collecting antique furniture and art that caught her eye. She didn't study art or go to galleries. She didn't follow any trends or themes. She just enjoyed making a room esthetically appealing and she did it in a cost-effective way.

Abandoning the case file she'd tried to read for the last hour now, she stood and walked to the open double French doors and entered a small reception area with early-century dark brown and beige Italian sofa and chair. Her receptionist was out to lunch and her assistant investigator was following a lead on a new case. There was a half bath off the reception area next to the front door. She sometimes wished she had a shower here, then she could stay the night…well, more than she already did.

Through the reception area, she went into the dark wood–floored kitchen, which she also used as a conference room. She kept the room showroom tidy. Passing the four-seater table, she went into an alcove and took out a water from the stainless steel refrigerator. White glass door cabinets hung above black granite countertops tastefully adorned with a bowl of green apples and glass canisters.

Her new case failed to divert her attention and so had her wandering into thoughts of her office decor. Knox had phoned earlier to let her know Rusty Nicholson had been put on unpaid leave for his role in Jamie's kidnapping. He had asked about her and Jeremy and told her Jeremy was lost without her. That had not helped her efforts to distract her from him and Jamie.

Hearing the door jingle, signifying someone had entered, she set down the water bottle on the table and stopped short when she saw Jeremy.

Closing the door, he held up his hand. "Before you tell me to get out of here, hear me out."

"No." She stepped firmly to him. "You need to leave."

"You won't answer my calls and I still haven't paid you for your work."

"I can't believe you think I want to be paid. And I don't want to talk to you." Jamie was her son, too. Being paid would feel just wrong.

He sighed and put his hands on his hips, staring at her awhile. "I could have done this over the phone."

But she hadn't answered and here he was. The sight of him did things to her she didn't want to like. She was glad to see him.

"I received your filing for visitation rights," he said.

She folded her arms. So he'd come here to fight her on that?

"You can come see Jamie whenever you want."

He'd said as much before, but what would happen if their relationship deteriorated further than it already had? He could deny her visitation on a whim.

"I prefer to have the legal right to see my son, not depend on your word." He'd proven his word could be dubious. She wouldn't go up against that without a court order.

She didn't know if he could sway her. It had been a while since she'd seen him and his presence gave her the same intense heat. She had to force herself to remain distant, lest the romantic side of her relent to desire.

"Come by and see him tonight. Any time after five. That's all I came here to say." With that, he turned and left.

Adeline stood there a moment, thrilled and happy with the prospect of seeing Jamie again. Tonight. She missed him terribly.

Would she wait the lengthy amount of time it would take to go through the courts to set up required visitation? She could take Jeremy up on his invitation and use his generosity as long as the offer stood. But she'd have to go to him to see her son. The courts might allow her to take Jamie with her for weekends. She wouldn't have to fight temptation with Jeremy close.

What to do…?

Jeremy finished his first investor meeting with Alastair Buchanan. They had a few more to go, but Alastair was excited about the new prospects. He'd be in town awhile longer. Jeremy was glad to have a friend while he adjusted to life without Adeline. Jamie had complained every day. He missed her.

Seeing Adeline this morning had only enflamed his feelings. He hadn't thought he felt this much for her. His obsession with Tess's accident could easily be blamed. He wished he hadn't said what he had. He had never spoken to anyone that way before and could only attribute the behavior to his inability to put Tess's memory to rest. Deep down, he'd known Livia hadn't killed Tess. He'd known Adeline proved that. He just couldn't let go, not until he realized what he'd done, how he'd hurt Adeline. She deserved better. He had treated her unfairly and should have given her more of himself all along. He wanted to now.

Alastair returned from the restroom, shutting the door to Jeremy's office. He stopped before the desk and eyed Jeremy. "You've been moping a lot lately. Are you sure you're on top of these investment briefings?"

Jeremy could spot a good start-up investment in his sleep. "Don't worry about that. I've been through a lot, that's all."

Alastair knew all about Jamie's kidnapping and the attacks on Adeline.

"Where's Adeline?"

"Don't ask."

Alastair smiled with a brief chuckle. "Women make men stupid sometimes. Find a way to apologize."

"I said some pretty stupid things. I was so sure Livia was involved with all that went wrong."

"And when Adeline proved you wrong you didn't take it well."

Jeremy leaned back against his chair, dejected. "I

asked her what kind of woman could give up her own child."

Alastair winced.

"I even accused her of working with Livia."

Alastair winced more. "Ouch."

"Yeah."

"Well, you have a lot of kissing up to do. I'd think of something good if I were you."

"Thanks," Jeremy said wryly. "Hey, did you go by Bluewood Ranch?"

"Not yet. I had to fly home to attend to pressing business matters. I thought I'd stop by there this week sometime."

Jeremy nodded. "I think you'll find the owner interesting. She's pretty, too."

"I'd go to try something new. Ranch life is definitely new for me."

Yes, Jeremy had always known Alastair as a sophisticated businessman. Luxury hotels and fine dining were more his personality, although Jeremy also thought he'd do well with a good dose of country. That's why he'd suggested a day at Bluewood. And maybe Halle Ford had something to do with the suggestion. She deserved a good man and Alastair needed a woman who interested him.

Why hadn't he thought the same for himself?

Adeline still hesitated when she drove up to Jeremy's big house. The chance to see Jamie had overruled her rationale every time she'd tried to talk herself out of going. She sat with the engine running, staring at the front door.

Jeremy opened the door and waited.

Caught, Adeline turned off the engine and headed for

the house. Jeremy didn't smile. He kept a neutral expression and Adeline sensed his tension. She believed he felt sorry for the things he'd said, but he must have meant them or he wouldn't have thought to say them. Just because someone kindly didn't share their uglier thoughts about someone didn't mean they weren't genuine. Jeremy thought less of her for giving up Jamie. He might have only been lashing out when he'd basically accused her of joining up with Livia. Did he actually think she'd try to help kill his wife so she could make inroads with her rich husband?

Adeline had given her ex-boyfriend the benefit of the doubt and she'd paid a high price. She'd had glimpses of the man deep inside and had ignored the signs. Had Jeremy given her a sign?

She eyed him as she entered, seeing him observe her with keen insight. He must feel her reticence.

"Mommy!"

Adeline forgot all about Jeremy and what he'd said when she saw Jamie running toward her, his bare feet pattering over the tiled entry. She crouched and took him into a crashing hug.

"Hi, Jamie. Oh, how I've missed you." She kissed the side of his head.

"I missed you, too." He moved back but stayed in her arms. "When are you coming home?"

"I'm home now, sweetie. And I'll come see you as much as I can, okay?"

"Mommies are supposed to live in the same house," he said.

She hadn't prepared herself for that insightful observation. "That's probably true most of the time."

"Why can't you live here with me and Daddy?"

How could she respond to that? She glanced up at Jeremy but he offered no help. In fact, she felt he waited for her response, as though he'd like to know, as well.

"Your daddy only asked me to stay with you for a short time." She glanced up at him smugly. He deserved that.

"Not forever?"

Forever was a long time. "No, not forever."

"But you have to be here so we can make pancakes."

She ran her finger down his little nose. "It's not good for you to eat pancakes too much, but I told you I'd come by some mornings to make them with you."

"Tomorrow?" he asked.

Adeline laughed softly. Only a kid would be so tenacious. "Probably not that soon."

She glanced up at Jeremy again, who watched with warm eyes and a soft curve to his mouth. He liked what he saw—her with Jamie. Or was it just Jamie?

When Jamie stood away and left the entry, she followed. He landed on his knees in the family room, where a cartoon played on the TV. He'd given up trying to get her to live with him for now, but Adeline suspected she'd hear more on that later.

"I want to apologize for the things I said," Jeremy said.

Adeline really did not feel up for this talk. "Well, too late—you said them."

"I didn't mean them."

Adeline glanced at Jamie, who had fallen entranced back into his cartoon. She turned and walked into the kitchen. Jamie didn't need to hear any of this.

Jeremy followed.

In front of the elegant kitchen island, she faced him.

"I don't think you would have said those things if you hadn't already thought that way."

Jeremy held a steady face and seemed to consider how to respond, or have some regret that he had to. "I did wonder how you gave up Jamie. I wondered how you felt. After seeing you with him, and talking to you and your mother, I know it was difficult. I didn't know that before, but I wanted to. I said that to hurt you and I'm so sorry."

"You thought I had no trouble giving him up and thought poorly of me?"

"I never thought poorly of you. I used that against you in the heat of the moment."

He'd hurled an accusation but hadn't meant it in his heart? "Then I suppose I should thank you. Now I know you're capable of being awful when you're angry."

Jeremy bent his head and rubbed his brow. After a bit he looked at her again. "I've never behaved that way before. I've never lost someone close to me before. I guess it made me go a little crazy. Finding out Livia didn't kill her, that no one did, was unbearable because I felt like I should have known she'd started drinking again. I could have prevented her accident by helping her stop. Guilt made me say those things. I swear to you I will never talk to you that way again. I feel horrible. I'm sorry. I really am."

She averted her gaze as she heard his sincerity. She would not let down her guard. He'd shown her how little she actually knew him.

"And the whole, 'you were working with Livia' thing. I definitely didn't mean that."

"More lashing out?" she asked, unable to keep her sarcasm out of her tone.

"Yes, unfortunately. I'm not proud of myself. I'm ashamed. I fought my feelings for you because I still felt beholden to Tess. When you uncovered proof she died in an accident and no one killed her, I couldn't accept that. I thought catching her killer would bury her and ease guilt—finally. I never once considered that she died in an accident, because I couldn't. Facing that would mean I helped kill her by not doing anything about her alcoholism, by not recognizing the signs. But now I can let her go. I have. Because of you. You've helped me cope with Tess's death. Her alcoholism. My guilt. You were right about that."

Adeline had already figured out he suffered from a severe guilt complex over Tess's death. "You don't sound as though you are over her death, Jeremy. You still feel guilty because you did nothing to save her. You aren't ready for a new relationship. You still aren't over your last one, one that ended in tragedy. I can't get involved with a man who still has that kind of baggage."

"I *did* feel guilty. I don't anymore, Adeline. I recognize now that there's nothing I could have done to save Tess."

That revelation caused a spark to smoke and light. If he was truly over Tess…

"I should have seen the signs. I could have talked to her, sent her to rehab, sent her to therapy, any number of things. But none of that would have mattered if she didn't decide to help herself. She didn't *want* to stop drinking. She didn't want to stop when she quit. I can't be held responsible for her choices. That would be the same as agreeing with Evan Sigurdsson that I deserved to have my son kidnapped and you murdered for firing him."

While she inwardly cheered his strong epiphany, Adeline held back. She had to be sure about him. Baby steps were in order for her right now.

"Mommy?"

She saw Jamie in the kitchen entry. "Yes, sweetie."

"Daddy wanted me to ask you something."

She eyed Jeremy. "He did?" What was he up to?

He held his hands out and shrugged with a mock virtuous look.

Jamie looked beguilingly up at her. The two were a pair, all right.

"My birthday is tomorrow," Jamie said, leading as though he expected her to deny whatever he was about to ask.

"It's next Tuesday," Jeremy corrected.

Adeline already knew that.

"I'm going to be four."

"Yes, I know." What was this all about?

"Are you going to come to my party?" Jamie asked. "Daddy wants me to invite you."

"Oh…" She looked at Jeremy. What had he planned? What would she walk into? Despite the risk to her heart, she couldn't turn down her cute son. While she sent Jeremy a reproachful look for using his son to lure her, she said to Jamie, "Your daddy put you up to this?"

He looked at Jeremy and then back at Adeline.

"Do you want me to come to your party?"

Jamie beamed a smile. "Yeah."

"Then I wouldn't miss it for anything."

Jeremy smiled, a wide grin that showed triumph. Then he sobered and moved closer to her. Taking her hands in his, he said, "Think about everything I said."

He'd given her just under a week to think about his apology. She was afraid that's all she'd think about.

* * *

Adeline arrived at Jeremy and Jamie's house with a giant teddy bear and another wrapped present. Jeremy opened the door, dressed casually in tan pants and a blue sweater that made his dark features stand out. After not seeing him for almost a week, she was starved for the sight of him.

Jeremy took the giant bear and the present. "Hi."

His warm, rich voice tickled her senses. "Hi."

"Mommy!" Jamie bounded to the entry.

Adeline crouched just in time to take the onslaught of his hug. She lifted him.

"I'm so glad you're here! Daddy made a special pot and a cake and he got me a new game." His young voice went high-pitched with his excitement.

"Well, you are the birthday boy." Wondering what *pot* Jeremy had made, she carried Jamie into the spacious family room, where he had a train set up in the middle of the room and construction equipment strewn over the floor.

"Daddy got me a train!"

"The family room has turned into a playroom," Jeremy said.

"I can see that." She put down Jamie and he ran to his train.

"See?" He turned the train set on and the train began to move around the track. They must have begun to collect village buildings and other props. She saw there were two more unwrapped presents.

"Spoiling him a little?" she asked Jeremy.

"I'm so glad to have him back." He smiled with his confession.

"I can relate to that."

Jeremy went to Jamie. "This is from Adeline."

His mouth gaped open and he took the bear, burying his head in the soft fur and then tossing it aside to continue playing with the train.

Adeline smiled. "I didn't buy it for play as much as I did for his room."

"He'll love it eventually. He's been asking for a train every day since I got him back."

"Jamie, why don't you open your other presents now?" They had decided to have this private celebration and scheduled a bigger one, involving all of Jamie's friends and Adeline's mother, later.

"Okay!" He jumped up and went to the two presents on the coffee table. Jeremy put Adeline's there, too.

Jeremy had a smartphone and started recording as Jamie tore open the first present. He examined the box with pictures of a campsite.

"It's a camp set. Maybe one of your train townspeople wants to go camping," Jeremy said.

"Cool!" Jamie put that aside, not very interested. Nothing compared to the train. He tore open the other present, a fishing set.

That Jamie liked. He tried to pry open the box. Jeremy handed her the camera and she took over filming.

Jeremy opened the box and Jamie began taking items out.

"Wow!" he exclaimed, holding up a fishing pole. "We can go fishing!"

He took out a magnetic hook, net, tackle box and, at last, a fishing vest. He put it on and began tossing the pole back and forth.

"Hey, kiddo. You mother has a present for you, too."

Jamie put down the pole and ripped open the last

present. He held the box up and studied the picture as he had with the fishing set.

"It's a tablet," Adeline said. "A learning tablet," she said to Jeremy. "I figured he'll probably take after you in business."

Jeremy grinned, so sexy her heart melted with adoration.

Then she moved to Jamie and pointed at the picture on the box. "It has letter buttons and the mode selector is a bear. It has a piano keyboard for music, and the arrow buttons are for game-play controls. These are the activities." She pointed to the eight buttons. "Those will help you learn letters and numbers, and lots of other things like puzzles and words." She opened the box and took out the tablet. "The bear will help you interact, play music, a camera, calendar and some games. You can even chat with the computer program."

"What's 'chat'?" Jamie asked.

"It's something people do when they want to let their friends know when they're doing something silly."

Jeremy chuckled. "Or something like that."

She smiled at him and fell into a warm moment. All they had to do was look at each other and the fire roared to life.

When Jamie took his new fishing set out into a wider space, Jeremy held out his hand to her.

She looked from his outstretched palm to his face.

"I have something for you, too."

"For me?" she put her hand in his and he led her out of the family room. "It's not my birthday."

"No, but you missed his first three. I'm going to make it up to you."

How? By giving her a present? She felt awkward

about that. It was Jamie's day. She glanced back and saw her son engrossed with his new toy, oblivious to them. He wouldn't even notice their absence, and Jeremy had thought ahead to take her to another room.

He led her to the formal living room off the main entrance.

Jeremy went to the seating area. An off-white couch with yellow and beige pillows faced a big square stone coffee table and two matching chairs.

He extended his hand, indicating she should sit on the sofa.

She did, growing nervous over why he'd taken her in here. She didn't see any presents.

When he slid his hand into his front pocket, she felt a singe of alarm and excitement.

With a jewelry box the size of a ring, he knelt on one knee before her.

"Jeremy...?"

"Adeline, forgive me for saying such stupid things, and believe me when I tell you I didn't mean them. Even if I thought them, I didn't truly believe you capable of any of them. That scared me, and not holding someone accountable for Tess's death scared me more. My mistake wasn't only saying the things I said to you. Please forgive me and say you'll marry me."

She felt his sincerity all the way to her core. She fought embracing his apology. "Marry you... Isn't this sudden?"

He shook his head. "It's you I should have married in the first place. These past several weeks have shown me what I needed to learn about myself. I love you. I think I've loved you ever since you were pregnant with Jamie. I just couldn't admit it until now."

Adeline watched him open the box and stared at the huge center stone sparkling with purity.

"Will you marry me? Will you be Jamie's mother for real?"

She slowly looked from the beautiful, stunning ring, to Jeremy. His dark eyes were bright with determination and passion.

"Be my wife, Adeline," he said.

When she continued to meet his eyes and not say anything—her mind was a jumble of questions and burgeoning love—he removed the ring and lifted her hand.

"I know this might come as a shock to you." He slid the ring onto her finger. "But somewhere inside, you must feel it's meant to be. I do."

She lifted her hand and admired the ring. "Jeremy, it's…beautiful." She breathed deeper to catch her breath and met his eyes again.

"Will you marry me?" he asked again. "Will you be Jamie's mother and my wife every day for the rest of your life?"

She would have her very own family. Her mother could come over for holidays. Jamie would grow up and bring his family here. She'd have a husband who loved her. Did she love him?

The burgeoning emotion expanded in her chest and she felt every cell of her body answer affirmatively.

"Do you mean everything you said this time?" she asked, already knowing he did.

"Yes. Every word. Forgive me, Adeline. I promise you will never regret trusting me."

She believed him…and trusted him. She did. The feeling felt wonderful. Heavenly.

Sliding off the couch, she drew her arms around Jeremy.

"Then, yes, Jeremy." She kissed him. "I'll be Jamie's mother and your wife for the rest of my life."

* * * * *

If you loved this suspenseful story,
don't miss these previous books in the
COLTONS OF SHADOW CREEK *miniseries:*

CAPTURING A COLTON by C.J. Miller
THE COLTON MARINE by Lisa Childs
COLD CASE COLTON by Addison Fox
PREGNANT BY THE COLTON COWBOY
by Lara Lacombe
COLTON UNDERCOVER by Marie Ferrarella
COLTON'S SECRET SON by Carla Cassidy

All available now from
Harlequin Romantic Suspense.

And be sure to check out these thrilling reads from
Jennifer Morey's COLD CASE DETECTIVE *series:*

RUNAWAY HEIRESS
TAMING DEPUTY HARLOW
COLD CASE RECRUIT
JUSTICE HUNTER
A WANTED MAN

Also available now from
Harlequin Romantic Suspense!

#1967 THE BILLIONAIRE'S COLTON THREAT
The Coltons of Shadow Creek • by Geri Krotow
One passionate night with billionaire Alastair Buchanan turns life altering when rancher Halle Ford finds out she's pregnant. But now that criminal mastermind Livia Colton's reach appears to extend from beyond the grave, will Halle and Alastair survive long enough to build the family they've come to dream of?

#1968 STRANDED WITH THE NAVY SEAL
by Susan Cliff
After a relaxing cruise goes horribly wrong, Cady Crenshaw and Logan Starke go from a vacation fling to partners in survival—luckily Logan is a navy SEAL. But even if they manage to get off the island alive, Cady isn't sure her heart will ever be safe with a proved heartbreaker like Logan.

#1969 PROTECTING HER SECRET SON
Escape Club Heroes • by Regan Black
When Shannon Nolan's son goes missing, she turns to firefighter Daniel Jennings for protection while the authorities dig into the case. But finding her son is only the beginning of their struggle...

#1970 HER ROCKY MOUNTAIN HERO
Rocky Mountain Justice • by Jen Bokal
Viktoria Mateev is on the run. Cody Samuels is a man in need of redemption. When Viktoria's son is kidnapped by her ruthless mobster relative, they'll do anything to get him back—before it's too late!

HRSCNM1017

"You don't think I can do it?" Her chin jutted out and her lips were pouty. Not that he was thinking about kissing her at this particular time.

"I know you can do whatever you want to, Halle. You pulled me out of a raging river, for God's sake. That's not the question."

"The river was still by the time I got to you. Tell me, Alastair, what do you think is the issue? What's your point?"

"The concern I have is how you're going to make enough money to not only keep Bluewood running, but to invest in its future. How will you ensure a legacy you can leave to our child? That's a full-time job in and of itself."

Tears glistened in her eyes as she bit her trembling bottom lip. Not that he was looking at it for any particular reason. "I'll do whatever I have to. It's how my daddy raised me. Fords aren't quitters. Although Dad always found time for me, always let me know that I was first, the priority over the ranch. He was bringing in a lot more money when I was younger, though. I don't know if the ranch will ever get back to those days." She wiped tears off her cheeks.

"Are you sure you want to take on another full-time job on top of the ranch? With a new baby?"

"That's the question, isn't it?"

"That's part of what brought me here, Halle."

She grabbed a napkin from the acrylic holder on the table and wiped her eyes, then blew her nose. He made a note to order the finest linen handkerchiefs for her, with the Scottish thistle embroidered on them. Her hands were long, her fingers graceful. Would their child have her hands?

Her long, shuddering breath emphasized her ramrod-straight posture. He was certain she was made of steel. She rested her sharp whiskey eyes on him.

"Go on."

"Marry me, Halle. For the sake of our child, marry me."

Find out Halle's answer in
THE BILLIONAIRE'S COLTON THREAT
by Geri Krotow, available November 2017
wherever Harlequin® Romantic Suspense books
and ebooks are sold.

www.Harlequin.com

HRSEXP1017

THE WORLD IS BETTER
WITH
Romance

Harlequin has everything from contemporary, passionate and heartwarming to suspenseful and inspirational stories.

Whatever your mood,
we have a romance just for you!

Connect with us to find your next great read, special offers and more.

f /HarlequinBooks

🐦 @HarlequinBooks

www.HarlequinBlog.com

www.Harlequin.com/Newsletters

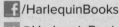

◆ HARLEQUIN®

A *Romance* FOR EVERY MOOD™

www.Harlequin.com